For Dave

The Followers

Also by Rebecca Wait

The View on the Way Down

REBECCA WAIT

The Followers

PICADOR

First published 2015 by Picador
an imprint of Pan Macmillan, a division of Macmillan Publishers Limited
Pan Macmillan, 20 New Wharf Road, London N1 9RR
Basingstoke and Oxford
Associated companies throughout the world
www.panmacmillan.com

ISBN 978-1-4472-2473-0

1 3 5 7 9 8 6 4 2

A CIP catalogue record for this book is available from the British Library.

Printed and bound by CPI Group (UK) Ltd, Croydon, CR0 4YY

Visit www.picador.com to read more about all our books
and to buy them. You will also find features, author interviews and
news of any author events, and you can sign up for e-newsletters
so that you're always first to hear about our new releases.

'Hearken not unto the words of the prophets that prophesy unto you: they make you vain: they speak a vision of their own heart, and not out of the mouth of the Lord.'

JEREMIAH 23: 16

After

In the visitor centre, Judith bundled her satchel and coat into the locker. She added the keys from her pocket and the ham sandwich she'd felt too queasy to finish, wrapped by her grandmother in about nineteen layers of cling film. 'For the road,' Gran had said, as she always did. Her gran, who never said anything that might be misconstrued as tender, who almost never smiled, still did what she could to fortify Judith against these visits, if only through the provision of snacks. During the search last time, the officer had fished out from Judith's pocket a single Hobnob, which looked like it had been shrink-wrapped. Judith was as surprised as the officer was.

'My gran must have put it there,' she said, which was met with raised eyebrows. 'At least it's not crack,' she added. An ill-judged comment, but the oxycodone she'd swallowed on the train had put her in an expansive, free-wheeling mood that made it hard to keep her thoughts internalized.

Now, clutching her passport and locker key, she joined the subdued band of visitors making their way over to the main prison. A couple of them she recognized, but she didn't greet them. Inside the first set of doors, she waited as she was patted down with rather unnecessary thoroughness – they probably remembered the crack comment – then followed the officer into the visits hall.

It was, she thought, the closest approximation to hell she was likely to experience. Neutral paintwork and plastic chairs, the smell of bleach; another scent beneath it, sour and harder to place. Judith tried not to look at the other prisoners as she made her way over to her mother. Stephanie was sitting in the far corner, hands folded neatly in her lap, eyes fixed determinedly on her hands. I don't like to look up too soon, she had told Judith once, in case you haven't come.

'I always come,' Judith had said, unsmiling. She was wary of people who teased out your sympathy and used it against you.

Now, her mother stood and hugged her. A strange embrace, one that pinned Judith's arms to her sides and left her unable to respond. They sat.

'It's good to see you,' Stephanie said.

Judith noticed that her mother's hair was looking thinner. Her face had taken on a dry, crumpled look. Stephanie had gone into prison young but she would come out old. Perhaps she would look at herself and be amazed.

Judith realized that her mother was speaking.

'Sorry?'

'How's Gran?' Stephanie said again.

'She's fine.' A pause, then she added, 'Thanks for the birthday card, by the way. I liked – the elephant picture.'

'You're welcome. Twenty-two. You're a real adult now.'

Judith had no reply to this.

'I'll get you a present,' her mother said. 'When I can.

You know, get it myself. I'll get you all the presents from your last few birthdays, OK? When I can.'

Judith tried to imagine being deluged with all the debts owed to her younger self, things she might once have wanted but no longer had any use for: My Chemical Romance albums, notebooks, Xbox games. Like unspooling time, being pulled back, back, back.

Searching wildly for a conversation topic, she came out with, 'I watched this old film with Gran the other day. *An Officer and a Gentleman.* I heard it was like *Top Gun*, which was shit, but it was OK.'

'Richard Gere,' her mother said. 'I fancied him when I was your age.'

'I didn't get why they had to make it so fucking depressing at the end. And then try to pretend everything was happy again.'

'You mean the bit where his friend—?' Stephanie said, breaking off as though afraid of spoiling the plot for invisible listeners. Judith glanced involuntarily over her shoulder, but the other people in the room were absorbed in their own visits. At a table nearby, a woman shared a bar of chocolate with an elderly man, meticulously measuring each of the pieces against the others.

Judith turned back to her mother. 'Yeah,' she said. 'When he kills himself.'

'I didn't like that bit either,' Stephanie said.

'It wasn't what happened that annoyed me. I just hated how they tried to have a happy ending afterwards. Like Richard Gere would just be fine again. And we could all just forget it.'

3

'Our film last week was *The Descendants*,' Stephanie said. 'Some of the others screamed whenever George Clooney was on screen.' She attempted a smile. 'Which was a lot. It was a bit distracting.'

'I saw that,' Judith said. 'It was alright.'

'I prefer Colin Firth,' her mother said. 'We had *The King's Speech* the week before. I enjoyed *that*. He's gorgeous.'

Judith nodded, suddenly tired of this topic. She said, 'I'm learning to cook. Last night I made a pork casserole.' She didn't add that she'd drunk too much in the afternoon, and bought all the ingredients except the pork. ('Ah. Tomato stew,' her gran had said drily. 'Very economical.')

'That sounds nice,' her mother said. 'And how's Nick?'

'Oh,' Judith said, regretting that she'd allowed this to be wormed out of her in the first place. 'Well, I haven't seen him for a while.'

Her mother seemed to deflate before her eyes. 'What happened?'

'Nothing.'

Of course, Nick had found out who she was. Judith still didn't know how, but she'd seen it in his face when he'd suggested coming to see her mother with her. Her mother, who lived so far away.

'It's a long journey,' Judith had said. 'And she's not that interesting. She's just my mum. Very ordinary.' She'd given him that bland, deflecting look she was so good at. But she knew what he was thinking all the same.

That was the end, because how could it not be? She'd done it over the phone the next day, and hidden upstairs in her room when he came round.

'She's not here,' she heard her gran saying over and over, until he finally left. Judith had allowed herself to cry for a little while. Then she'd gone downstairs and it hadn't been mentioned again.

Her mother said, 'If he's upset you in some way, or if you've upset him, perhaps you could talk to him about it. Find a way to forgive each other.'

Judith shrugged. She wanted to say, 'I don't believe in forgiveness,' but the words stayed in her head. She turned her eyes to the window instead. It was too high to see anything except a square of light, framed like it had been hung there. They were almost out of time.

When Judith got up to go, her mother said quickly, 'See you next month?'

Judith hesitated, letting herself imagine, just for a second, that there was more than one answer.

'Of course,' she said.

I

Before

1

Stephanie didn't know what it was about the man in the corner because as far as she could see he just sat there quietly and read his book. But the other girls jostled for position on Thursday mornings to serve him, and then competed again for who would clear his table.

'He usually has a cappuccino,' Helen told her on her first Thursday, as though she were revealing the secrets of the universe. 'But sometimes, just occasionally, he switches to breakfast tea.'

'Right,' Stephanie said.

She decided to leave them to it. Plenty of other customers to serve and plenty of other tables to clear. She hadn't been here long and she wanted the other girls to like her. The risk of losing your job was ever-present these days, everything so shifting and unstable that it was best to keep your head down and get on with it. Three years she'd been at the bookies, had made the mistake of thinking she was safe – why worry about losing a job you hate, anyway? – but as it turned out, she'd been the first to go.

The rent was a problem, as constant as her exhaustion. She still remembered a time when she'd actually relished the idea of rent payments. On those nights in her early twenties when she'd left Judith with her mum and gone out for a drink, she'd enjoyed dropping it into conversation with her friends: 'Better not have another, or I won't make the rent this month,' or, 'No, it's a rubbish job, but you have to pay the rent somehow, don't you?' It was a magic word back then, transforming her into someone she wanted to be: adult, bold, a little haphazard, perhaps, but making it all work. Her friends – many still sleeping in their childhood single beds – had been impressed.

She was thirty-one now, and the charm of paying rent was long gone. Too many moves. Too many cramped, dreary towns, each time hoping for better. Everyone was paying rent now, and much less precariously than she was, it seemed. And Judith's dad had never been much help, either with money or with anything else. No sign of him for ages now. It wasn't Sean who had to worry about paying the rent, or finding the cheapest way to make bolognese without Judith complaining it was grey.

It seemed to happen as you got older that instead of expanding, the world shrank around you, so in the place of all that freedom you'd been promised you got breathlessness and fear and the daily drudge of making ends meet.

Stephanie began to hate the man who sat in the corner every Thursday, who had nothing better to do than drink coffee and read a book on a weekday morning.

'What does he actually *do*?' she said to Helen on her third Thursday.

Helen was vague. 'I think he's a teacher.'

'Where? St Joseph's? The FE college?'

'Don't think so.'

'There's nowhere else.' Not in this wasteland, she added silently; nothing but the moors and the wind and the rain.

'Well, then,' Helen said, 'he probably works further afield, doesn't he? Bradford, even.'

'Bradford? Right.'

Stephanie looked over at him again. Early forties, maybe. Dark hair that curled a little. He was OK-looking, she'd give him that, but nothing special. The others were welcome to him.

Then, an accident. Helen had gone out for a cigarette and Liz was wiping down the tables by the door so that somehow Stephanie was alone at the counter when he came up, his polite half-smile already in place. She didn't smile back.

He said, 'Please could I have a chocolate croissant?'

Soft-spoken, with quite a posh accent – a little like he was about to read you the news. Mainly, she noticed his eyes. A strange pale green, too light for his colouring. Stephanie had never seen eyes like that before. They unsettled her.

She focused on the pastries instead, lifting the plastic lid and using the tongs to retrieve a croissant for him.

'That'll be 90p, please.'

He said in his gentle voice, 'You're new, aren't you?'

'Been here nearly a month.' She wasn't sure where her irritation came from. Maybe because he made it sound like he was the one who belonged here, like he was welcoming her onto his territory.

'Nice to meet you,' he said. Then, 'My name's Nathaniel.'

Her 'Stephanie' sounded silly coming after his curiously old-fashioned name.

He had paid and was holding the little plate with the croissant on it. But he didn't walk away.

He said, 'I come here every Thursday.'

'I know.' She regretted saying it immediately. Made it sound like she'd been watching him, same as all the others. A short silence, during which she felt those pale eyes on her again. She'd been staring down at the cash register, but now she made herself look up and meet his gaze. There was something patient in his expression that made her feel like she was being unreasonable.

'I'll let you get on,' he said, and the next moment he'd gone back to his table with the croissant and picked up his book. He didn't look at her again after that, not when he'd finished his coffee, not when Helen went over and they seemed to be chatting away, laughing together, not even when he left.

'What's so special about him?' she said to Helen later, as they were closing up. 'Why do you all fancy him?'

Helen snorted, gave her a shove. 'I don't *fancy* him. He's just nice, that's all. Nice manners, you know?'

Must be the polish of Bradford, Stephanie thought. She just managed not to say it out loud.

Shrieks of laughter greeted her from the front room when she got home. A moment later, Judith burst out into the hall, and Stephanie thought, as she often did, that it was a peculiar gift on Judith's part that she could make even school uniform look scruffy.

'We've made a talk show, Mum,' Judith said. 'I'm the interviewer, and Megan's my guest, and she's a pop star, but she's off her head on drugs and keeps answering with stuff that doesn't make sense. Do you want to see it?'

'Not just now, love.' Stephanie stuck her head round the living-room door, where Megan seemed to be conducting some kind of elaborate mime by herself. 'Megan, hadn't you better be getting home? Your mum will be wondering where you are.'

'She knows I'm here,' Megan said placidly.

'She means she wants you to go home,' Judith said, coming back into the room. 'She's not being rude. She just wants to make our supper and watch *Coronation Street* in peace. Come on. I'll walk with you.'

'Judith!' Stephanie said, but the girls had already gone to get their coats.

When Judith returned, Stephanie had the beans heating up on the stove, and was buttering toast. Judith came and leant against the counter next to her. She seemed to be getting bigger at a rate that Stephanie found alarming, taking up more and more space as Stephanie felt herself diminishing. It struck her as extraordinary, when she thought about it, that she'd produced a child like Judith: this bright, self-assured person who seemed like no one but herself.

Judith said, 'You know, Mum, you should see people more. It'd do you good.'

'I see Megan often enough, don't I?'

She hadn't meant to snap, but Judith seemed unfazed.

'I mean friends your own age, Mum. Why don't you invite Megan's mum round for coffee?'

'Kay is *not* my age, Judith. She's in her forties, for God's sake!'

'Yes, but you're both mums, aren't you?' Judith said, as though that settled it.

Stephanie closed her eyes briefly. 'Shall we have supper in front of the telly?'

Another accident: this time, entirely his. She was wiping down the tables the following Thursday when she heard a quiet sound of frustration behind her, and looked up to see that he'd knocked his mug over, sending a wave of coffee over the table and soaking the paperback that rested on it.

She went over with her cloth, and did her best to absorb the worst of it before it flooded his lap. He picked up the book and flapped it uselessly, as though he could shake out the coffee that had already sunk into its pages.

'I'm such an idiot,' he said.

'We all do it.' He was looking at the book so sadly that she added, 'If it's ruined, you can get another copy, can't you?' She couldn't see what the book was, but it looked old and tattered, the pages yellow where they weren't stained with coffee.

'Well, yes,' he said. 'Only—'

When he broke off, she found it impossible not to prompt him. 'Only what?'

A quick, rueful look. 'Sounds stupid. But it was my mother's book.'

'Oh – sorry.'

'No use being sentimental though, is there? It's only a book.'

'Did you lose your mother recently?' she said. Was this OK to ask? Did people ask things like this?

He didn't seem to mind. 'No. Back when I was a kid.' He remained thoughtful a moment longer, then gave her an unexpectedly charming smile. 'Sorry about the spill.'

'It's fine. It's nothing. It's just a shame about your book.'

'It's my own clumsiness,' he said. 'I sometimes wonder if my brain's failed to understand the length of my arms. I'm always misjudging distances when I reach for things.' He had placed the book back on the table now, and she was able to read the title: *Murder in the Cathedral* by T. S. Eliot, which sounded like an Agatha Christie novel, though wasn't he the one who wrote poems about cats?

'Is it any good?' she said, gesturing to the book.

He looked up at her, and those pale eyes locked on hers so that for a moment it was as though the rest of the world stilled and receded and there were just the two of them there. He said, 'This is one moment, but know that another shall pierce you with a sudden, painful joy.'

It took her a couple of beats to realize he was quoting. She didn't know what to say, but she couldn't drag her eyes away. He seemed clever, she thought.

He freed her by giving a small huff of amusement and looking down at the book. 'It's a bit strange, to be honest.'

'Sounds it.' A pause, then she said, 'I'd better get on.'

Back at the counter, she made him a replacement cappuccino and took it over to him, with a breezy, 'On the house,' and then winced inwardly, because this expression belonged to television, not real life. She brushed off his thanks and walked away, not trusting herself to linger any longer.

The following Thursday was her day off. She started out by cleaning the flat, then gave up and went to bed with a magazine. It was hard to focus, though. She wasn't used to having time to herself; felt she was wasting it.

On Friday, Liz said, 'He asked about you yesterday.'

Stephanie could tell who Liz meant from her sidelong look. She felt something in her stomach, a wriggle of excitement.

She affected nonchalance. 'Oh?'

'He asked where you were, if you were ill. I said you were working at the weekend instead. That he'd have to make do with me and Helen.'

Stephanie didn't comment. She told herself it was weird he'd asked.

He was there again the next Thursday. She wasn't at the counter when he placed his order, but he made a special point of bringing his empty mug up himself later, when she was replenishing the pastries. The coffee shop was quiet that day, so she was able to pause in her work and say, 'Did you dry your book out OK?'

'It's not too bad,' he said. 'The pages have gone quite an attractive shade of brown. I think I prefer it. Before long, everyone will be doing it.'

'I'm not sure about that.'

As she turned to wipe down the coffee machine, he said, 'So have you always lived round here?'

'No. Leeds, originally.'

'What made you come here?'

Stephanie shrugged. She'd followed a boyfriend here a few years back, only he hadn't stuck around, and now there seemed neither anything to keep her here nor any reason to move on. 'You know,' she said. 'Life.'

'And are you happy here?'

A strange question. 'It's alright,' she said. But, feeling his directness required a more honest answer, she added, 'It's not where I imagined I'd end up.'

'Things don't always turn out the way we expect, do they?'

He said it softly, almost to himself. Something made Stephanie ask, 'Are *you* from round here?' It already seemed obvious he wasn't.

'No, I grew up with my uncle in London.'

She wanted to ask about his parents, but didn't know how. Perhaps his father as well as his mother had died when he was a child. Stephanie's own father had been killed in a road accident when she was six, and though she hardly remembered him, though her mother never spoke of him, Stephanie seemed to carry with her a physical memory of his death, a pain in her chest when she thought of him that was like being winded.

'Everyone's always telling you that things turn out for the best,' she said. 'But don't they just *turn out*, without any scheme behind it? And anyway, we can't say things have turned out for the best or the worst because we don't know what the other options would have been.' She had taken herself by surprise – the words seemed to burst out of her in his presence. She risked a glance at him. 'What?'

'Oh, nothing,' he said. 'I had a feeling about you, that's all. And I was right.'

'What feeling?'

'I suppose – that you think about things more deeply than other people.'

'Oh!' she said, trying to hide her pleasure. 'Hardly. Look where I've ended up. Working in a cafe.' A single mother, she almost said.

'It's not about what we do,' he said. 'It's about who we are.' When she didn't answer, he added, 'Actually, I think there is a scheme to it all. But we can talk about that another day. I'd better leave you in peace now. People will think I'm making the world's longest and most complicated coffee order.'

She smiled at him. 'See you next Thursday.'

But the next week he didn't come. Stephanie told herself she didn't mind, she would see him again the following Thursday. But he didn't appear then either.

'Maybe he's found another coffee shop,' Helen said gloomily.

'Maybe he's *dead*,' Liz said.

Stephanie didn't comment. Isn't this typical, she thought. It was almost worse than if he'd never spoken to her. This was what they did, men: made you think it meant something to them as well, when really it was just a passing fancy, throwaway remarks.

That evening, she stood in the kitchen stirring pasta sauce, thinking of nothing. She was dimly aware that Judith was talking to her, relaying with an unnecessary level of detail the plot of the film she'd watched with Megan the night before. Stephanie had given up trying to follow, and stared down at the pan instead, letting her mind go quiet.

Judith's voice broke in, strident. 'Did you hear what I just said, Mum? About the man with the hook?'

'Yes.'

'OK, what does he do, then? What does he do when he comes up behind Ryan Phillippe on the balcony?'

Stephanie stirred the sauce. 'He kills him,' she said.

'Oh, *Mum*. That was a lucky guess. I can tell you're not listening.'

'I was.'

'You weren't. You never listen.' She paused, then delivered the devastating blow. '*Megan's* mother always listens to *her*.'

'Well, why don't you bloody well go and live with Megan then?' Stephanie said.

'You shouldn't say "bloody",' Judith said. 'It's undignified.'

'I don't fucking care,' Stephanie said, feeling even more of the moral high ground slipping away from her. 'Anyway,' she went on quickly, 'it doesn't sound like a suitable film. I'm surprised Megan's mum let you watch it.'

'We watched *Sleepy Hollow* when Megan came round here a few weeks ago,' Judith countered. 'Remember? You screamed your head off and spilled the popcorn. Megan said she was going to have nightmares until the end of her days.'

'Get the plates out, will you?'

'What are we having?'

'Pasta with mushroom sauce.'

'I hate mushrooms,' Judith said.

'Since when?'

'Since about a *year*. See? You never *listen*.'

It was true, really, Stephanie thought later. She was a failure as a mother, even though it was about the only thing she'd ever done with her life. And even that had been an accident. She remembered her own mother saying once, 'Some people shouldn't have children.' It had appeared to be an idle comment, a response to something they'd seen on the news, but Stephanie had taken it personally and couldn't shake off the suspicion that it had been intended that way.

She and her mum didn't speak these days. There hadn't been a falling-out, exactly, but somehow they seemed to have nothing to say to each other. Stephanie could feel the waves of disapproval coming from her mother even down the phone line. Her mother had a point, anyway. Stephanie had got everything wrong.

She sometimes thought about the time she went to the Fens with a boy from college, long before Judith was born. She didn't know why this trip stood out so vividly in her memory, except that it had felt like a moment in someone else's life. They'd stayed with the boy's sister, a romantic getaway of sorts, only instead of a hotel in Paris it had been a dingy back bedroom in the Fens.

The Fens had scared her to death. Flat like an unfurled ribbon, all that sky, fields going on forever and nothing to stop you slipping right off the edge of the world. There'd been no other houses around the cottage, just the farmhouse it backed on to, and beyond that just emptiness, empty fields and empty sky, for miles and miles. When it got dark, you could see a glimmer of light in the distance, a small, lighthouse pinprick floating somewhere across the vast expanse of black.

'Our neighbours,' the sister said, with no apparent irony.

Still, you could breathe in the Fens. You could see a glimpse of something else opening out before you. You felt like nothing, but you were part of all that other nothing, and somehow it helped.

Callum, the boy had been called. Spots.

2

Thomas came out of work to find Nathaniel leaning against the bonnet of his car.

'Nice badge,' Nathaniel said.

Thomas hastened to remove it – *Thomas Salter, Store Manager* – but it was too late.

Nathaniel was grinning. 'Don't be embarrassed. It makes you look important.'

'Ha ha.'

'Is it in case you forget who you are?'

'It's so customers know who to shout at.' Thomas unlocked the car.

'Does everyone wear badges these days?' Nathaniel said, getting into the passenger seat.

'More or less.'

'Maybe I should get one.'

Thomas looked at him, decided not to comment. Nathaniel like this was thrilling, his exuberance bleeding into everyone around him. But Thomas was on his guard, waiting for the switch, the tilt.

'Long day?' Nathaniel said.

He should have remembered how easily Nathaniel could read him. 'Very.'

Thomas made to turn on the engine, but Nathaniel put

his hand on his arm and said, 'Not yet. I want to talk to you. Before we pick up the others.'

Thomas tried to relax his shoulders against the seat. Waited. Why were his responses never correct these days? He couldn't seem to get himself under control.

Nathaniel said, 'God spoke to me again.'

His hand was still on Thomas's arm. All of Thomas's consciousness was centred on that point of contact: Nathaniel's hot palm, his spread fingers, pressing against Thomas's body, thrusting their warmth deep below the skin. Thomas was almost trembling beneath that hand. It did something strange to him.

He said, mouth dry, voice failing on the last syllable, 'What did He say?'

'It's been hard,' Nathaniel said. 'I haven't been sure. I've been struggling with it. But it's becoming clearer now.'

'Yes?'

'He's found someone else.'

'What?'

'He wants me to bring in someone else.'

'Into the Ark?'

Nathaniel nodded. He was watching Thomas, registering every flicker of his expression. Thomas took the cue, fought to make his reaction appropriate.

'I thought—'

'So did I. We were wrong.'

'Why now?'

'I don't know.'

Silence. At last, Nathaniel said, 'I don't need to tell you to keep this to yourself.'

'Of course.'

'I need to prepare the others a little. But I wanted you to know first.' He smiled at Thomas. 'You know you're my right-hand man.'

Thomas felt some of the old warmth, the kind that didn't make him tremble. But it was battling with something else.

He said, 'Seth and Joshua will be waiting.'

'Let's go, then.'

Thomas turned on the engine and they headed towards the town centre. To his relief, Nathaniel didn't try to talk any more. He knew that before long he would have to ask for guidance, even if it resulted in a session. Somehow it was as though he'd given the devil a way in, however careful he'd tried to be.

Nathaniel had told them the Ark was already filled, sealed off from the outside world. So had God changed His mind? But no, Thomas could see that was a stupid thought. This must have been part of God's plan all along.

It was a woman. Thomas didn't know how he knew, but he was certain it was a woman.

Again, he struggled with himself. Something was askew. The revelation of God's will, where once it had filled him with excitement, now brought nothing but unease.

3

Three Thursdays had passed with no sign of him. But it didn't matter, Stephanie thought. None of it mattered in the long run.

She had taken to awarding herself little treats in the evening. A glass or two of wine (or, more often than not, three). Chocolate. Crisps. Just something she could look forward to throughout the day. She'd always been slim, but she noticed she'd been putting on weight recently, a small roll of fat forming around her stomach. She hated the idea, but couldn't bring herself to do anything about it. Men had used to look at her in the street once. It seemed a long time ago. She assuaged her anxiety by drinking more, eating more.

'Mum,' Judith said, 'you watch a lot of television. Do you think you should take up a new hobby?'

'I don't watch that much.'

'You do. More than other mothers.'

'How do you know? Have you done a survey?'

'There's no need to be sarcastic,' Judith said.

Meanwhile, a mouse in her kitchen was driving her mad with its quiet, unseen scuffling. It upset her more than she might have expected, the horrible moments when she glimpsed it out of the corner of her eye, this small dark thing, obscenely alive and *fast*, shooting across the floor by her feet.

She ordered traps from the Internet, the kind with a bar that snapped down to break the creature's neck. The idea seemed brutal, but she didn't want to risk the mouse returning, and at least this way its death would be quick. When the traps arrived, she laid them behind the fridge.

Finally, one evening she heard the crack of a trap. Judith was at Megan's, and Stephanie was pleased that she would be able to dispose of the mouse without her daughter ever knowing.

But then, turning her cold, a scrabbling started up, the click of the trap on the floor as it was dragged.

It took her a while to force herself to pull the fridge out to look. She saw that the bar had snapped down on the mouse, snaring it in place, its neck pushed grotesquely flat. But it had come down at a slant, or rather the mouse had approached the trap at an angle, so the bar had caught only one side of it. Its tiny legs were paddling frantically, its back bucking in a useless bid to free itself.

It was going to die, but it was going to die slowly, in terror and in pain. Stephanie knew she would have to put it out of its misery, but the idea appalled her. What would be the best way to dispatch it, the fastest and most painless? She would have to stamp on it, she realized in despair.

It was more difficult than she expected, picking the trap up in a plastic bag to take outside. The dying mouse wriggled inside. She was again glad Judith was out of the house, because she found it impossible to suppress the whine that burst from her as she rushed to the back door with it.

When she had laid it down on the concrete, she took a few moments to compose herself. She looked at her shoes: navy pumps, one of her favourite pairs. Feeling faintly ridiculous, she went back inside and returned in her wellingtons. Then, stiffly, she made herself raise her leg, but couldn't bring it down on the twitching bag. It took her a few more minutes to work up to it.

Finally, with a strangled cry, she stumbled forward and stamped, too gently at first – why wasn't it already dead from pain and shock, why was it still *moving*? – and then with more force, again and again, until the translucent white of the bag was smeared red. She stopped, breathing hard. No movement from the bag. A sob was trapped in her throat and now she let it out: an ugly, embarrassing sound.

Picking up the bag by the edges, she took it to the wheelie bin, arms held out squeamishly in front of her. She left her wellingtons outside the door, and went straight to the bathroom to shower.

When Judith came home later, Stephanie was weighing up whether to tell her about the mouse after all. It might make that red smear inside the bag seem less terrible. Judith was a tough kid; it would hardly stop her in her tracks.

But Judith rushed straight through to the living room

to put the TV on because she didn't want to miss *Spooks*. Stephanie went and sat beside her.

'Did you and Megan get all your homework done?' she ventured at last.

'Yes.'

A proper mother would have worked out some way of checking, Stephanie thought, rather than just taking Judith's word for it. But even if she did find out Judith hadn't done her homework, what could she do? Her daughter became more formidable every day.

'You need to go to bed straight after this, OK?' Stephanie said.

'If I'm tired enough,' Judith said, not taking her eyes off the TV.

Without a word, Stephanie got up and left the room, not entirely sure where she was going. In her bedroom, she climbed under the covers still wearing her clothes and put out the light. Had enough of this day, she thought, feeling childish and angry. She ought to go back and say a proper goodnight to Judith – she hadn't even checked if she'd had supper, had just assumed Megan's mum had fed her – but she didn't have the energy to get up again. She closed her eyes.

A while later, she was woken by the door being pushed open, bringing in light from the landing. Judith came a little way into the room.

'Mum?' she said in a small voice.

'Yes?' Stephanie didn't bother to raise her head.

'I thought you were coming back. I thought you'd just gone to the loo.'

'I'm tired, Judith. Go to bed.'

'Mum?' Judith said again. When she got no reply, she said, 'Are you OK?'

No, Stephanie thought. 'Yes, fine. Just tired.'

'Are you ill?'

'Perhaps a bit.'

The door was pulled shut again and Stephanie thought she'd been left in peace, but after a few minutes Judith was back, this time making her way carefully over to the bed in the semi-darkness, and depositing a mug on the bedside table (slopping some of its contents over the edge, by the sound of it).

'I've brought you some hot water with honey and lemon,' she said. Then, after a pause, 'We didn't have any lemons, so I used a satsuma instead.'

Stephanie made herself sit up. 'Thank you, love. I'll make sure I drink it all.'

'You should.'

'Now you'd better go and brush your teeth and get in bed. Will you be alright?'

'Course.'

Judith departed, and Stephanie forced herself to drink as much of the concoction in the mug as she could bear. There was a segment of satsuma bobbing on the top, as if for garnish. She placed the mug out of sight in case Judith came to check the next morning, contemplated getting up to brush her teeth and take off her make-up, then simply let herself fall into unconsciousness.

*

And suddenly he was there after all, even though it was a Friday, even though she no longer cared, not about men like him who thought they had some kind of power over you.

He didn't order a coffee this time but came straight over to the table she was clearing. Stephanie pretended not to see him standing there, but he moved a little closer and touched her arm.

'Stephanie. How are you?'

'Fine, thanks.' She didn't pause in her stacking of plates, nor even look up at him. But when she took the dirty crockery over to the counter, he followed.

'When's your break?'

'Already had it.' She had gone behind the counter to load the plates into the dishwasher.

'Don't you get more than one a day? When's your next one?'

She shrugged. 'Not for ages. Sorry.' She suspected Helen and Liz were both watching them from across the room.

'I'll wait,' he said.

'We're very busy today.'

There was a pause. He said, 'You know, I've been away these past few weeks.'

She wanted to say something icy and formidable, like *And?* or *What's it to me?* but nothing came. She carried on stacking the plates instead.

He put his hands on the counter. 'My uncle died,' he said. 'I had to go back to London to make arrangements for the funeral. There was a lot to sort out.'

'Oh! God.' She turned to face him. 'I'm sorry.'

'Thank you.'

She looked at him helplessly. 'I could see if Helen will swap with me. If you like. See if I could take a break sooner?'

'That would be great. Perhaps we could go for a walk. Or go to a coffee shop.' He stopped, then smiled. 'That was a stupid thing to say.'

'I'll go and talk to Helen.'

In the end, they walked away from the town centre and up the hill a little way, stopping to sit on a bench beside the road. Beyond the houses scattered at the edge of the town you could just see the moors looming up on the horizon, shadowy and vast, trying to block out the light.

'Was it very hard?' she said.

'In some ways. It was partly the fact that I *didn't* feel all that much grief for him, and then of course that made me feel terrible.'

'You weren't close, then?'

'Well.' Nathaniel glanced up towards the moors. 'He brought me up. He was all I had. So yes, I suppose we were close.'

Stephanie caught herself wanting to touch him, and resisted.

'But – he didn't like children much,' Nathaniel said. 'And he ended up stuck with me after my parents died, so that was difficult for him. He did his best.'

She noted the reference to his parents – both dead, then. Awful for him. She said, 'He must have cared about you.'

'Yes, I suppose so. And anyway, I was all *he* had, as well. Hardly anyone came to the funeral. That was sad, too.'

'I'm sorry.'

'I was thinking while I was down there,' he said, 'about whether I should just stay in London. I get restless sometimes. And this town can feel small.'

'That's true.'

'But it was strange,' he said. 'When I thought about settling down south, and never coming back here, I kept—'

When he stopped, she leaned forward a little. 'You kept what?'

'It's funny,' he said. 'I kept thinking of you.'

The first time they went out to dinner, she was amazed again at how easy it was to talk to him, and how interested he was in her. They went to an Italian restaurant, and both chose the pizza with ham and mushrooms, and shared a bottle of white wine. Stephanie found herself swigging it at first, looking for the familiar soothing lull, but soon noticed he wasn't drinking much and managed to slow down.

Nathaniel sympathized when she said she disliked working in the cafe and told her about a job he'd had once in a canning factory ('Even now I turn pale at the sight of a tinned peach'). He'd had an office job for a while, too, which he'd also hated.

'I lasted even less time there,' he said. 'Though it was much better paid than anything else I'd done, and there were opportunities for career progression and so on. My uncle was furious when I resigned.'

'How long did you stay?'

'Only about three weeks.' He smiled. 'And by "resigned", I really mean went out for my lunch break and never returned.'

'You didn't!'

'Afraid so. I know. Not great behaviour. I didn't even intend to, really. I went out for my sandwich, and then found my legs carrying me further and further away. I ended up getting on the train and going to the seaside.'

'*Nathaniel!*' She was laughing, enjoying being able to scold him. 'But you're a teacher now?'

'Who told you that?'

'One of the girls at the cafe.' She felt herself blushing.

'Well, she's right.'

'What do you teach?'

He paused for a moment. 'Philosophy.'

He was even cleverer than she'd realized, then. 'Adults or children?' she said.

'Both, actually. But I'd rather talk about you – I'm very boring. Tell me something else about yourself.'

She had to bring up Judith at this point. But incredibly, he didn't seem perturbed; just exclaimed that she looked far too young to be mother to a twelve-year-old. She didn't mind the line from him.

'I don't like him,' Judith said, a few weeks later. 'Why's he round here all the time?'

'Sweetheart, he's hardly ever round here. He's only been over *twice*, for God's sake.'

'I don't like him.'

'Don't you want me to be happy?' Stephanie said, playing her trump card.

Judith considered. 'Yes, I do. But there are other ways.'

'You don't know him, love. You haven't given him a chance.'

'I have,' Judith said. 'He has chest hair coming out of the top of his shirt, and he doesn't know how to talk to children.'

'If you're rude to him again,' Stephanie said, 'I'll take away your Game Boy.'

Judith narrowed her eyes and left the room.

When Nathaniel stayed over for the first time, Stephanie was nervous; she hadn't slept with anyone for a long time. Judith was having a sleepover at Megan's, and Stephanie knew she should get it over with now; there might not be another opportunity for a while. She was half afraid he would turn her down when she suggested he come over that evening ('and bring a toothbrush', she added awkwardly), but he had accepted calmly, as though it weren't such a big deal.

It was, though. She'd been on a clandestine shopping trip in her lunch break to buy new underwear – dark purple, matching; rather cheap, but it couldn't be helped – and spent a long time shaving her legs, underarms and bikini line, the first time she'd bothered in ages. The whole process felt clinical and absurd.

She was so anxious when he started kissing her after dinner that she felt sick. But he took things slowly, and once they were in her bedroom, she began to relax.

As he pushed her back onto the bed, he said, 'I wish this was your first time. I wish I was the only one.'

'Me too,' she said. No man had ever been this romantic with her, not even Sean in the very early days.

All the same, she was afraid the moment before he entered her, though she couldn't say why. She tried to touch his face, but he gently took hold of her wrists and moved her arms back to rest on either side of her head. He kept his hands on her wrists as he pushed into her and she couldn't think at all any more, not even to be afraid. He looked down at her, stilling for a moment. Time stretched itself out before them.

Then he began to move again, and Stephanie had a strange sense of being taken over, that something formless and unseen was moving inside her as well as his body. There was an ache low in her stomach but it became warmth, moving up into her chest and then into her head, making her ears ring.

When he came, shuddering and easing himself down on top of her, she felt his breath hot in her ear as he whispered, 'Thank God I found you.'

Pinned there beneath him, her limbs trembling and her thighs wet, she said, 'Yes.'

*

Later, when they were lying with their arms round each other, he said, 'What do you think is meant for us, Stephanie?'

Her head on his chest – slightly uncomfortable – she said, 'I don't know.' She wasn't sure if he meant *us* as a couple or *us* as the human race, and was waiting for more of a prompt.

He said, 'Do you think we're meant to be miserable?'

'I don't know,' she said again. 'Are we *meant* to be anything?'

'You're an extraordinary person. I hate seeing you so unhappy.'

She raised her head. 'Who says I'm unhappy?'

'Anyone can see it. Anyone who sees you properly, that is.'

He saw her, she thought. She said, 'The last few years haven't been easy,' and was surprised to find a thickness in her throat.

'I know, my darling,' he said. 'I know.'

'I love Judith to bits, but – she's a handful. And I haven't had any help.'

He pulled her closer. 'But you've got me now. Haven't you?'

She nodded against his chest, closing her eyes.

4

A few weeks later, Nathaniel suggested introducing her to one of his friends.

'Thomas has heard so much about you,' he said. 'But it's possible he thinks I've made you up. My reputation's on the line.'

'Your reputation as what?' Stephanie said. 'A ladies' man?'

'Why have you adopted an ironic tone?'

Stephanie looked forward to this further glimpse into Nathaniel's life. There had been tantalizingly few so far, but this wasn't surprising given that he had no family left and had moved around a lot. She was excited about meeting Thomas, even if it did mean another argument with Judith.

'We were supposed to be spending Saturday *together*,' Judith said.

'But love, we hadn't arranged anything.'

'I'm your *daughter*. We're not supposed to "arrange" things. You're supposed to want to spend time with me. But now you're gadding off with him again!'

Where on earth, Stephanie wondered, did she pick up expressions like this? She said, 'It's only for a couple of hours.'

'You're not supposed to leave me alone at *all*. I'm only a kid. I might set the house on fire.'

'You probably won't even have been awake long by the time I'm back. I'll be home by twelve. Then we'll do something nice in the afternoon. OK? Rent a film and – make our own popcorn,' she added in a burst of inspiration. This seemed to mollify Judith, but she still went off muttering about 'that man'.

Stephanie arrived at the cafe – a rival establishment – a little early, but Nathaniel was already there, along with a man with fair hair, wearing a white, long-sleeved shirt even though it was the weekend. He seemed to be regarding her rather seriously as Nathaniel introduced them. Stephanie reached out to shake hands, made formal by Thomas's own air of polite reserve.

The conversation did not flow easily, but Nathaniel appeared untroubled by this, sitting back comfortably in his chair with his arms folded. Thomas asked Stephanie about her job and about Judith, with an awkwardness that discouraged long answers.

'How long have you two known each other?' Stephanie said when there was a lull.

'More than fifteen years,' Thomas said.

'Where did you meet?'

She saw Thomas glance at Nathaniel before he answered. 'Church.'

'Church?' She didn't mean to parrot him in this stupid way, but Nathaniel had never mentioned religion before.

'We went to the same meetings,' Thomas said. 'In London. Many years ago.'

She would have liked to know more about this, but it was always difficult to talk about religion. 'You're from London too?' she said instead. 'How come you both ended up here?'

There was a short silence.

Thomas said, 'We all needed a change. It was the right time.'

Stephanie was confused by his use of 'all', but she didn't have a chance to ask about it because Nathaniel was speaking.

'There wasn't much to keep us in London,' he said. 'We'd outgrown it.'

Stephanie nodded, though she had only been to London twice, and it had seemed vast and sprawling to her – a place that would swallow you up before you outgrew it.

'Where do you live round here?' she asked Thomas.

'A little way from Fosswick,' he said. 'On the moors. It's a bit secluded, but very beautiful.'

Sounds cold, Stephanie thought. She knew Nathaniel lived near Fosswick as well, though she hadn't visited his house; it was easier for him to stay at her place, because of Judith. She asked Thomas, 'Do you go walking a lot, if you live on the moors?'

'When I have time.'

Another long pause. She said, trying for playfulness, 'What was Nathaniel like when he was younger, then?'

Thomas seemed at a loss. 'He was – like he is now,' he said.

Stephanie knew when she was defeated. As the silence opened up again, she began to feel annoyed with Nathaniel for contributing so little. But at that moment, he reached across the table and took her hand, saying to Thomas, 'Well? Do you see what I mean? See why I love her?'

Stephanie felt her face growing hot with pleasure, though she tried to appear calm.

Thomas got to his feet not long afterwards, murmuring something about errands. 'It was nice to meet you,' he said to Stephanie.

'I'll see you in the usual place,' Nathaniel said. 'Forty minutes, OK?'

'No problem.' Thomas nodded to Stephanie and left.

She remained quiet for a few moments, thinking Nathaniel might tell her he loved her again, or begin to explain a bit more about his friend. But Nathaniel seemed content to sit in silence, staring thoughtfully down at his mug.

Eventually, Stephanie said, 'I didn't know you went to church. Do you believe in God, then?'

He put his head on one side. 'Don't you?'

'No. At least – I don't know.'

'Perhaps you haven't given yourself space to think about it.'

'Perhaps not.' She reached for her handbag. 'Anyway, I'd better go. I've left Judith on her own.'

He put his hand out to still her. 'Just a little longer. Come for a quick walk with me. Judith will be alright.'

They left the cafe and wandered up the hill to sit on their usual bench, Nathaniel holding her hand.

He said, 'Look at these people.'

She looked, but couldn't see what had drawn such a

tone of despair from him. One or two of the passers-by were overweight, perhaps. Some were badly dressed.

Then she got it. 'They all look so miserable, don't they?'

'Exactly.' She could tell he was pleased with her. 'And why?'

'I don't know. They – don't like their lives, I suppose.'

'Yes. They're worried about money, their relationships, their jobs. They're suffering, but there's no purpose behind it. Without a greater purpose we're just animals, dressed in our people clothes, trying to forget our dying bodies.'

She shivered in the cold wind. He didn't sound like himself. Must be the philosophy teacher coming out.

He put his arm around her and pulled her closer. 'I'm sorry to talk like this. I just feel sorry for them. For everyone who's unhappy and can't change it.'

She leaned her head on his shoulder.

'I don't want you to waste your life,' he said.

She was startled at this, and turned to look at him. 'Well, I don't either. But like you said, there are lots of things you can't change.'

'What if *you* could change things for yourself in a way that other people can't? What if there was a way for you to be happy?'

She kept her eyes on his face.

He said, 'If you were offered an opportunity for real happiness, wouldn't you be mad not to take it?'

'Well – I suppose so,' she said.

'I see you, Stephanie. Remember that.'

She nodded.

'And I love you,' he said. 'I've loved you from the moment you came over to wipe up my coffee spill.'

'So romantic.'

He laughed. 'I don't know why I haven't said it before – only I thought you must know.'

'I love you too.' Incredible, she thought, to say these words to a man and realize that for the first time you truly meant them.

'I'm not going to let you waste your life. You're too extraordinary for that.'

She looked ahead and tried to imagine the tunnel walls coming down, life spreading out before her in a wide, glorious sweep.

Nathaniel's hand rested on her shoulder. 'Are you ready for something better, my love?'

'I think so.'

'I want to take care of you,' he said. 'If you'll let me. I'm going to do everything in my power to give you the happiness you deserve. I feel so lucky to have met you.'

She leaned forward to kiss him. 'I'm the lucky one,' she said.

5

There was no getting away from him these days. Judith could always sense him before he arrived: a prickle in the air, her mum taut as a stretched string.

He brought them both presents. For her mum, a thin little book with a glossy cover that she wouldn't let Judith read; two long skirts, one dark blue and the other green, to replace the jeans she usually wore; and a silver ring which she now wore on the fourth finger of her right hand.

For Judith, there was a hairbrush made of carved wood to look like a hedgehog, and a skipping rope with purple-painted handles.

'Honestly,' Judith said to Megan as they sat on the steps behind the canteen. 'A *skipping rope*? He'll be getting me a doll's house next.'

'Or tin soldiers,' Megan said. 'Or one of those big hoops to push along.' (They were doing the Victorians in History that term.)

'He says modern society's broken,' Judith said. 'He says people have lost their way. And now Mum's taken away my Game Boy.' She stopped. The loss was still too raw to talk about.

'It's pretty, though,' Megan said, picking up the skipping

rope to inspect it. 'I love purple. You know my purple jeans? It matches them.'

'You can have it if you want,' Judith said.

'Better not. He might ask about it next time he's round.'

Judith's mum was different now, bursting with energy, whirling round the flat, dusting, cleaning and polishing. Judith was amazed at how neat the place had become.

'I didn't know the carpet was this colour,' she commented in honest wonder, but for some reason this made her mum snap at her.

Stephanie had also started insisting Judith take off her shoes at the door when she came home.

'You've never made me do that before,' Judith said.

'It stops you walking dirt in,' Stephanie said.

'Since when do you care about that?'

'Since always,' Stephanie said firmly. 'If you're lazy about the small things, who's to say you won't be lazy about the big things as well?'

Judith had no answer for this.

On the days when he was expected, her mum put on her rubber gloves and apron as soon as she got back from the cafe and set to work, and if she had any time left after cleaning she would rush to the kitchen and set about chopping vegetables or baking a cake – he apparently had a sweet tooth.

On the days when he didn't come round, her mum seemed to flag, and sometimes Judith would come home from school to find her sitting on the sofa staring into space – she didn't even have the TV on.

'Mum?' Judith would say. 'Are you alright?'

'Just a bit tired,' her mum would reply.

One night, when the whole flat seemed to be crackling with her mum's excitement, Judith was surprised to hear he wasn't expected. Her mum had made spaghetti carbonara, Judith's favourite. They sat at the kitchen table for once, and her mum had even bought Judith a can of Coke.

'Just as a one-off, OK?' Stephanie said.

Judith nodded and quickly cracked it open before her mum could change her mind. She was hoping Stephanie had come to her senses and there would be no more of him. Perhaps this was their way of celebrating.

She realized her mum was staring at her. 'What?'

'There's something I need to talk to you about,' her mum said.

Judith saw her take a deep breath, her chest moving up and down beneath the thin blouse.

Stephanie said, 'I want you to know something. I want you to know that everything I do is for us. For you and me. To give us a better life.'

Judith clasped her hands around the chilled can, making herself keep them there as long as possible before the cold became unbearable.

Her mum said, 'There are some things you might not understand as a child. Things you might never have thought about.'

Was she talking about sex? Judith wondered. She very much hoped not.

Her mum said, 'Sometimes you can't see what's really important until someone else shows you. Having a sense of purpose, for instance. A sense of community. Feeling safe and loved.'

Judith felt her face twitch into a frown, as though her facial muscles were one step ahead of her brain. Her mum sounded like she was reciting from memory, like the time Judith had had to learn that poem about a cat for school and perform it in front of the class. She'd been so nervous about forgetting the words or making a mistake that she'd rushed through it without any expression and got a rubbish mark.

Her mum said, 'You might get used to managing without the things you need, and managing without people who care about you. But that doesn't mean it's a good way to live.'

Judith kept quiet. She was finding this difficult to follow.

'If there was a way to be happy,' her mum said, 'wouldn't you be mad to ignore it? If you have an opportunity for a better life, shouldn't you take it?'

Why was she making everything into a question, Judith thought, but never waiting for an answer? 'I like my life,' she tried to say. The words felt too big for her throat. She took a sip of Coke, swallowing carefully. The cold burned.

'We're going on a special trip,' her mum said. 'A day out.'

'With him?'

'With Nathaniel, yes. There's something he needs to show us.'

'What?'

'You'll see.'

'I don't want to,' Judith said. But her voice was so weak
it seemed to dissolve in the air.

After

On the final leg of her journey home from the prison, Judith listened to her iPod and tried not to think about her mother. It had started to rain shortly after she'd boarded the bus, and now she watched the streaks of water travel down the window and remembered the end of the Ark, as she always did when it rained.

My mother sleeps a lot in the daytime, Moses wrote in one of his letters. *Nobody mentions my father.*

Judith disliked buses. If she had any money, she would take taxis everywhere. She distrusted what it did to your mind, being in a confined space with other people. It made you part of the group; allowed you to erase yourself.

A few years ago, sitting on the bus back to her gran's one evening, she'd seen a girl being harassed by three men. It was around 6 p.m., not even dark, but the men were drunk. Perhaps later they blamed it on that, but in Judith's opinion, alcohol only freed people to do what they secretly wanted to do sober.

The girl had bare shoulders, wore a black strappy top. It looked good on her. They'd say she was asking for it, obviously. When the bus stopped at traffic lights, the men moved in from their position at the back of the bus, two of them sliding into the seat behind the girl and the other taking the empty space next to her.

Judith watched carefully. The girl didn't look round, but her body had taken on a rigidity, like a spider freezing when it knows you're watching. They can still see you, Judith wanted to tell her.

'Alright?' one of the men behind the girl said.

He slid a finger, insolent and invasive, beneath the strap of her top and she shuddered.

Judith tried not to stare. She was acutely aware of the other passengers, a scattering of men and women, young, elderly, middle-aged. She waited for one of them to intervene, knew instinctively they would not.

'Where are you going, darling?' the man beside the girl said.

She replied too softly for Judith to hear.

He put his arm around her shoulder and she shrugged a little, a half-hearted attempt to shake him off, and then leaned away from him as far as she could, resting her shoulder against the window.

'You got a boyfriend, love?' the man said.

Minutely, the girl nodded.

'Lucky bloke.' His hand on her shoulder was slipping down now, over her exposed collarbone. She tried to pull away from him, but there was nowhere for her to go.

'Please,' she said. 'Don't.'

The men laughed, and Judith saw – as everyone else on the bus surely saw – that by acknowledging at last what was going on, the girl had sealed her fate.

'Come on,' the man said in a wheedling voice. 'Be a bit more friendly.'

Judith had a bottle of vodka in her satchel which she was planning on smuggling up to her bedroom when she got back to her gran's. For reassurance, she opened her bag and closed her hand around the cool bottle-neck. Then she got up, and moved over to the group of men.

'Leave her alone,' she said to the man with his arm round the girl.

The two in the seat behind were looking away now, as if trying to absent themselves from the situation, but the third faced Judith belligerently.

'Jealous?' he said. The girl had managed to twist away from him whilst he was looking at Judith, ducking out from under his arm, and now it lay limply between them.

'Go and sit somewhere else,' Judith said to him.

'We'll come and sit with you, shall we?' he said, turning to his friends, trying for a laugh.

And Judith, because she didn't give a shit, swung the bottle into his face and broke his nose.

They'd almost pressed charges, which had amazed her. Her gran had been furious, and for once not with her. Judith liked to think afterwards it was the incandescent rage of this elderly woman that had diverted the CPS from its righteous course. Nevertheless, Judith felt herself more closely observed after that; she wondered if her gran suspected her of carrying within her the same seed of violence as her mother.

*

It was still drizzling when Judith got off the bus. She put her hood up and walked home with her head down. She felt rough, as she often did after a prison visit: that drained, pale feeling she associated with a temazepam hangover or with having cried for a long time. She wanted a drink, but her gran would be waiting for her in the kitchen when she got back, with her careful, 'Was she well?' and her ritual offering of cheese on toast. So there would be no opportunity to sneak upstairs for a while. I could ask for a sherry, Judith thought desperately. A soothing, medicinal sherry . . . ?

She was only metres away from the house when she spotted the woman at the gate. For a second, her heart flared in her chest. The spectre of bad news, the threat of catastrophe, was always with her. She saw it again, the bloodstain on the dirt floor. It seemed to follow her wherever she went; could leak into her eyes at any moment and turn the world red.

But the woman didn't have the look of the police about her – too relaxed, the way she was leaning against the wall like that – and Judith hadn't caught a glimpse of a social worker for years now, not since first going to live with her gran. Besides, she reminded herself, she was twenty-two now. Nobody was coming to take her away.

The woman was blocking the gate, so Judith had to stop and say, 'Can I help you?'

The woman said, 'Hello, Judith.' She was wearing jeans; but fitted, expensive-looking ones in dark denim, definitely not the kind Judith wore. She had a confident, vaguely official air about her.

Judith had no choice but to say hello back and wait for more.

'Grim day, isn't it?' the woman said, giving her a smile. 'I'm glad I ran into you.'

Ran into me? Judith thought. You're waiting outside my house.

'You're looking extremely well,' the woman said.

'Thanks.'

'My name's Jo Hooper,' she said, holding out her hand. Judith took it: cool and dry. 'I was hoping we could have a quick chat,' the woman added. 'Is there somewhere we can go, out of the rain?'

'A chat about what?' Judith said. If she really were being given bad news, she would rather have it out here in the rain, not in her gran's sitting room over tea and cake.

The woman said, 'Well, about you, mostly. I'd love to hear how you're getting on. How's your mum doing these days?'

And finally, the penny dropped. Judith pushed past her, but the woman pursued her to the front door and stood there whilst Judith struggled to get it open.

'Go away,' Judith said.

'There are a lot of people out there who care about you, Judith,' the woman said, her voice gentle and reasonable. It reminded Judith of Nathaniel and made her shudder. 'People who've wondered about you over the years, and would love to know how you and your mum are getting on.'

Judith had unbolted the deadlock and was wrestling with the stiff latch.

The woman said, 'Your mum was a victim too, Judith. Plenty of people would say she wasn't responsible for her actions.'

Why did they always wheel this line out, Judith thought, as though it were a defence and not the most damning thing of all? She opened the door and flung herself through it, allowing herself the small luxury of turning back at the last minute. 'Why don't you fuck off?' she said to Jo Hooper. Then she slammed the door.

II

The Ark

1

They'd been waiting all morning in the schoolroom. All week, they'd been waiting, but these last few hours seemed the longest. The mist had crept up on them sometime before daybreak. The moors were hidden from sight and only the tops of the forest trees were visible. The world was white and its walls looked solid.

'It's cloudy, like heaven,' Abigail had said at breakfast.

Moses had kept quiet. He didn't think heaven would be so cold and dark.

As they waited, they discussed the newcomers.

'They'll look different to us,' Ezra said.

'How?' they asked him.

'They just will,' Ezra said. 'They're from Gehenna.' When he saw them all looking at him, he added, 'They'll be impure.'

'What does that mean?' Abigail said.

Ezra said, 'Impurity has its own colour.' He sounded like he was repeating something the prophet had said, so no one could argue with him. Ezra was the son of the prophet and Ruth, so he was especially close to God. Sometimes, before he could stop the thought, this made Moses feel sorry for God.

When they heard the car, the children crept out of the

schoolroom to get a better look. It was hard to see much through the mist, but Moses caught a flash of bright-red hair in the back seat before the prophet got out of the car and sent them away. Moses hadn't even known hair came in that colour.

In the kitchen of the big house, when they were finally allowed in, Moses stared at the girl's hair until she caught him looking and scowled. He wondered if red hair could be a mark of the devil. No one had spoken about it, but he wouldn't judge. He carried his own mark.

The red-haired girl hardly said a word during lunch. Moses knew this because he was sitting next to her. He had jumped in quickly before Abigail and Mary and taken the seat beside her.

'*Moses*,' Abigail said, 'she doesn't want to sit next to you. She's a *girl*. She wants to sit next to us.'

They all looked to the girl for clarification, but she provided none, so Moses stuck out his tongue at Mary and Abigail and stayed where he was.

When the sisters had stomped away, Moses tried to get the girl's attention by using her name. The prophet always said that names were important. The girl's name was Judith, which Moses liked; it wasn't in the Bible, but it was holy. Judith the slayer. The prophet had told them the story once. Sometimes killing was necessary, even glorious, if done in the name of God.

He said, 'Judith, I like your hair.'

She didn't reply.

'Judith, would you like some orange squash?'

Still nothing. Moses studied her carefully. He said, 'Judith, I could get you a whole glass of orange squash if you want.' When this too got no response, he added kindly, 'Don't you have orange squash in Gehenna? It's very nice.'

Finally, the red-haired girl turned to him.

'Shut up,' she said.

Moses didn't speak for the rest of the meal.

That afternoon, they left to go back to Gehenna.

Moses followed his mother from the dining room to the kitchen and back again as she cleared up.

'When will they visit again?' he said.

'I don't know, sweetheart,' his mother said. 'Soon, I think.'

'Tomorrow?'

'Probably not tomorrow, Moses.'

'Next week?'

'Perhaps,' she said. 'If all goes well and they let God fully into their hearts, they might come and live with us here forever. Just be patient.'

'Forever?' Moses' eyes were wide. 'From Gehenna?'

Ruth's entrance in a clatter of plates and cutlery prevented him learning any more.

'You shouldn't answer all his questions, Rachael,' Ruth said to Moses' mother. 'You'll encourage him to whisper.'

Moses went outside, ashamed to have got his mother into trouble. The mist was beginning to clear and the other children were playing Jericho on the moors, but he didn't think they'd let him join in. It was always Ezra or Mary who started it, but the others didn't help, not even Peter, his own brother.

He went instead towards the forest to show them he didn't care. The others thought the devil was hiding in the darkness but Moses knew better. The devil was everywhere, and he was no more likely to approach you in the forest than out on the moors, or in your bedroom.

The forest belonged to him. Even in the daytime, it was dark. The branches at the edge were so thick and so close to the ground that you had to bend down and crawl in between the gaps. Inside, the branches began to thin and die because no light could reach them. Moses liked to watch the little wiggles of sunshine trying to work their way through near the tops of the trees; they soon faded and fell apart.

He pushed through to his usual clearing and sat down on a tree stump. Judith and her mother would be out in Gehenna again by now, back in the town. Moses tried to picture them there and failed. He had never seen a town, but he knew they were places where lots of people lived together in houses like the big house and the small house. There was killing and stealing and everyone was full of sin. In Gehenna, they lived without purpose and without truth.

Some days, when he had walked as far as he could across the moors and reached the highest point, he would stand and stare down into the valley. He knew the town was there because that was what he'd been told. On the clearest days, he thought he could almost see the outline of houses. Eventually, Peter and Ezra and Jonathan would join their fathers and go and work in the town amongst the sinners. But you had to be strong to do that, complete against the devil. Moses could never leave.

2

When the red-haired girl and her mother did come back three weeks later, they had cases and bags with them.

Moses had felt certain something was about to happen because the grown-ups made them move bedrooms the day before, so that Ruth could move into their old room in the big house. That meant Ruth's bedroom in the small house would be empty.

Now Moses and Peter were sharing with the other boys. They had a mattress on the floor because Jonathan and Ezra wouldn't give up the bunk beds, but Moses didn't mind. He and Peter went top-to-tail for more space. He found it comforting to wake from a nightmare to find his face pressed against the warmth of his brother's calves.

Another reason he knew something was coming: the wind had dropped. Everything was very still and soft, and it excited Moses with its strangeness. Even in summer the wind hardly rested, the breeze rippling over the heather and grass like a snake. When the wind was at its strongest, you had to stay inside. It could carry you off your feet, and make the tops of the trees bend and jerk. Sometimes it sounded like a huge fire, rushing and roaring around you. They always knew when it was coming because the white cloud bank built at the edge of the forest. Then they retreated inside, closed all the windows and doors and listened to the wind as it burst against the house.

Once when Moses was very young, the wind picked him up and threw him against the side of the barn. When he woke up, he'd been taken inside and everyone was praying. Moses had never seen his father cry before. They asked Moses if he had seen the face of God but Moses couldn't remember. Perhaps he had whilst he was sleeping.

The prophet said, 'Didn't I tell you that if you believed, I would show you God's glory?'

Only a true prophet could raise a child from the dead. Elijah had done it once; so had Elisha. Now Nathaniel.

Where the wind had gone now, Moses did not know. God might have rolled it up in the palm of His hand. The long grass on the moors appeared to be sleeping. Moses watched and waited, knowing God was preparing the way.

When he saw Judith getting out of the car again, he had to force himself to stay still and not run over to her. She didn't seem angry this time. She was frowning, but looked as though she was deep in thought. Perhaps she was reflecting upon God's glory. The woman with brown hair went straight into the small house with the prophet. Moses wanted to go over to Judith but he felt too shy. He had to watch as Mary and Abigail claimed her, taking her bags and leading her off to the big house. Moses trailed up the stairs after them, keeping at a safe distance. He stopped outside the door of the girls' room and listened to what they were saying.

'This is your bed,' said Mary's voice. 'And you can put your things here. We share all our clothes.'

'Even *knickers*?' Judith said. In the corridor, Moses felt himself blushing.

'No. Not underwear,' Mary said, her voice chilly. 'But dresses and blouses we share. And tights.'

'I want to wear my own clothes,' Judith said.

'You can't,' Abigail said, but she sounded kinder than Mary. 'They're going to throw them away.'

Moses pictured Judith's scowl but didn't dare look round the door.

'These are the books we have,' Abigail said. 'You can share them now.'

A silence.

'I'm not interested in Bible stories,' Judith said at last. 'And flower books. I have my own books, but he wouldn't let me bring them.'

'They were probably full of sin,' Mary said.

Judith didn't reply to this. After a moment, she said, 'Why can't we wear trousers? I want my jeans back.'

'Girls don't wear trousers,' Abigail said.

'That's stupid.'

'Don't say that,' Mary said, 'or the devil will come for you.'

Moses waited in the barn with the others whilst Judith and her mother were taken into the prayer room. Jonathan and Peter were sitting with their backs against opposite walls, bouncing a ball between them, but Ezra kept deliberately getting in the way, so the game became keeping the ball away from Ezra. Abigail and Mary had retreated into the corner to talk in hushed voices.

'If they were chosen all along,' Jonathan said, hurling the ball over Ezra's head, 'why weren't they in the Ark already?'

It was a bad throw, and it hit the wall next to Peter and bounced towards Moses. Moses caught it without really meaning to, and threw it to Peter, who tossed it back to him again. Excited to be included, Moses threw it carefully, underarm, to Jonathan.

'You sound like you're whispering,' Ezra said to Jonathan. He was out of breath and angry, but Moses could see it was about the game, not about what Jonathan had said. 'You sound like the devil's speaking through you.'

'I just wondered,' Jonathan said quickly. 'I wasn't whispering.'

'It must have been what God wanted,' Moses said, to help him out. 'He wanted them to take longer to get here.'

'So might there be more chosen people out there?' Jonathan said.

Moses was pleased to see Jonathan was looking at him for an answer. 'God might not have told the prophet yet.'

This seemed to satisfy Jonathan, but Ezra said, 'You don't know anything, Moses. You're marked by the devil.'

The others were quiet now. No one was looking at Moses, which was good, because he felt his face going red, the good side matching the bad side. Jonathan threw the ball to Ezra, who threw it to Peter. Moses hovered for a while in case he was included again, but the others ignored him.

He went to sit by himself in the opposite corner to Mary and Abigail, drawing up his knees and wrapping his arms round them. It gave him some comfort, a bit like being hugged. He wished he could go and find his mother because he liked to talk to her best, but they'd said he was too old to do that now.

From where he was sitting, he could still hear the boys' conversation.

'God sent her as a reward for the prophet's struggles,' Ezra was saying. When Peter made a scoffing noise, Ezra added, 'It's true. I heard my mother say it. And she's young.'

'Esther's young, too,' Peter said.

'Yes, but the Lord closed her womb,' Ezra said.

They all fell silent at this. Moses, too, considered the matter. They had never been told what Esther had done to deserve this punishment. Moses' mother had said to him once it was the greatest affliction for a woman, and although Moses had barely understood the word 'affliction', it fixed in his mind as something mysterious and ancient and sad.

All the same, he sometimes envied Esther. Her punishment was invisible, but he took his everywhere he went, the stain on his face that the others no longer noticed but never forgot.

When Judith and her mother came out of the prayer room with the prophet, Moses was waiting outside the door.

The prophet said, 'Hello, Moses.'

Moses said hello back. It was thrilling to be spoken to by the prophet.

Then the prophet said, 'Don't stare, Moses,' so Moses directed his eyes to the floor.

The prophet said to Judith's mother, 'Let's go and get you settled in,' and she nodded. She looked back at Judith and said, 'Go and play with the others now, Judith. OK? I'll be back soon.'

Judith stood where she was. She said, 'I don't want to.'

Her mother said, 'Judith—'

And Judith said over the top of her, 'I want to stay with you.'

Her mother hovered where she was and Moses started to worry he would lose his chance. But then the prophet said, in a sharper voice than before, 'You can't take up all your mum's time, Judith. She has things to do. You'll see her again soon, so there's no need to worry.' Moses thought it was kind of Nathaniel to add the last part. The prophet was always kind. It was painful to him to punish people, but better to do that than to give up their souls to the devil.

Moses was so busy thinking about the prophet's kindness that he almost didn't hear him say, 'You'll look after Judith, won't you, Moses?'

He caught the words just in time, and swelled with pride. 'I will.'

'Good lad,' the prophet said, and for a moment his hand rested lightly on the top of Moses' head. Moses felt the love of God moving within him, despite his sin, despite his mark.

Then the prophet and Judith's mother went up the stairs together, his hand on her back, and Moses and Judith were left alone together in the hallway.

Moses searched for a suitable conversation topic. He said, 'Do lots of people in Gehenna have hair like yours?'

'What the fuck's Gehenna?' Judith said.

'Gehenna is the burning place,' Moses said. 'The valley of the son of Hinnom. What's the Fuck?'

Judith paused thoughtfully for a moment, then said, 'Why don't you ask him? Ask Nathaniel. He'll explain it better than me.'

Moses watched her carefully. He sensed a trap, but wasn't certain of its nature. He said, checking for her reaction, 'I don't think I will ask him.'

Judith shrugged and seemed to lose interest.

Moses said, 'You're not like Mary and Abigail.'

She didn't answer.

He said, 'Are other girls in Gehenna like you, or like them?'

'Go away,' Judith said.

'Do you want me to show you the forest?'

'No.'

Still he lingered. 'Be careful if you go for a walk on the moors. You have to watch out for bogs and the devil. You can drown in a bog.'

She frowned. 'I hate the moors.'

'Why?'

'They're ugly.'

Moses considered this. He didn't think they were ugly, but he didn't know what Judith was comparing them with.

Besides, when you knew something as well as he knew the moors, it was hard to see it properly so you could explain it to someone else.

He said, 'Would you like to see the river, which is on the other side of the forest?'

'No.'

Moses thought for a bit longer. He could see he was approaching this from the wrong angle. 'What *would* you like to do?'

'I'd like,' Judith said, 'to go home.'

'This is your home,' he said. 'It's much nicer than Gehenna.'

'Shut up!' she said. 'How would you know, anyway? You haven't been. You don't even know what you're talking about, you stupid *freak*.'

Moses didn't know what a freak was, but it didn't sound complimentary. He said, 'If you fall into a bog on the moors, you'll drown.'

She looked at him. 'Shut up. You already said that.'

'I'm answering your question,' Moses said. 'About how I know what Gehenna is like. It's the same way that I know bogs can drown you. I've never actually seen anyone drown in a bog. But I know it's true.'

Judith didn't reply for a while. When she did, all she said was, 'Just go away. Go away, OK?' And when he didn't move, 'Alright. I will, then,' and pushed past him and went out of the front door. He followed her a little way, but then saw Mary and Abigail joining her as she went towards the big house. He decided that it would be better to stay away for now rather than risk the sisters saying something horrible to him in front of Judith.

He headed towards the forest alone instead, still thinking about her. He wasn't very happy with how their conversation had gone, but Judith had only been in the Ark a few hours so far. He would have plenty of time to make friends with her before the end times came.

3

Sometime after dawn the next morning Stephanie woke suddenly, unable to remember where she was. Slowly, the knowledge came back to her. The bare room, the mattress on the floor. Nathaniel's warmth beside her.

Careful not to wake him, she eased herself up and went across to the window, tiptoeing over the floorboards to avoid splinters. The glass was misted up from two people's breath in the small space, but she could still see out a long way across the moors. They were ragged and vast, stretching on until their edges blurred, sheets of grass struggling beneath gorse and bracken clumps, jagged rocks standing out at intervals like shark fins.

'Beautiful view, isn't it?' Nathaniel's voice behind her.

Stephanie turned. He'd raised himself up on one elbow on the mattress and she wondered how long he'd been watching her.

'It's a bit desolate,' she said.

'Well,' he said. 'Maybe. But don't you think there's a kind of cleanness to it? All the irrelevancies of modern life stripped away, all the ugliness gone.'

She looked again, trying to see it through his eyes. Yes – perhaps.

He beckoned to her and she rejoined him in bed,

enjoying the feeling of his arms around her, the firmness of his chest. He murmured into her hair, 'It makes me so happy to think I'll wake up next to you every day from now on.'

'Me too.' She let herself savour the moment a little longer, then said, 'I'd better go and check Judith's OK. She might be awake already.' She made to get up again, but he held her back.

'She'll be fine, my love. Mary and Abigail are looking after her.'

'I know. But it's her first night in a new place. It's a big change.'

'And a wonderful one,' he said. 'I hope you can still see that.'

She twisted to look at him. 'Of course.'

'You've done what's best for Judith. Don't forget that.'

'She might need a bit of time, though. She's angry with me.'

'She'll get over it much faster without you fussing over her.'

'I'm not *fussing*,' Stephanie said, mildly indignant.

He held up his hands. 'Sorry. Not fussing, then. Please don't kill me.' She was still sitting up, and he leaned forward to press his chest against her back, kissing her neck. 'I know you're a bit unsettled, darling. But I wish you could relax and enjoy the first morning of your new life. You might look back on this one day and wish you'd savoured it.'

She leaned back against him.

'You'll see Judith at breakfast,' he murmured. 'Very soon. Can you wait until then?'

Stephanie nodded at last, and allowed him to pull her down to the mattress again. His hands moved to toy with the buttons at the neck of the nightdress he'd given her, delicately slipping them open.

'Do we have time?' she said, afraid of Ruth's stern expression if they came down late for breakfast.

His hands stilled abruptly, and she was afraid she'd hurt him. He didn't reply for a moment, and when he did his voice was distant. 'I do wish you'd stop worrying so much.'

'Sorry.' She made a conscious effort to relax and focus on him. Sensing he still needed reassurance, she said, 'I'm so happy to be here, Nathaniel. It's just a bit new, that's all.'

'You'll adjust quickly enough,' he said, and his hands began to move again.

There wasn't much time to worry, anyway. Even a single day living amongst them made her realize how much time she'd wasted in her old life, often just slumped in front of the TV or staring into space. Every moment here was accounted for, from the thanksgiving meeting in the prayer room before breakfast, to the meal itself, served and cleared by the women (Stephanie soon noticed and got up quickly to help), to the work tasks allocated to them for the remainder of the morning whilst the men

– Thomas, Seth and Joshua – set off in the car for work. There was such a sense of energy and purpose here.

Still, she was relieved to hear she would be spending the morning with Nathaniel, since it was only her first full day in her new home. Judith had been led away to the barn with the other children for morning lessons, so at least Stephanie wouldn't have to worry about her for a few hours. Her daughter had been stony-faced at breakfast, seated between Mary and Abigail and wearing a new pink dress that clashed strikingly with her hair. Stephanie had tried to catch her eye, but Judith wouldn't look at her.

'I hope she's alright,' she said to Nathaniel now.

They were walking across the moors together, Stephanie wearing the brand-new, sturdy boots Nathaniel had bought her, and picking her way carefully around the boggy patches. The wind was calm, which was a relief; when Nathaniel had driven her up here the first time for that special lunch, it had been so strong she could barely stand up straight, and they'd had to battle through it to the safety of the house.

'Of course she's alright,' Nathaniel said. 'She'll have settled in before you know it. Trust me.' He took her hand. 'Listen, how did you find the meeting this morning? I know it's not the sort of thing you're used to.'

'It was OK,' she said cautiously. 'I think I felt more peaceful afterwards.' She stumbled on a hidden dip in the ground, and he caught her, holding her upright. They paused for a few moments, his arms around her. 'The thing is,' she said, 'I'm still not sure I believe in God.' She made a face. 'Sorry. I'm not saying I don't think I ever could, but I don't really feel it at the moment.'

'You don't have to apologize,' he said. 'All I want from you is honesty.' They began to walk again, turning their steps back towards the narrow track that led towards the two houses and barn. 'But I'll let you in on a secret,' he said. 'You said you felt peaceful afterwards, didn't you? When the rest of us talk about God, we don't mean anything very different to the feeling of peace you've just mentioned. The others talk about heaven and the Bible because that's how *they* come to it, that's how they've always understood it, the kind of calm you felt. The paths may be different, but the end point's the same. And there's nothing wrong with the path you're on. You're doing brilliantly. God will reveal Himself in whatever way is most suited to you.'

She tried to take it all in. She thought she understood, but she wished, not for the first time, that she were a bit cleverer, that she'd tried harder at school and college, got herself a proper education, so that following Nathaniel's train of thought wouldn't be such an effort. She'd never experienced this before – loving someone so much you were afraid of disappointing them.

They were back on the rough track now, and she was able to walk more easily without watching her step. As the houses came back into view, the dark outline of the forest rising up behind them, she said, 'Does anyone else ever come this way?'

'Outsiders?' he said. 'No, it's private property. We see

the odd walker from time to time, but they mostly don't make it this far.'

'It's lovely and remote,' Stephanie said. She remembered again the drive up here on her first visit, the way the mist had seemed to bleach the colour out of everything, giving the scene a mythic feel.

Before they went back inside, he said, 'One more thing. It might be best if you avoid mentioning any uncertainties about what we mean by God in front of the others. Don't worry if you feel you don't quite see things the way they do. Just trust me, OK?'

She nodded. 'Always.'

He led her into the smaller of the two houses and up the stairs to their room.

Afterwards, he said, 'There may come a time when you think of me as having saved you.'

'I already think that.'

'Oh, my love,' he said, touching her face. 'That's what I'm trying to say. I don't want you to think like that. The truth is, *you've* saved *me*. I didn't know I could love someone as much as I love you. I don't think I could manage without you now.'

'You won't ever have to,' she said.

It had been surprisingly easy in the end, unravelling her life. There weren't really any friends she needed to tell. No one close enough to care much. Stephanie wasn't quite sure how this had happened – she'd been popular once. But in any case, it hardly mattered now.

Her mother, too, had been easy to deal with. Stephanie had written her a letter, with Nathaniel's help, explaining that she and Judith were moving away to get a fresh start; and since their relationship had been difficult in recent years, Stephanie wrote, it would be best to make a clean break.

Her possessions were quickly disposed of. Some things she had given to charity shops, but other things Nathaniel had managed to sell – the TV, Judith's Game Boy, the antique oak dresser that had belonged to her grandmother. She was grateful to be able to make this small financial contribution since, as Nathaniel gently pointed out, he would be providing for her from now on. He had already made it clear that he didn't want her to carry on at the cafe, and she secretly agreed with him that it was beneath her.

'But the money won't last for long,' she said. 'I could try to find a proper job. Something more worthwhile.'

He reached out to touch her cheek. They were in bed, as they always seemed to be. One of the last evenings they spent in her flat. 'There's no need. I've said I'll take care of you. This is how it works, with our little group. We're a family, so we look after each another. If there's enough money, why should people work for the sake of it, when it doesn't make them happy? What's the point?'

It was strange, the idea that she wouldn't need to worry about money any more: that familiar grind of anxiety, the agonizing in the supermarket over what could be afforded, eyes always trained for the red flash of a special offer, all those coupons carefully saved – suddenly she was delivered from it all.

'But what will I give in return?' she said.

'You'll make me incredibly happy,' he said. 'Providing a roof over your head and food for you to eat seems a small price to pay in return.' He laughed. 'Especially as the food, I expect, will mostly be cooked by you. You've seen me in the kitchen.'

She grinned. 'I haven't forgotten the boiled egg.' This had been Nathaniel's single foray into the kitchen since they'd been together. He'd insisted on making her breakfast in bed after one of their nights together. She'd been amazed at the egg: it was as tough and rubbery as a bouncy ball.

'I didn't even know this could happen,' she'd said, pressing it between her fingers in fascination. 'How long did you give it?'

'Not sure,' he said vaguely. 'Maybe around twenty minutes. I didn't realize it was an exact science.'

She'd begun to laugh, but then, seeing his face, stopped herself. 'Let me cook us breakfast,' she said. 'I love cooking for you.' He'd laughed as well then, and allowed her to get up and go to the kitchen.

Her first task was preparing supper with the other women that evening. She met Rachael, Deborah and Esther in the kitchen; only Ruth was absent, having a meeting with Nathaniel in the prayer room. Stephanie was nervous to begin with, but it was difficult not to relax when Deborah and Rachael were so warm and friendly, chatting brightly to her about their daily routines and the weather on the moors as they chopped vegetables.

Esther, however, seated herself in the corner and barely spoke. Stephanie wondered if she was shy, or if she was always like this. Esther seemed a bit of an anomaly, about ten years younger than the other women, probably no older than Stephanie herself. Very pretty, too, with an unusual combination of blonde hair and dark eyes that Stephanie envied.

When she'd finished peeling and slicing the carrots, Stephanie tried to endear herself to Esther by asking if she wanted any help with the onions. But Esther simply murmured 'No, thanks,' without looking up from her chopping board.

'I'd love some help with these peppers, Stephanie,' Rachael said, at the same time as Deborah said, 'Do you think you might help me score the meat?'

Stephanie was startled, but Rachael and Deborah looked at each other and laughed.

'You see how in demand you are,' Rachael said as Stephanie went over to help chop the peppers.

She was relieved by the distraction provided when Judith came in, trailed by the boy called Moses with the birthmark staining half his face. He hovered in the doorway as Judith came forward.

Judith was scowling, but had clearly decided that ignoring her mum wasn't going to get her anywhere. She said, 'What are you doing?'

'Making supper, love,' Stephanie said. 'Do you want to help?'

Judith paused a moment. 'Alright.'

But Rachael said to Moses, 'Sweetheart, you know you're not supposed to be in here whilst we're cooking. Why don't you show Judith your books?'

'I don't want to see his books,' Judith said. 'We're not friends. He keeps following me.'

'We're not friends *yet*,' Moses said, prompting Judith to sigh with impatience.

'I want to stay with you, Mum,' she said, and Stephanie saw that underneath the sulkiness she was close to tears.

'Can't she stay with us just this once?' she said to Rachael. 'The move's been a bit of a shock for her.'

Rachael looked at Deborah. 'But Ruth—' she began, and Stephanie began to see that Judith would have to be sent out of the room. She felt like crying herself.

But then Esther spoke, addressing Judith. 'If you stay in the kitchen, Judith, will you be very good and do as we say?'

Looking resigned, Judith nodded.

Esther turned to Rachael and Deborah. 'Let her stay just this once. It's not easy when you first arrive.' She smiled for the first time. 'Remember what I was like?'

Rachael and Deborah seemed to consider for a moment. Then Rachael said to Moses, 'But you don't have the same excuse, darling. You're not new, are you? So be a good boy and run along and find Peter. See if he'll play cards with you.'

'He won't,' Moses said over his shoulder as he left, but he spoke without resentment.

Judith sat down on the workbench beside her mother. Stephanie wanted to give Esther a grateful smile, but Esther was looking down at her chopping board again. Stephanie slipped her arm round Judith, squeezing her tightly for a few moments. Usually, Judith would have resisted, but now she leaned into the embrace, burying her head in her mother's shoulder.

'Hey there,' Stephanie murmured. 'Hey. This isn't like you. It's alright, love.' She was talking to her softly, soothingly, as she hadn't since Judith was little. She felt her daughter's tears on her neck. 'Come on, Judith. Everything's fine.'

Judith got herself quickly under control, wiped her arm once across her face, and then sat in an uncharacteristically docile manner amongst the women as they continued to get the meal ready.

After dinner and the evening prayer meeting, Stephanie made a point of going upstairs to check on Judith as the girls got ready for bed, ignoring Nathaniel's disapproving look. She found her daughter showing Mary and Abigail how to do a handstand against the wall of their bedroom, and was relieved to see them all on friendlier terms.

She was afraid Nathaniel would reproach her again for 'fussing', but when she returned to the smaller of the two houses and joined him in their bedroom, he held out his arms to her. 'Seeing what a wonderful mother you are only makes me love you more,' he said.

As she fell asleep, she thought that perhaps there was some truth in what he said; perhaps she wasn't as bad a mother as she'd always thought. Although it was obviously going to take some time for Judith to adjust to living here, wouldn't she have a far better life overall? She would be safe and happy and fulfilled, just as Nathaniel promised, just as Stephanie herself already felt. Judith would be able to become the best version of herself. In Shipdale they'd only ever had each other, but here they would be part of a large, loving family, and Stephanie wouldn't be tired all the time, wouldn't be irritable, would always be patient and cheerful with her daughter. She hoped that Judith would be able to understand all this one day.

4

Moses breathed out a big gust of relief when the naming ceremony was announced, because this meant Judith and her mother would definitely be staying.

As the followers knelt together in the prayer room, the prophet revealed that the God-given name of Judith's mother was Sarah.

'Sarah, an obedient and virtuous woman,' the prophet said, placing his hand on her head. 'You are reborn.'

Moses almost wriggled with excitement as he waited to hear what Judith's God-given name would be. But when the prophet asked if she was ready to hear it, Judith said no.

Moses felt the room go still. A cold shudder in his chest; the feeling he got when he knew someone was going to have a session.

Judith's mother began to say, 'Judith, it's just a special—' but the prophet held up his hand and she fell silent.

When the prophet spoke again, his voice was soft. Moses knew this was the most dangerous voice of all. The prophet said, 'Do you refuse what God offers?'

'I have a name,' Judith said. 'It's Judith.'

The prophet's eyes closed and his mouth moved, so

Moses knew he was praying. He could feel Peter standing rigidly beside him and wanted to look at him, but he didn't dare take his eyes off the prophet.

Then the prophet's shoulders relaxed and he opened his eyes. He said, 'I thank God for His gift of patience. He's reminded me that shaking off the narrowness of Gehenna is no easy matter.' He smiled at them then, that gentle smile that Moses liked best. 'I'm going to pause things for now, and pray. We need to ask for God's help on this, OK? Sometimes He sends us a challenge, but there's always a reason for it.'

Moses delighted in the prophet's mercy, and the new warmth in his voice. At times like this he felt he didn't love anyone more, not even his own mother. As the adults began to drift away to go about their work tasks and the children went off to play, Moses saw Judith's mother, who was now called Sarah, go over to Judith and try to hug her. Judith pulled away. The prophet came over and said something and placed his hand on Judith's head, then he and Sarah went out of the room together. Moses heard their footsteps on the stairs overhead.

He looked at Judith. She was staring at the floor, her lips pressed tightly together. He thought he recognized the expression; it was what he did when he was trying not to cry. Even Mary and Abigail hadn't waited behind for her.

He asked God to make him brave.

He said, 'Hello, Judith.'

She didn't look at him. She said to the floor, 'Just as soon as they know where I am, social services will be round here. They'll be round here quick as a flash.'

Moses waited to see if she wanted to say more. When she didn't, he said, 'I like the name Judith.'

She looked up at him quickly, as if checking he was serious. After a moment, she said, 'I like it too.'

'It's a good one,' Moses said.

'Did you ever have a different name?'

Moses shook his head. 'I was born in the Ark, so I've always had the right name.'

'You've always lived *here? Really?*'

'Yes,' Moses said. 'Really.'

Judith absorbed this in silence. After a moment, she said moodily, 'I'm not having a different name.'

'But it's a nice thing,' Moses said, 'to be given a special name from God. It shows He's chosen you, like He chose all of us.'

'I don't believe in God,' Judith said.

Moses was so astonished he couldn't speak for a few moments. Then he said weakly, 'There's no such thing as not believing in God.' When she didn't reply, he pushed for reassurance. 'You do really.'

'I don't.'

'You must do,' Moses said, common sense reasserting itself. 'You wouldn't be alive if God hadn't made you. The moors wouldn't be here. Nothing would be here. The world would be empty.' Feeling slightly dizzy, he pursued this thought to its logical end. 'There would be no world at all.'

'Yeah, there would,' Judith said. 'Science did it.'

'What do you mean?' The only lessons they had in the schoolroom were Arithmetic, Reading and Writing, and

History, but Moses knew what Science was. It was what people called the way God had put their bodies together, and the way God had put the land and the sea and the sky together. It was the way God made everything work. Now he could see Judith's mistake.

'God made Science,' he said. 'Science doesn't exist without God.'

'Oh yeah? Prove it.'

This was a bizarre demand, and Moses looked at his new friend in increasing bewilderment. He could see she was on very dangerous ground, however many allowances the prophet said they must make for her. He wasn't sure how to help her, since she seemed unmoved by warnings about the devil. 'Heaven is high,' he said. 'We mustn't look into God's affairs.'

Judith shrugged and walked away from him and he saw that somehow, once again, he'd lost her.

Moses worried for the rest of the day about the problem of Judith's name, but when the prophet called them to a special meeting the next morning, he said that God had resolved the matter for them. Judith, it turned out, already *had* her true, God-given name. She had been living under it all along, as a sign that she and her mother were always destined for the Ark. It was further evidence, the prophet said, of the neatness of God's plan.

Moses was vastly relieved, and delighted with God. But he could see the others hadn't forgotten Judith's rebellion. Once again, Mary and Abigail didn't wait for her after the meeting, and nor did any of the other children. Judith's mother went over and touched Judith's shoulder, but then she followed the prophet out of the room.

Moses watched as Judith wandered outside on her own. He made himself wait a few moments before going after her.

She had walked a little way onto the moors. 'Hello,' he said as he approached.

She looked at him warily, but didn't seem as angry as before. She had tears on her face, though she wasn't crying properly.

Moses searched for a way to comfort her. 'Do you know the story of Judith?'

'What are you talking about?'

'Judith the slayer. It's a story from God. We learned it in the schoolroom when we were little.' Seeing that she was actually listening to him, he continued. 'Judith was a Jew, who were a good people once and now are full of sin like everyone else in Gehenna. The Jews were attacked by a wicked army, and Judith wanted to protect her people. She went and made friends with the general of the wicked army, and when he fell asleep in his tent – ' he paused, glad to have got her attention properly – 'she got a huge knife—'

'Did she stab him?' Judith said.

'Not quite.'

'Gouge out his eyes?'

'No. She cut off his head. And the blood of God's enemy went everywhere.'

'Cool,' Judith said.

'And then she carried the head back to her friends and they all celebrated.' Seeing that she was still listening, he capitalized on his advantage. 'Would you like to see the forest now? It's dark and scary. The other children are too scared to go in by themselves, even Peter. But I'm not, even though I'm nearly two years younger than him. He's the oldest, and Jonathan's the second oldest, and they're both scared.'

'How old are you?' Judith said.

'Twelve.'

'You're *twelve*?' she said. 'You seem younger. You seem like a baby.'

'I'm not,' Moses explained. 'I'm twelve.'

'*And* you're weird.'

He thought he was beginning to understand how people talked to each other in Gehenna. 'Your hair's weird,' he said, to make her feel at home, and gave her his best smile. 'But I also like your hair,' he added, because it was true. 'Shall I show you the forest?'

He expected her to tell him to shut up again, but suddenly she shrugged her shoulders: a big, loose shrug. Moses wanted to copy it immediately.

'Alright,' she said.

5

'I just want her to be happy,' Stephanie said to Rachael and Esther as they cleaned the kitchen a couple of days after the naming ceremony. 'But she's so angry with me at the moment.'

'I wouldn't worry,' Rachael said. 'Children are very adaptable, aren't they? Before long, she won't remember things were ever different.'

Esther, as usual, said nothing. Stephanie tried not to mind.

'Did your children have any problems when you first came here?' she said to Rachael, deliberately avoiding names since she couldn't remember which of the children, apart from Moses, actually belonged to Rachael. She was having enough trouble getting to grips with the adult relationships – Rachael married to Seth, Deborah to Joshua, Esther to Thomas, Ruth on her own. Specific families in the Ark were not clearly demarcated. Stephanie had found this strange at first, but now she was coming round to Nathaniel's way of thinking, that it was better this way; everyone belonged to one much larger family.

'All the children of the Ark were born here,' Rachael said.

Stephanie tried to hide her shock. 'They've never lived – on the outside?'

'No, they were born where they belong.'

Stephanie digested this in silence. 'It's harder for Judith,' she said at last. 'She misses Megan a lot. Her best friend from school.'

'It's healthier not to look back,' Rachael said. 'We have to cleanse ourselves of the old, negative influences. You must try not to talk about your former life. We're not supposed to.'

'I know. But there's bound to be an adjustment period, isn't there?' She paused, deciding to try out on Rachael an idea she'd been weighing up for a couple of days. 'I think if I took Judith back to see Megan next weekend it might cheer her up. Help her feel that life isn't so bad after all. And afterwards I could get her a treat in town, a hot chocolate or something. A bit of time just the two of us, to make her feel special.'

Rachael had been scrubbing away at the oven throughout their conversation, but now Stephanie noticed that she'd gone still.

Rachael said after a few beats, 'I don't think that's a very good idea.'

'I know it's important to cleanse ourselves of the old influences,' Stephanie said. 'But perhaps if Judith was allowed to do it a bit more gradually—'

'No,' Rachael broke in, gentle but firm. 'Take my advice and put that thought out of your head, Sarah. It won't do any good.'

Stephanie was surprised to be addressed by her new

name like this, so casually in the middle of a conversation. Nathaniel had given her the impression that it was a special extra name rather than a replacement, a name 'for best' as her mother might have said, and a symbol of her acceptance here. But there didn't seem to be a way of explaining this to Rachael without it being awkward.

She decided not to raise the subject of a visit to the town again until she was alone with Nathaniel, but somehow he seemed to know about it before she had a chance to mention it. When she was preparing supper that evening with Rachael, Deborah and Esther, he appeared in the kitchen with Ruth by his side.

'Can I borrow you for a few moments?' he said.

Stephanie wasn't alarmed until they reached the small house and it turned out he wasn't leading her upstairs to their bedroom but to the prayer room. Inexplicably, Ruth was still with them.

But when he told her to sit down, his voice was as gentle as ever. She sat on the wooden chair that was placed in the middle of the room and he pulled up another close to hers, sitting with his hands resting on her thighs. She would have been comforted by this gesture were she not acutely aware of Ruth standing stiffly in the doorway.

'Now,' Nathaniel said, looking at her intently. 'What's all this about you wanting to go back to the town?'

'Oh!' She rushed to reassure him. 'No, you've got the wrong end of the stick. I don't want to go back. I love it here.'

'Be honest with me,' he said. 'Be honest as you always

91

have been. What's all this you've been saying about taking Judith to visit her friend?'

So which of them had told him? Remembering Esther's silence in the kitchen, Stephanie thought she knew. 'Well, yes, I did, but I wasn't talking about *staying*. I just meant a quick visit, for Judith's sake. She's having a really hard time, Nathaniel. There's no one *I* want to see, obviously.' She felt tears rising in her, brought on by his obvious disappointment, by Ruth's silent, disapproving presence, and by the sense that she had been deliberately betrayed. 'This is all just a big misunderstanding,' she said, trying to keep her voice light.

'I think it must be, my love,' he said, and she was grateful for his softened tone.

She reached out to touch his face, deciding she didn't care that Ruth was watching. 'Of *course* I don't want to leave you,' she said. 'I love you.'

'And I love you,' he said. 'But you must see that you can't go and visit the town. The whole point is that we've saved you from that.'

Slowly, she did begin to see. 'You mean – I'm not supposed to leave here *ever*?'

He seemed taken aback by her question. 'But how can you have thought you could?'

She could only shrug helplessly.

He said, 'What would be the point in making the kind of commitment you've made if it could be so easily undone? I thought you knew all this from the start. How can you not have known?'

She tried to swallow down her dismay. 'I'm not sure.'

'You're not a prisoner here. Just say the word and I'll drive you and Judith back to town. Anytime you want. But you must see that once you've left you can't come back. That's how it works. You commit to this life totally or you don't commit at all. Your choice.'

'If I left, would I ever see you?'

He seemed unable to answer at once. 'I – no, you wouldn't. Half-measures don't work. I can't be only *half* with you. I can't be only half in love with you.'

She leaned forward, resting her forehead against his. She had nothing to go back to, anyway.

'If you left me,' he murmured, 'I don't know how I'd bear it.'

'I'm not leaving you.' She felt his slow exhalation of relief, soft against her face. She said, 'But – what about shopping and things?'

He leaned back. 'Little one, are you really telling me the thing you're going to miss most is trips to Tesco? You'll simply tell Seth or Joshua or Thomas what you need, and they'll do the shopping for you after they've finished work. Does that sound so bad?'

She let him kiss her, though Ruth was still watching. 'No,' she said. 'That doesn't sound bad.'

And the more she thought about it, the more stupid it seemed not to have realized the women never left. Whether or not she could remember anyone actually *telling* her, it had been right in front of her from the start. Nothing had been hidden. Nathaniel had said the women were looked after properly here – and she'd been so relieved at the idea, however old-fashioned it might have sounded, that she could hardly start complaining now.

She said, 'It seems strange to think I'll never see anything except the moors, and the two houses and the barn.'

'But what would you have seen if you'd stayed in the town?' he said. 'The same streets every day, the same miserable concrete buildings, the same unhappy people. Everyone out there is trapped in their tiny, confined space. Perhaps the scenery here is just as limited in a way, but now your mind can expand so much further than it ever could in the town. You can experience true happiness for the first time.'

She nodded, and he kissed her again. She reminded herself how lucky she was that he'd found her.

But as she rejoined the other women in the kitchen, she couldn't help giving Esther a quick glance. Esther met her gaze neutrally, but Stephanie was beginning to distrust her blankness. It alarmed her that without even realizing how or why, she already seemed to have made an enemy within the Ark.

6

When Thomas went up to their bedroom, he found she'd been crying again – Esther's was a face that always showed it. But she would never admit it, nor let him comfort her, so he didn't comment.

She said, 'Was work alright today?'

'Yes, thanks.' (It hadn't been, not really; the super-market seemed to grow more depressing every day.) 'How's your quilt coming along?' She'd shown it to him the previous week, rather shyly, when everyone else was still in the kitchen. Thomas had been entranced. The other women's quilts lay folded in the corner and he could admire their neatness, the soothing wash of pastel shades, lilacs and creams and soft blues. But when Esther unfurled hers, it looked like it was on fire. Triangles of bright gold were sewn into a star in the centre, with an explosion of vibrant reds, oranges and yellows fracturing outwards from it, the spiked edges of the blast eventually turning back to gold before the pattern began again.

'That's incredible,' had been his – inadequate – response.

'Ruth says it's too "loud" to sell,' Esther had said. 'I'm hoping that means I can keep it. Is that sinful of me?'

He had wondered if perhaps it was, but she looked so

cheerful that he didn't pursue the thought, saying instead, 'I think it's beautiful.'

But now Esther said, coming towards him and taking his hand, 'It's nearly done, but Ruth says Seth has to take it to the market with the others.'

'Oh,' Thomas said. 'Well, perhaps no one will buy it.'

'Thanks!'

'I didn't mean that,' he said quickly, but she put her hand to his face.

'I know.' At last her smile was back. 'Don't look so worried.'

She stepped back and began to undress, not bothering to turn away from him. He adored her ease with him, the grace with which she pulled her dress over her head and unbuttoned her blouse, the delicacy of her shoulders and collarbones. Her lack of self-consciousness amazed him as she slipped off her underwear and walked naked to the chest of drawers to fetch her nightgown. It was a source of secret shame that he couldn't match her. He turned away to fumble with his shirt buttons.

He didn't hear her coming up behind him – her steps were as quiet and soft as a cat's – but then her arms went round him and he felt her cheek against his back. He turned, awkwardly pulling his pyjama trousers all the way up, wanting to be hidden.

When he looked down at her face, he felt a rush of love that was almost painful. He was struck once more by how extraordinary it was that a woman like this could be married to him – that he of all people had been chosen for her. Noticing again the redness of her eyes, he said tentatively, 'You haven't done anything wrong, Esther. You know that, don't you?'

She looked down, giving a small shrug.

'It's not because of any failing in you,' he said.

She murmured something, too softly for him to hear. He leaned closer. 'What?'

'I did fail,' she repeated.

'That was God's decision, not something you did.'

'I must have been unworthy.'

'No,' he said. 'You're not unworthy. Stop it. God has other plans for you, that's all. Trust God and the prophet.'

'Of course I trust them,' she said, and he saw that the wall had gone up again.

He said, 'It's a gift, I think. That He's giving us back to each other.'

Finally, she looked up, and the brightness was back in her eyes. 'I love you,' she said.

He couldn't say it back to her; the feeling didn't fit into the frail words.

The prophet sought Thomas out alone the next day and led him away from the houses.

'Look at this,' Nathaniel said, gesturing out across the uneven tracts of moorland that shambled away from them in every direction. 'We're lucky to have this reminder of God's glory.'

Thomas nodded, but he was shivering. Although they were still in autumn, the wind was sharp today, and they hadn't stopped to get their coats.

The prophet said, 'We're all adjusting to change, aren't we?' He laid a hand on Thomas's arm.

'Sarah seems to be settling in well,' Thomas said.

'Yes. I'm pleased with her.' A silence, then he added, 'How's Esther doing?'

'She's fine.'

'Things will go back to normal soon enough,' Nathaniel said. 'I hope Esther knows that.'

Thomas nodded without thinking, then saw what Nathaniel meant. His dismay was so strong and so painful that he couldn't have resisted it even if he'd thought to try. It must have shown in his face.

Nathaniel said, 'What, did you think I'd just abandon her? Thomas,' he chided softly, 'don't you know me better than that?'

'Of course,' Thomas said. But in his mind, his treacherous mind, the devil sent his reply: Why do you need them both? Why Esther as well, when it's clear she can't give you a child? She's my wife.

He tried to rein in his thoughts. *Satan, I refuse you.*

'You must see I can't undo what God's done,' Nathaniel said. 'He gave me Esther. I won't cast her aside as though she's worthless.'

Thomas made himself nod. But he thought, I would walk through fire for her. Why do you need them both? Why both?

Satan, I refuse you.
Satan, I refuse you.
Satan, I refuse you.

After

Judith finally caught up with Nick as he was going into the pub for his evening shift. Swinging her satchel off her shoulder, she smashed it into his arm. 'Bastard!'

'What the hell?' He caught it and pulled it away from her.

'You piece of shit,' Judith said. She'd misjudged this, was angrier than she'd realized on the way over here. Too angry to do this, too angry to talk to him without breaking down and crying in the street. God, she actually wanted to kill him. If she could get him onto the ground, she thought she might kick him to death with her size-four combat boots.

What had Nick said to her once? We're all capable of killing. Circumstances shape us.

They'd been wasted, were in their first year at university and hadn't known each other long. Nick had reached the stage of drunkenness where he was throwing his words out carelessly; he'd probably never even thought about it before. But Judith had had to get up from the sofa and make for the door. In the street, she had retched.

'Judith!' Nick said, still holding onto the strap of her satchel. 'You scared me. I thought I was being mugged.'

She wiped the tears away furiously. 'I can't believe you

did it.' But shouldn't she have known better than this, better than to be so hurt? If she'd learnt anything, it was surely that nothing people did ought to surprise you. With renewed energy, she pulled her bag free from his grasp and swung it at him again.

'Stop it. What have I done?'

She couldn't answer him. Nick took her arm. 'Come inside. You need to sit down.'

She let herself be steered into the pub and through to the back room, where he deposited her on the sofa. He returned a moment later with a pint of water and pushed it into her hand. Judith sipped it and tried to take some deep breaths.

Nick went to sit beside her, then appeared to reconsider and pulled up a chair opposite her instead, out of the satchel's range.

'OK,' he said. 'What's going on?' When she didn't speak, he said, '*Please*, Judith. Just tell me what I've done.'

She ground the heels of her hands into her eyes and then made herself look at him. 'You know what you've done.'

'I don't. Honestly.'

'You told them,' she said. 'A newspaper. You told them about my mum. You *bastard*.'

His eyes widened, his face almost a parody of confusion. He said, 'What about your mum? I've never met her. I don't know anything about her.'

Judith watched him, wrong-footed. His bewilderment looked put on, but all Nick's expressions came out that way. He was like a child in that respect, everything in his mind played out extravagantly across his face. She'd always thought he'd be the last person to lie to her; he wouldn't be able to pull it off. Belatedly, Judith realized why she'd been drawn to him in the first place: he reminded her of Moses.

Nick said, 'What happened to your mother? What have I told a newspaper? Judith, what's *going on*?'

His shock seemed genuine. She said slowly, testing him, 'Have you heard of the Ark of God? The group that lived on the moors?'

There it was on his face, the dawning horror.

She said, 'My mother's in prison. Been there eight years.'

Nick didn't speak for a moment. At last, he said, 'Fucking hell. That's awful. *Fuck.*' Then, when Judith didn't reply, he added, 'I swear I didn't know. I swear I didn't. I mean – I always thought there must be something. Because you were so private about everything. But I thought maybe it was a nasty divorce or some kind of family feud. Not *this*.'

Gradually, she realized that she believed him. She stood up.

'Where are you going?' he said.

'Home.' A pause, then she added, 'Sorry I called you a bastard.'

'It's OK.' He stood up too. 'You gave me a dead arm. I didn't tell you before in case it encouraged you.'

'Sorry,' she said again.

She made for the door but he stopped her. 'Judith, don't

go. If this is why you've been acting weird, can't we just – go back to how things were?'

She shook her head but didn't answer because she was afraid of crying again. She got herself out of the door but he came with her.

'Please stay,' he said.

'Can't.'

She forced herself to walk away from him. He was steady and he'd been a good friend to her. But she would manage without him. She was so used to missing Moses that it would hardly make any difference.

Perhaps it was better for us because we were only children, Moses wrote. *I hope you're OK. That's what I hope the most.*

III

Heaven is high

1

'The wages of sin is death!' Moses shouted with something close to delight when Ruth finally picked him. Beside him, he felt Judith wince, but he knew she was putting it on.

'Good, Moses,' Ruth said, though she always seemed to mean it less when she said it to him. 'Can you give us another example?'

Moses stood up.

Ruth said, 'You don't need to stand up.'

He sat down again, blushing as the others snickered. He said, 'The story of Samson and Delilah.'

'Go on.'

'God made Samson mighty from birth, but told his parents that they must never cut his hair or he'd lose his strength. But he fell in love with a woman called Delilah and told her the secret about his hair. Delilah betrayed him, and cut off his hair. He lost his strength because he'd broken his promise to God, and the Philistines captured him and blinded him. Then he pulled down the temple and destroyed them all, but he died too. Because the wages of sin is death,' he finished with a flourish.

'Good.' Ruth turned towards Judith. 'Do you have an example, Judith?'

Moses tensed. He didn't want Judith to get in trouble

again, especially as he really thought she might get a session this time. But he didn't know how to help her whilst Ruth was staring at them both. Luckily just then there was a wild burst of wind outside which made the windows of the schoolroom rattle. Whilst Ruth turned towards the noise, Moses was able to lean over and hiss, 'Lot's wife.'

Ruth turned back towards them.

'Lot's wife,' Judith said.

'Yes,' Ruth said, as if she was disappointed Judith had got it right, which made no sense. Moses disliked Ruth, but dislike was sent by the devil, patience and obedience by God.

'Can you expand on that, Judith?' Ruth said. 'Why did you choose Lot's wife?'

Judith stayed quiet, and Moses began to feel frightened again. But just as Ruth's lips were going into a hard line, Judith said, 'She was turned into a pillar of salt.'

'Why?'

'Because she sinned.'

'How?'

'She didn't listen.'

'She was prideful and rebellious!' Ezra shouted out from his seat at the back. 'She disobeyed her husband and God.' Anybody else, Moses thought, anybody who wasn't Ruth's son, would have got in trouble for speaking when it wasn't their turn and showing off. But Ruth just made a little gesture at Ezra to shush him and turned back to Judith.

'She was prideful and rebellious,' Judith said.

'And the wages of sin is death,' Ruth finished for her.

'God punishes us if we rebel against His will. We've seen this ourselves. We're fortunate to have a reminder always amongst us.'

Moses looked quickly down at his desk. He could feel the others' eyes on him, but thankfully Ruth didn't pursue the subject.

'Is today's lesson clear, Judith?' she said.

'Yes.'

'You're improving,' Ruth said. 'I'm pleased to see you're learning to be governed by the Spirit.'

She didn't look very pleased, Moses thought. And neither did Judith.

After the lesson, he and Judith went to the forest and pushed their way through the branches at the entrance. It had been raining on and off all week, and the children were banned from going out onto the moors. The others had stayed in the schoolroom to play Daniel-in-the-lions'-den, but Moses sensed Ezra was in a combative mood and didn't want to take any chances. He'd said he was going for a walk, and had been amazed and delighted when Judith had said she'd come with him.

Inside the forest, you hardly noticed the rain. The ground stayed dry, few drops making it through the tangled canopy.

'You remembered,' he said to Judith, as they picked their way carefully between the trunks and spiked branches, 'about Lot's wife.'

'It's one of the better stories you've told me,' Judith

said. 'The bit about the pillar of salt stayed in my head. Because it's so stupid.'

'It's not stupid,' Moses said.

Judith glowered at him. 'Let's go to the river,' she said, and they headed to where the forest sloped downwards. You could always hear the river long before you reached it, the rumble and rush of it, and Moses felt a burst of excitement as they drew closer. When at last they came out into the light and rain, he looked at the river as he always did, torn between fear and wonder. The water bucked against its banks as though it might escape. It made him think of a spitting, rippling monster.

'The river marks the furthest boundary of the Ark,' he'd told Judith the first time he showed her. 'We're not allowed to go further than here. And anyway, the river's dangerous.'

'Can't you swim?' Judith had said.

'It goes too fast and the current's too strong,' Moses said. He didn't want to lie, but he didn't want to admit he couldn't swim either. He hadn't known it was something they did, out in Gehenna. And why would you? People belonged on dry land. Look what happened to Jonah.

They stood in silence for a while, staring at the churning water. The rain had eased off, speckling their clothes and hair with light drops.

Judith said, 'I can't believe you've never left the Ark. That's so weird.'

'It's dangerous in Gehenna,' Moses said.

'No, it isn't.'

'It is.' He didn't want to argue with her but the truth

was the truth, as his mother said. 'The people out there are sinners. They steal and lie and kill.'

'My best friend's out there,' Judith said. 'She's called Megan. When we finally go home, I'll see her again.'

Moses was about to tell her that she would never be allowed to go back and that Megan would burn in hell, but it didn't seem a very cheerful thing to say and he didn't want to annoy her again.

Instead, to steer her in the right direction, he said, 'I don't want to leave the Ark. Gehenna is full of sin and all my friends are in the Ark.'

'You mean the others?' Judith said. 'If they're your friends, why do they always tell you to go away?'

Moses looked at her. He couldn't tell if she was just saying it to be nasty or if she was really curious. He said, 'They don't.'

'Sometimes they do.'

'It's on account of my face.'

Judith snorted. 'Is that all?'

'I was marked by the devil when I was born.' It was a shameful thing to say, especially in front of Judith.

She wasn't laughing any more. 'What do you mean, marked by the devil?'

'Because of the story of my birth,' Moses said.

'Is it a good one? Like Lot's wife?'

'I don't want to tell it.'

'Alright.' Judith patted his arm, which seemed like a kind gesture, though he could never quite be sure. She said, 'If my mum won't take me home, I'll go on my own. How many miles is it across the moors?'

He had no idea. 'You can't go on your own.'

'I'll manage.'

'You can't go anywhere on your own. You're a woman. A girl,' he amended.

'What?'

'Women are weak and open to the devil,' he said. 'They need to be guarded.'

Judith shook her head. She was smiling, but not in a nice way. 'That's so stupid,' she said. 'You think women are weaker than men? Men are crap. My mum always said we were better off without them, only now she's pretending she didn't. Megan's cleverer than all the boys at school, and I'm better at football.'

'Everyone's weak,' Moses said. 'We need God to make us strong. But women are weakest of all.'

'Stop repeating stuff,' she snapped. 'You're just repeating stuff *he's* said. You're stupid and wrong.'

'It's the truth,' he said. 'Women need men to protect them.'

That was when she hit him.

'Is *that* weak?' she said. 'Am I weak?'

He stumbled backwards and put his hand to his face. She had caught him on his cheekbone, and it hurt. Her hand had been half closed as though she couldn't decide between a punch and a slap, but she'd got him with the knuckles all the same. The blow made his eyes water.

'I thought only girls were supposed to cry,' she said, but her voice was lower now.

She walked away from him and back into the forest. Moses followed her a little way and then gave up and sat down on a tree stump. He stared at the ground, which was covered with fir needles and moss and broken twigs, until his eyes went out of focus and his thoughts quietened. Then he rubbed his hands over his face to make sure there weren't any tears left, and got up.

During the Arithmetic lesson that afternoon, he didn't look at Judith and she didn't look at him. When it was over she went away with Mary and Abigail.

By the end of the day, his cheek felt swollen. Peter pointed it out when he found Moses behind the barn.

'It's almost suppertime,' he said. 'What happened to your face? It's purple below your eye.'

Moses stood on tiptoes to look at himself in the barn's one small window. He could just about make out the bruise. It showed up more because it was on the good side of his face.

Now Judith was going to get a session, he thought. They probably wouldn't mind if one of the other boys had done it, but Judith wasn't a boy, and she was new, and Ruth didn't like her. They'd punish her. And she deserved it.

He said, 'Nothing happened to my face.'

'Did Ezra do it?'

'Nobody did it.'

'If it was Ezra, I'll get him back for you,' Peter said.

'It was a tree branch. I ran through the forest too fast and a tree branch hit my eye.'

It amazed him, how simple it was to lie. He began to understand why people in Gehenna did it all the time. The words just fell out of you without you even having to think about them. As he followed Peter inside to lay the table, his eyes went to every corner of the room, wondering if the devil was lurking there, waiting to take him.

And during the meal, when his mother suddenly looked at him and said, 'Sweetheart, what have you been doing to yourself?' it was strangely easy to repeat the lie, even into the silence his mother's words created, even with the prophet's eyes upon him.

The prophet said, 'You must be more careful, Moses. We'll get some ice on it after supper, but it's probably too late now to do much about the bruising. I hope it's not too painful.'

This was worse than if he'd asked more questions, because it reminded Moses you obeyed the prophet not because you were afraid of him but because you loved him.

After the evening meeting, Moses went to stand behind the barn again so he could pray for forgiveness. You weren't supposed to pray with your own words because it created doorways for the devil, so he couldn't explain to God about the lie. Instead he used the words the prophet had given them for protection against their wicked thoughts.

Satan, I refuse you.

Satan, I refuse you.

Moses repeated it over and over and his mind was finally starting to go still. Then he opened his eyes – and shouted, because Judith's face was right up close to his.

She shouted too.

'You *scared* me,' she said.

'You scared *me*!' he said. 'You crept up on me.'

'I didn't creep,' Judith said. 'I walked normally. You were being all weird with your eyes closed so you didn't notice.'

'I was praying,' he said. 'Because I lied.'

She went quiet at that, and thrust her hands into the pockets of her dress. 'Why did you lie?'

It was difficult to answer because it was difficult to know. 'I didn't want you to get in trouble.' That was the surface answer, but what lay beneath it was the important part, and that was the part he couldn't see.

'You didn't have to lie,' she said, and she sounded angry again. 'You could have just told them.'

He shrugged, as he'd learnt from her.

There was another long silence. Then Judith said, almost too quietly for him to hear, 'Sorry I hit you.'

'It's OK.'

'You shouldn't have said that stuff about girls.'

'I was only repeating what God said.'

'You were repeating what Nathaniel said.'

He looked at her blankly, and she rolled her eyes.

Then she said, 'Tell me another story. Tell me a good one, like Lot's wife, or the one about Judith.'

Moses thought for a few moments. 'Alright,' he said. 'I'll tell you about Jael, who killed the enemy general with a tent peg.'

'Spoilers!' Judith said, giving him a push.

He had no idea what she meant, but assumed it was an expression of excitement in Gehenna. He launched into the tale.

2

Although she had been living in the Ark for more than two months now, and was growing better at quietening her former, worldly reactions, Stephanie was shocked when Nathaniel told her he would no longer be sharing a room with her.

'Sorry, Sarah,' he said, 'but the truth is, I've always found it hard to sleep properly when I'm sharing a bed with someone else.'

She noticed that he was using the other name again, as he seemed to do more and more often these days. She'd commented on it the week before, saying it felt strange, but Nathaniel had said, 'Darling, it's my special name for you,' and seemed hurt. She hadn't mentioned it again.

'I'll only be just down the corridor,' he said now. 'It's not really anything to get upset over, is it?'

'But you said when I first came how much you were looking forward to waking up next to me every day. You *said* that.' She'd treasured those words ever since. But she sounded petulant now, even to her own ears.

'No, I didn't.' He smiled down at her. 'I might have said how much I was looking forward to *seeing* you every day.'

'You said "waking up".'

His smile was gone. 'Why would I have said something that wasn't true?'

This was difficult to argue with, and she was afraid that she'd offended him again. 'I'll be lonely,' she said more softly.

'Don't be silly. I'll be close by, and so will Esther.'

'Esther?'

'She'll be taking over the other room,' he said.

It took Stephanie a few moments to process this. She'd never given the spare rooms along the corridor much thought, had taken it for granted that only she and Nathaniel would ever sleep in the small house.

'I thought Esther shared a room with Thomas,' she said.

'Don't look into other people's business.' The sharpness in his voice startled her.

'But what about us?' she said.

'Well, what *about* us?'

'I mean – we need some privacy, don't we?'

'Privacy from what?'

'I don't know,' she said, faltering in the face of his incredulity. 'Just some private place where we can – be a couple. Without people watching.'

'I think you're overestimating the others' interest in you, my love.'

It could have sounded unkind, but he was smiling now so she knew he was teasing her.

'It's just a bit of a shock,' she said.

'But I did mention it before, darling. A couple of times. Weren't you listening?'

She opened her mouth to protest, then closed it. She wasn't absolutely certain it hadn't been mentioned.

'What's got into you, little one?' he said. 'You were never difficult like this before.'

'I don't know,' she said. 'It seems weird, that's all.'

'We have a habit,' Nathaniel said, 'when we've lived in Gehenna for a long time, of thinking we know best, of thinking our view on things is always the right one. It's a habit I can see you're trying to shake off, but there may be times when you need to try a little harder. I know it's not easy.' He looked at her, and she felt herself weak before those searching eyes. 'Don't let me down,' he said.

She shook her head and didn't speak.

Perhaps dissatisfaction with her attitude was the reason Nathaniel didn't want to sleep with her as often as he used to. For the first few days after he moved out of her room, he visited her every night, holding her in his arms afterwards until she was almost asleep, and only then slipping back to his own room.

But then there was a night when Stephanie lay waiting for him and he never came. She chided herself the next day for her disappointment. Did she think it would go on like that forever? Give the poor man a break, she told herself, trying for humour. No couple had sex every night. It wasn't sustainable. But two more nights passed without a visit, and it wasn't mentioned between them. In the daytime he was as courteous as ever, but also rather distant, she began to think. He would take long walks on his own whilst the other men were at work, and in the evenings he would sometimes remain shut up in the prayer room with Thomas or Ruth for several hours. Stephanie hardly saw him, and even if she did have a moment alone with him, she wasn't sure how to raise the subject of sex.

The following night, lying alone again as hope turned to disappointment, she grew tired of her own passivity. She didn't want to seem clingy, but there was no reason why Nathaniel should have to do all the running either. Perhaps that was why he'd stopped visiting; he might think Stephanie had cooled off because she never initiated anything herself. She would go to him now, she decided, and slip into bed beside him. He would be pleased. It would be like the early days again.

She got up and put on the old dressing gown Ruth had given her, then padded along the corridor, already anticipating the warmth of his body against hers.

But at Esther's door, she paused. There were faint sounds coming from within that at first confused her, then made her blush. A rhythmic squeaking of bedsprings. A woman's breathy gasps. Thomas must be paying Esther a visit, though Stephanie had assumed they no longer slept together. Perhaps it was an occasional thing. Perhaps Thomas, like Nathaniel, found it difficult to get to sleep with his wife in the room. Stephanie carried on along the corridor and tapped gently on Nathaniel's door. No answer. She didn't want to knock more loudly and risk Esther and Thomas hearing, so she gently twisted the handle and opened the door a crack.

'Nathaniel?' she whispered.

There was no reply. She was nervous now. Her plan didn't seem as sound as it had done a few moments earlier. Perhaps he wouldn't thank her for barging uninvited into his room. If he was asleep, she could still retreat without him ever knowing she'd been there. She pushed the door open a little further to check, and saw the empty bed. But even then she didn't understand – not immediately. She went back into the corridor. A midnight walk? she thought. A few moments alone in the prayer room? She was only thinking these things to distract herself, because the truth was already pushing at the edge of her thoughts. She took a few steps back along the corridor. Closer to Esther's door, she heard the sounds again. The truth slid into full view.

She returned to her own room and closed the door, getting back under the covers and pulling her knees up to her chin. She wrapped her arms around them and failed to sleep.

Stephanie forced herself to wait until the following afternoon to confront him, so she would have a chance to get things straight in her head. But the longer she waited, the more muddled she felt. Her rage and misery were the only clear things – but how she could adequately express them, and how he might respond, remained beyond her.

The values of the world, Nathaniel had shown her, were fatally distorted; sometimes her reaction felt like a trap she'd fallen into. And however carefully she tried to prepare what she would say to him, the words she practised seemed flat and meaningless, flimsy beneath Nathaniel's imagined scrutiny.

She caught up with him outside the houses after lunch, when he was setting off for his afternoon walk.

'Aren't you helping the others clear up?' he said.

'No. I need to talk to you.'

He didn't say anything to help her, just continued to look at her levelly, with that deliberate patience of his that wrong-footed her before she'd even spoken.

But the rage came back to help her. 'I *heard* you,' she said. 'I heard you last night. You and Esther. You *bastard.*'

'What did you hear?' he said.

'I heard – you know what I heard. You were sleeping with her, weren't you?'

She'd expected him to deny it and had steeled herself against this, but Nathaniel was calm. 'Yes,' he said. 'Sometimes I visit Esther.'

He put his hand on her shoulder and it felt like a weight. She shrugged it off.

'But you're supposed to be with me! You bastard,' she added again, but it came out feebly.

'I *am* with you,' he said. 'You're the centre of my life.'

'Don't say that!' she said. 'Not when you're having sex with someone else.' He put out his arms to her, but she moved out of his reach. 'You're a liar,' she said. 'I thought you loved me.'

'I do.'

'You can't *say* that,' she said. 'You can't say that now.'

'Why not? What have my visits to Esther got to do with my feelings for you?'

The gentleness in his voice was almost too much for her. 'You're cheating on me,' she burst out.

Nathaniel raised his eyebrows. *'Cheating on you?* A stupid, empty phrase. Have you thought it through at all? What does it even mean?'

She felt foolish, but pushed the feeling down. 'It means you're being unfaithful.'

'How? I promised to love you, and I promised to look after you. I haven't broken those promises, and I'll never break them, not as long as I live. Anything I have with Esther is entirely separate. It goes back to long before I knew you.'

'But you can't be with two women at once,' Stephanie said.

'Why not?'

She was bewildered. 'You just *can't.*'

'Oh, I see,' Nathaniel said. 'Because the shallow rules of the world say so. Because it's what your women's magazines say, and bitter, unsatisfied wives who've never been taught anything different, and an old, corrupt marriage institution that has no true links with God.' He paused, seeing her face. 'I'm not attacking you, my love. I'm just trying to make you see where your views come from. Just because you've been told something all your life doesn't mean it's true. Didn't I say I'd free you from all that?'

The more she tried to hold the tears back, the more insistently they filled her eyes and overflowed down her cheeks. 'I thought I was enough for you.'

'You are,' he said. 'It isn't that. Stop thinking about our

relationship in the narrow terms of the world. If you need an example, look to the Bible instead. Just because Abraham had Hagar as well doesn't mean he loved Sarah any less. Sarah was the love of his life, Hagar simply a helper. God gave me Esther many years ago, but He never intended her to be my love, to be my life. He wanted me to wait for you. I had to wait a long time, but now I'm so thankful I did.'

Stephanie was confused, as she always was, by his mention of God. She didn't believe. She didn't think she believed. But so often these days she thought she felt God watching her. His eyes were pale and fierce; they followed her everywhere.

All the same, she looked up at him and made herself go on. 'But now I'm here, aren't I? Doesn't our relationship change things?'

'It changes everything. I've never been happier. But Esther still needs me. I can't abandon her.'

'But – she has Thomas. She's his wife.'

'That's different. She was my helper before anything else. But she was young and unsteady, and needed a husband to guide her. It was decided she should marry Thomas. That doesn't eclipse her other role.'

Stephanie was at a loss for how to answer. 'But you didn't tell me,' she said at last. 'This isn't fair.'

'It had nothing to do with you,' he said. 'There was no reason to tell you. You must see that.'

Must she? She could no longer tell which of them was being unreasonable.

'Little one.' He touched her chin, tipping her face up towards him and then, when she didn't resist, kissing her. 'I love you. You know that. But I have certain responsibilities I can't turn away from. Sometimes I wish I could, sometimes I wish it could just be you and me, but that's wrong of me. It would be selfish to put my own desires ahead of everything else. I can't turn my back on God's will. I can't turn away from my followers.'

'But I can't bear it,' she said. 'I can't bear thinking of you with someone else. It makes me so jealous.'

He said, 'Jealousy is a sin.'

'I know, but – I can't help it. It's instinct. Isn't it? When you love someone.'

He shook his head sadly. 'Have I failed you? I believed so strongly in you. But you haven't learnt a thing. You can't bring yourself to trust me, even now. You're still letting the world whisper to you. You talk about instinct. Don't you realize that every single one of your instincts is wrong? You've been shaped by the world you lived in, and it's almost ruined you. Do you know what God tells us in the book of Jeremiah? He tells us that, "The heart is deceitful above all things, and desperately wicked." I thought I could save you from that, free you of your broken instincts and wicked heart, and give you something better in their place. Maybe I was wrong.'

He'd leant in close to her throughout this speech, and she felt his breath on her neck. Now he moved away, putting a gulf between them. Stephanie put out her hand to him.

'Nathaniel—' She didn't know what else to say. She couldn't pretend she wasn't distraught. But perhaps that was where this feeling of wrongness lay, not in what he was doing but in her reaction to it. If she could just get her reaction right perhaps things wouldn't feel so awful any more. She needed a moment to be alone, to think clearly again, but she knew she couldn't risk losing him when she'd come so far already, when she'd given up so much.

And if her own view was so wrong, being alone would only give her mind a chance to twist things further.

She said, 'I don't understand. I don't know what to do.'

He took her hand. 'Repent. Learn that just because a thought comes into your head doesn't mean it's pure or true. For the most part, our thoughts exist to torment us, to lead us away from what's right. You have to learn to master them.'

'I want to be good,' she said.

'I know you do.'

'This is – difficult for me.'

'I know. And it's partly my fault. I should have realized how trapped you still are in the mindset of the world.'

She nodded.

He put his arms round her. 'I said I'd free you and I will. I said I'd make you happy, and I will. Trust me.'

'Alright.' She was so exhausted she felt she could sleep for days.

'I wonder if I've been too hard on you,' he said. 'It's a lot of change for you, all in one go.'

'Yes,' she said gratefully.

'But there's something you should remember,' he said. He dipped his head to whisper in her ear. 'I'll always love you best.'

Stephanie became watchful after that. Every movement Esther made caught her attention, every look that shadowed her face. Stephanie watched her across rooms, across the table, until she had learnt her features by heart. She couldn't pretend, even to herself, that Esther wasn't beautiful. It was only her nose that marred the picture; narrow and neat around the nostrils, but bumpy at the top, pushed slightly to one side, throwing the rest of her face off-kilter. It had been broken, Deborah had informed her in passing, some years before.

It seemed absurd to Stephanie that she'd once thought she and Esther could be friends. Esther had known better. No wonder she'd been suspicious of Stephanie, and no wonder she'd taken the chance to report her when she could. Esther had understood the situation, and Stephanie had not – until now. They were set against each other, not because they wanted to be, but because that was the way things were.

Stephanie longed to know more about Esther's life before the Ark, how she and Nathaniel had met, why she had been chosen. But no one would enlighten her. Rachael and Deborah reminded her gently when she tried to fish for information that it was sinful to dwell on their lives before the Ark. The past had been wiped out, the fol-lowers of the Ark reborn. But it wasn't entirely wiped out,

Stephanie thought. It hovered there still, half forgotten, mostly disregarded. Somehow it had led them all to this point and she would never know why. She saw that this was once more the whispering of her wicked heart, and she tried to curb it. But it made her feel disorientated, missing this knowledge the rest of them carried, as though she had stumbled out of the mist to meet them without ever having found the path they had used.

She felt God's eyes on her again, and tried to close off the whispering.

Heaven is high, she recited, as Nathaniel had taught her. *Heaven is high.*

3

Where did he find her, anyway?

Esther had tried, as gently as possible, to discover
this, but Thomas wouldn't say much. She kept picturing
Nathaniel going up to Sarah at a bus stop, but she could
see this was absurd; just because it had happened this way
for Esther didn't mean people could only be saved whilst
waiting for the 47 towards Catford.

'God asked it of me,' Nathaniel said, as they lay together
that night. 'What should I have done, Esther? Ignored
Him? "No thanks, God. We've got our hands full at the
moment"?'

She didn't reply. He was trying to shake her out of
her sadness; but she knew it would be a mistake to laugh.
Remember the way he saved you, she told herself. Although
she tried not to think about the old life, Esther couldn't
forget its misery and chaos. She hadn't cared about anything after Toby died, and neither had her parents, so there
was no one to notice that Esther had stopped going to
school, was drinking in the daytime, sleeping with anyone
who asked. She didn't know what would have happened to
her if she hadn't met Nathaniel. So how could she begrudge
someone else the same lifeline?

She remembered asking Nathaniel where he thought

Toby was, not long after they first came to the Ark. 'I know he wasn't saved,' she'd said. 'But he can't be in hell. Not Toby.' Then, when Nathaniel didn't reply, she added, 'You'd have liked him if you met him. He was special.'

Though probably he hadn't been that special. He'd just been her brother.

Nathaniel said, 'Modern society has turned its back on God. People will suffer for it.'

'No,' Esther said. 'He can't be in hell.' It was strange to remember this now, that there was a time when she'd openly defied him. Even the distant memory of it made her fearful, but Nathaniel hadn't been angry. She'd been very young back then, and perhaps he'd taken pity on her.

He said, 'I don't have all the answers, Esther. But I think if I pray very hard for your brother, and if you make sure you always submit to God's will, God may exempt him from the punishment He's saved for other sinners.'

'So I might see him again eventually?'

'Perhaps.'

Tonight, remembering the peace he'd given her back then, Esther laid her head in the curve of his neck and kissed the skin behind his ear where it was soft and pale.

'Love you,' Nathaniel murmured.

'Me too.'

They lay drowsily together for a while, then Nathaniel raised her gently off him and turned on his side to face her.

'There's something I need to say to you,' he said.

She waited.

'God wants me to have another child,' he said. 'It'll be

a symbol of hope.' Then, when she still didn't speak, he added, 'I have to think about the others, as well as you.'

'I know.'

'We have to accept God's will.'

'I know. I do.'

'Oh, my love. Don't feel slighted. You have a different role here.' He reached out, touched his fingers to her cheek. 'Do you think I could carry on even for a single day without you? Leave the children to others. God clearly doesn't want that from you.'

But if she's just here to bear children, Esther thought, why does she have to be so pretty?

Stop.

Heaven is high.

Heaven is high.

Then she didn't have to fight her thoughts any longer because he was pushing up her nightdress again. Esther was grateful for sex as a reminder of her true role. (Did you know vagina comes from the Latin word for sheath, he'd asked her once. And what purpose does a sheath have except to house the sword?)

After he'd left her to go back to his own room, she struggled for a long time to fall asleep. It was childish, but the truth was she was still afraid of the dark – even at her age. It didn't seem to matter when she was with Thomas. Though she was relieved Nathaniel had called her back, she missed her husband on the nights the prophet asked for her. As long as she and Thomas were coiled together, a shared weight and warmth, the darkness backed off. But when Esther was alone it returned, gaining in strength and malevolence, hissing like a serpent.

She should tell Thomas things like this, that in his presence she didn't fear the darkness. Now was the time when he most needed to hear it, because she knew he was suffering, knew also that he would never admit it in case it seemed like a reproach to her. Thomas had believed they would belong only to each other from now on. He hadn't realized that Nathaniel still needed her as well. Esther wished there was a way to comfort him, but she couldn't find the words.

It had been easier, she thought, before she came to love him so much. When she was first given to Thomas, back when she was eighteen, she had always been blurting out whatever came into her head. She'd confused it with honesty, saying everything out loud, as though transparency excused you from having to exercise control over your thoughts. ('I don't love you,' she'd told him early on. 'Nathaniel has all my love, all of it. But I'll try to be a good wife to you.' Remembering this, she winced at her cruelty.) Now she found that the more you loved someone, the harder it became to say what you really meant.

Going for her shower the next morning, she met Sarah in the corridor, both of them still in their nightdresses.

They smiled cautiously at each other and said good morning. Esther added after a slight pause, 'Did you sleep well?'

Sarah's expression became guarded, and Esther regretted the question. Somehow, she could see, Sarah had interpreted this as a taunt; because it was Esther who'd spent the previous night with Nathaniel.

'Yes,' Sarah said. 'Thanks.'

'Bit of a storm, wasn't there?'

'I didn't hear anything. I was asleep.'

Esther wrapped her arms around herself. She nodded to the shower door. 'You go first. I'll wait.'

'No, it's alright. You were here first.'

Esther was disconcerted by Sarah's air of suspicion. She had a sudden, mad urge to do something to make Sarah like her, but she knew it wouldn't help in the long run. Best if they kept their distance. And anyway, it would be too disloyal to mention it had been Rachael and not Esther who'd reported Sarah for wanting to take Judith to the town.

Esther said instead, 'I think we're on work task together today. Cleaning the downstairs rooms.'

'OK.'

There was another pause. Esther was trying to work out which of them *should* have the first shower, which outcome would be less likely to annoy Sarah, when Sarah said suddenly, 'How old were you when you met him?'

Esther studied her carefully. How long had she been waiting to ask that? She weighed up possible responses, and decided to play it safe. 'We're not supposed to talk about before. It's unhelpful.'

She tried to soften her answer with a smile, but Sarah looked back at her coolly and didn't reply.

4

Alone in the barn, Judith pressed her hands against her eyes and wept. She understood it all now: her mum was never planning on leaving. These sagging, dirty houses in the middle of the moors were supposed to be their *home*. Judith would be a grown-up before she was able to return to her real life. Nobody would remember her. Megan would have a new best friend.

The wind rattled the windows and slid through the gaps in the wooden walls. Everywhere was gloomy and damp and cold. Her mum claimed it was 'lovely and peaceful'. But there was no peace here. True, you couldn't hear the traffic any more, but there were different noises, ones that disturbed Judith more than the sound of cars. The wind, howling and whistling and banging against the sides of the house. The creak of the old floors and the gurgle of pipes, footsteps on the floors above you, voices in other rooms – you could never be alone for long – doors groaning open or banging shut, a clatter of pots in the kitchen where one of the women was always working.

And away from the old houses, even when the wind had dropped, there was no quiet. On the moors when the weather was soft, you could still hear the rustle of the grass as the wind slithered through it. When you were walking through the forest and the wind was up, you could hear the creak and whine of branches moving high above, and when things were still, the cries of birds and the crackle of small creatures amongst the fir needles on the ground. Judith didn't believe she would ever hear silence again.

She had given up trying to get her mum on her own to talk. There was always someone guarding Stephanie; Rachael demonstrating how to hem the bottom of one of those stupid long dresses they all wore, Deborah showing her a new recipe, Esther helping her do the laundry with silent efficiency. Nobody was allowed a moment to themselves. Or perhaps the others didn't *want* one, Judith thought, remembering how sickly-sweet the women were with each other, as if they were dearest friends and couldn't bear to be parted even for a second. And her mum went along with it, even though she'd only known them a couple of months. They all called her Sarah now, and her mum didn't correct them, which annoyed Judith so much she thought she might die.

She had no one to talk to when she was upset except for Moses. He wasn't Megan, but he was better than the others. If she ever complained to Mary or Abigail, they would say they'd pray for her, like pious, pint-sized Nathaniels. Then they'd go straight off to tell their mother, so that Judith would have to go and have a special chat with Deborah about her feelings, and would have to play down her misery so that Deborah wouldn't tell Ruth she was struggling against the Spirit. That usually ended with Ruth saying she was ungrateful or shouting at her.

If she told Moses she was unhappy, at least he kept it

to himself. But he would try to comfort her by going on about heaven, which was irritating in its own way. Judith had got rid of him today by saying she had a headache and wanted to be alone for a while.

'Another one?' he said. 'Is it bad?' His half-stained face peered anxiously at her, as though assessing her symptoms.

'It's OK,' she said. 'I just need to sit by myself for a bit. That always makes it better.'

'OK,' Moses said. 'Where will you sit?'

'The barn.'

'Watch out for the devil.'

Judith looked at him carefully, but he was serious. Like the other children, Moses believed the devil would materialize out of the shadows to tempt him the moment he was alone.

'That's how he tricked Eve into sin,' he'd explained to her once. 'He waited until she was alone. We're most vulnerable when we're alone. Especially me.'

'Why especially you?'

As usual, he refused to explain.

When she was younger, Judith had been frightened of ghosts. A boy called Tommy Reynolds had told her about them in Year 2. He said they were always watching you, waiting to take revenge for the way they'd died. The terror had stayed with Judith for years. Sitting on the dirt floor of the barn this afternoon, she remembered that fear, and experienced a moment of panic in case the devil was real, was spying on her right now. Perhaps she really would end up in hell, as Ruth had suggested, her skin being peeled off and her eyeballs melting in the heat.

Judith forced the thought aside. She'd never been scared of the devil in her life, and they couldn't force her to believe he existed now. But what she was discovering was that it was harder to hold on to all your normal thoughts when everyone around you believed something different. You started to doubt yourself. But Megan didn't believe in the devil, Judith reminded herself. Nor did any of her friends from school. Nobody in the real world did. It was just a scary story like the one Tommy Reynolds told about ghosts. But if you'd heard it all your life like Moses, you probably would think it was true.

She had to get out before it was too late, before all these horrible ideas about hell and the devil seeped into her. She'd tried suggesting to her mum that social services would come and rescue her, but Ruth had interrupted, snapping at her not to be so silly. If she were going to be rescued, she would have to rescue herself.

Judith got to her feet, newly invigorated.

She waited until their afternoon lessons were over to put her plan into action. The other children had gone to the barn to play Philistines and Israelites. Moses, as usual, hovered near her.

'Shall we go to the forest?' he said.

'Yeah,' Judith said. 'But I have to ask my mum some-thing first. I'll meet you in the clearing.'

Moses nodded and went off, and Judith waited until he was out of sight, then looked around for any adults. There were none. Ruth had joined Nathaniel on his afternoon walk, the women were 'quilting' (whatever that was) in the workroom, and the men were in the town. Judith felt almost giddy at this unaccustomed freedom.

She took one last look at the hated houses, then set out along the track, wondering what she'd say to Megan when she saw her again. Megan would laugh in amazement when Judith turned up on her doorstep!

She tried not to think of Moses, waiting alone in the forest, tried not to wonder how long it would be before he realized she wasn't coming.

By the time the track met the main road, the houses were almost out of sight. Judith decided it would be best not to walk along the road. It would be quicker to get back to the town if she descended in a straight line across the middle of the moors, since the road became so winding as it dropped down into the valley. And if they came looking for her before she made it to safety, they'd probably look along the road first. She turned and headed out across the moors, keeping the road in sight for now.

The wind was fierce. Judith zipped her coat up to her chin and kept her head down. She tried to look where she was going, but the ground was a mess of different grasses, clumps of bracken and springy heather that came up past her knees, hidden hollows designed to catch your foot and twist your ankle. Rocks stuck out from the ground like bones breaking through skin. She longed to be back in the town where the ground didn't fight back. The pools of standing water and dark blotches of peat brought to mind Moses' warnings about bogs, and Judith gave them a wide berth, although this didn't stop her accidentally splashing into them from time to time. Soon her boots and socks were soaked.

She battled on, but began to feel she wasn't making much progress. The wind beat against her, trying to force her back to the Ark, and she was quickly out of breath.

Though she thought she must have come a long way, she still couldn't see down into the valley where the town should be, and she felt a shiver of panic at the idea she might have gone the wrong way. But surely she couldn't have when she'd just walked in a straight line away from the houses, and then almost alongside the road for the rest of the way? As Judith looked around her, she couldn't see any landmarks to help. In fact, she couldn't see any distance across the sloping grasses in front of her. The valley, which she'd kept in her sights for most of the walk, had been swallowed up. So had the road. With a sinking horror, she realized the mist had come down, descending so gradually she hadn't noticed until it was too late.

So now what? Judith put her freezing hands into her pockets and tried to stay calm. What had Moses said you were supposed to do in this situation? She heard his voice, soft and slightly anxious: you have to stay where you are, find some shelter if you can, and wait for it to lift. Don't keep going, because that's how people get sucked into bogs and drown.

Judith stumbled on for a few more metres until she came to a large rock, about the size of a person crouching. She sat down behind it on the damp ground, grateful for this small shelter from the wind, and wrapped her arms around her body for warmth. The mist curled around her and she felt it trying to blur her edges, rub her out. She would die here, she thought. They would find her body many weeks later and her mum would almost die herself from the grief and guilt. This idea comforted Judith for a little while, but then she began to feel even worse. She didn't want her mum to be miserable forever; she just wanted her to be sorry. And she didn't want to die.

She was considering allowing herself to cry when she spotted something strange. Two circles of light just breaking through the mist up ahead. As they came closer, the orbs turned to strips spearing through the mist. Judith stared at them without comprehension for a few moments, then realized that they were car headlights. She sprang to her feet and ran towards them.

The car almost hit her. The brakes slammed on as she leapt into the road, and Judith just had time to lurch back, out of the way. The car jolted to a stop alongside her. The doors opened and people were getting out, and then she recognized Moses' father Seth, and Joshua and Thomas.

'What on earth are you doing?' Seth said. 'We could have run you over.' He took hold of her arm roughly, and looked at her hard, apparently checking she was unhurt. He'd sounded angry when he spoke, but his anger seemed to disappear in a moment. 'Are you alright?' he said.

Judith was close to tears of misery and relief. She said, 'The mist came down.'

'You shouldn't be out this far alone,' Thomas said. 'It's lucky we came past.'

Judith's relief was turning to dismay as she realized how much trouble she was in.

Seth was still holding her arm. Seeing her tears, he said, 'You're safe now.'

'Seth, she was running away,' Joshua said.

Judith searched desperately for a cover story, but none presented itself. She rubbed the tears off her face with the back of her hand.

Joshua said, 'We're going to have to tell the prophet. This is very serious, Judith.'

There was going to be a lot of shouting, Judith thought. She hadn't had a session yet, but she'd heard about them from Moses. She began to cry properly.

Then Thomas spoke up again. He said, 'She's had enough of a fright already, hasn't she?'

'Thomas, he'd want us to tell him,' Seth said.

'Tell him what?' Thomas said. 'That Judith went for a walk and strayed a bit too far? That she got lost in the mist? I don't see that there's anything to tell. He has much more important things to deal with than a lost child. A lost and *found* child.'

'She was running away,' Joshua said again.

'Do you know that? Have you asked her?'

Judith dared to look up at Seth and Joshua, who were both staring at Thomas. There was a long silence. Then Seth crouched down in front of her. 'Did we get it wrong, Judith? Were you just going for a walk?'

She looked quickly at Thomas, then nodded.

'And you got lost?'

'The mist came down,' she said again.

'She's lying,' Joshua said.

Seth didn't answer. He was still looking at Judith.

Thomas said, 'I think she's telling the truth. Seth? She's just a child.'

'Alright,' Seth said at last. 'Alright. I don't see any harm in believing her.' He was speaking to Joshua now.

Joshua shrugged and turned back towards the car. 'If you say so.'

'Wait,' Seth said, and Joshua turned. 'Are we all agreed?'

The other men nodded.

'Come on, trouble.' Thomas opened the car door and gestured for Judith to get in the back. He climbed in alongside her.

They drove slowly along the road towards the Ark. With a flicker of despair, Judith saw the shadowy houses take shape and emerge from the mist. When they pulled up, Seth and Joshua got out of the car and went straight into the big house, but Thomas paused as he held the door open for Judith. He said, 'It'll get better. I promise.'

Judith nodded, but only to be polite. She watched him go inside. Then she thought she'd better look for Moses.

5

The mist had thinned, but it hadn't gone the next day. A light furring lay over the moors like down. Moses didn't know anything was wrong until breakfast was over. The men had already left the table, and he was about to turn to Judith to ask what she wanted to do after lessons, when Ruth stood up.

She said, 'Judith, you need to come with me.'

Mary and Abigail stopped their whispering and turned to watch. Across the table, the boys sat up straighter.

Judith didn't look back at Moses as she followed Ruth out.

He waited all day for her to reappear. He waited outside the barn, and outside the big house, and in the school-room. It reminded him of how he'd waited once before, the first time he ever saw her, when he hadn't been able to believe how red her hair was.

Ruth didn't reappear either, so there were no lessons. Moses didn't know how to fill the time. He was no longer used to being alone.

'Go away, devil boy,' Ezra said when Moses hovered near the other boys, who were playing on the path by the small house, but Moses hardly cared.

By the time the men came home in the evening and

they were told to gather in the barn, he knew there was going to be a session. The feeling of sickness had been building in him all day and now he was too frightened to open his mouth in case it came out.

When he followed the others into the barn, he saw that they'd put Judith on a chair in the middle of the room. Thomas had a chair next to hers, which was another shock; they almost never had two sessions at the same time. The prophet stood before them with his arms folded as they came in. His eyes seemed to blaze out of his face and Moses could almost feel the heat on him as he took his place next to Peter. There was that shiver in the air, the fear that took on a presence of its own before a session. Moses was afraid to look at Judith in case she cried and it made him cry. But he should have known better than to think she would cry.

She looked pale and tired, which wasn't surprising – they'd had her in the prayer room all day by then. One of her cheeks was red so it looked a bit like his. She was chewing her lip and looking at her mother, who stood with the other women, her arms wrapped round her stomach and tears dripping silently down her face and onto the floor. She said to Judith, 'It's alright, darling. It'll be alright.' The prophet gave her a look and she went quiet. But she continued to stare at Judith.

Moses kept his eyes on Judith too, because after he thought about the way her mother was looking at her, he realized it was a kind of comfort, not to turn your eyes away like the others, not to leave her sitting all alone on that chair.

The prophet let them stand for a long while in silence. When Moses' heart beat as fast as this, he got a strange light feeling in his chest like he was turning to water, like he might collapse and pour all over the floor at any moment.

Finally, the prophet spoke. Very softly, he said, 'The devil has come amongst us.'

A pause, as they took this in.

The prophet said, 'He has tried to tempt one of us away. We could have fallen, all of us, were it not for the righteousness of one of my followers. Joshua, thank you. Next time, I only urge you to obey the promptings of the Spirit sooner.'

Moses looked across at Joshua, who nodded solemnly in response to the prophet. Moses' own father was looking at the ground.

The prophet said, 'And you, Seth. You allowed yourself to be led astray.'

Moses saw his father nod, still not raising his eyes.

The prophet said, 'Your contrition has saved you. It satisfies me, and it satisfies God – this time.'

With a shudder of relief, Moses realized his father was to be spared. The prophet had already turned his attention to Thomas. 'You instigated this. You instigated this *lie*.'

On his chair, Thomas kept his head bowed. Into the silence that followed, he murmured, 'Forgive me.'

'Fortunately,' the prophet said, 'God worked through Joshua, and then through Seth, and brought them to their senses. They realized that having the devil walk amongst us is no *small matter* after all.'

The silence began to grow heavy. Moses felt it pressing in around him, restricting his breath. He sent his eyes back to the floor and kept them on the toes of his shoes, willing it all to be over.

Eventually, the prophet spoke again. 'Thomas,' he said, his voice gentle. 'I'm disappointed in you. Your lack of judgement. I expected so much more from you.' Thomas raised his head slightly, and his eyes met the prophet's. Unexpectedly, the prophet reached forward and touched Thomas's face. Thomas seemed to flinch a little, then steady himself.

'I know your intention was to *help*,' the prophet said, his hand laid against Thomas's cheek. 'I know you believed you were doing the right thing. You didn't wish to trouble me. You wanted to help Judith regain the true path on her own. That's right, isn't it, Thomas?'

'Yes.'

'You trusted your own instincts above my word and above God's word. You've accepted your guilt and your punishment will be swift and merciful.' He turned to Esther. 'Your wife will act as the rod.'

Esther stepped forward. When she hesitated, the prophet said, 'Do as God asks you. Esther, this is hard for all of us.'

Moses reminded himself that this wasn't the worst part, the waiting was the worst part; that the sooner it was over the better.

Esther raised her hand and slapped Thomas's face. The blow was half-hearted, and he didn't even turn his head.

'Obey God,' the prophet said, and Moses felt his nausea

returning. He remembered watching his own mother, when he was younger, being made to hurt his father. He understood it had to happen. God wanted the husband or wife to act as the rod to remind the sinner of whom they were hurting the most when they sinned. But it made the punishment especially difficult to watch.

Esther slapped Thomas again, harder, and this time his head snapped sideways. Esther began to sob, a strange harsh sound. Crying louder, she lifted her hand and held it there, but couldn't seem to bring it down a third time. Moses saw Thomas raise his head slightly and murmur something to her, but he couldn't hear what it was. Esther slapped him again, and then again, as hard as she could, so the noise rang out through the barn like the crack of a tree branch. When she'd finished, Thomas's lip was bleeding. His head hung down on his chest. Esther stepped back, shoulders heaving.

There was a long silence, broken only by Esther's dry gasps.

The prophet said at length, 'The will of God is not always comfortable for us. It doesn't always suit our own desires. Well done, Esther, for serving Him.'

Esther went back to her place alongside the other women. Deborah placed a hand on her back and said something in her ear.

The prophet turned back to Thomas. 'You've taken your punishment well, Thomas. I absolve you.' When Thomas didn't respond, the prophet put his hand under Thomas's chin and raised his head so he could look into his face. 'Let this be an end to it, yes?'

Thomas gave a small, exhausted nod.

'Rejoin your brothers, then.'

Thomas got shakily to his feet and went to stand with Joshua and Moses' father. They didn't look at one another.

The prophet said, directing his words at all of them, 'Did you not come to me, all of you, looking for answers? Will you then turn away from the answers I've given you?' He looked round at them. 'Give yourselves up,' he said. 'Give yourselves up to God and He will save you.'

'We do,' Ruth said. 'We give ourselves up!'

They all murmured it after her. Moses tried to find reassurance in the familiar words.

'Now,' the prophet said. 'Judith.'

All eyes went to Judith, who was still sitting on her chair in the middle, her hands folded in her lap. She had winced and closed her eyes whilst Thomas was receiving his punishment, but now she looked up again.

Judith's mother had been crying quietly the whole time. Now she stepped forward as though she might speak. The prophet turned to her and shook his head, but Judith's mother didn't step back. She was clasping her hands in front of her, staring at the prophet's face.

The prophet said, as though she'd asked him something, 'This is her first session. God will be merciful.'

When she carried on standing there, as though she'd been fixed in place, the prophet said, 'I've asked you to trust me. Can you do that?'

Judith's mother looked at Judith again, and finally gave a small nod. Ruth reached out and took hold of her elbow, forcing her to step back into the line of women.

Moses was trying to work out what they would do to Judith. He wanted to unravel time and go back, to prevent her sin or hide it so she wouldn't have to be punished. But the wish to hide it, he knew, was a sin in itself. His thoughts were a tangle.

The prophet turned towards Judith very slowly. He said, 'Are you afraid of hell, Judith?'

Moses silently urged her to say yes, but he already knew she wouldn't. At least she didn't shake her head, though. That was something.

The prophet carried on as though she'd given a response. 'You should be. It's where you'll end up if you listen to the whisperings of the devil, like you did when you tried to leave the safety of the Ark.'

Judith muttered something.

'What?'

She repeated it, more loudly. 'I was just going for a walk.'

'Liar!' He spun round to Ruth. 'Ruth, remind us what happens if someone puts the Ark at risk through their sin.'

Ruth said steadily, 'Their blood shall be upon them.'

Moses closed his eyes and begged God that Judith wouldn't be badly hurt.

'Do you think there won't be consequences for your behaviour?' the prophet said. 'Do you think we harbour sinners in the Ark?'

Judith remained silent. Speak, Moses thought. Please speak.

Eventually: 'No,' said Judith.

The prophet said, 'I'm moved to mercy today. You're

very young, and you haven't been with us long, whereas you've been amongst sinners your whole life. God reminds me that someone may not be saved at a single blow.' His voice became low like when he was leading the prayer meetings: soft and soothing. It floated up and down like music, so that sometimes you could almost forget that what he was saying was frightening. 'Judith, there are things you need to learn if you're not going to give way to the devil and put us all at risk. You have to learn to stamp out your wicked thoughts. You have to learn to close down your mind when the devil seeks to enter. It's our only defence against him.'

He was quiet for a moment, meeting their eyes one after another. He stopped at Peter. 'Peter, what does God tell us in the book of Genesis?'

Out of the corner of his eye, Moses saw his brother stiffen. Peter said, 'The imagination of man's heart is evil from his youth.'

'Yes,' the prophet said. 'The imagination is *evil*. Your thoughts are wicked *from the day you are born*. And where does the root of that wickedness lie? In our first parents, Adam and Eve.' He was addressing all of them now. 'Our first parents, unlike us, were free from sin. Until, that is, they gave the devil a way in, allowed him to foster in them his own wicked thoughts and vicious jealousy. Satan brought them challenge and rebellion. Satan taught them to think and act against the Spirit. He taught them to *question* and to *whisper*.

'In eating the fruit, Eve showed that she had strayed from the true path, just as you've strayed, Judith.' He had turned back to her now, and Moses saw her sit up a little straighter, as if readying herself once more for battle. 'Eve elevated her own independent will above the will of God. In doing this, she brought ruin on us all – just as you, Judith, risk doing now. Never again will humankind be pure and free from sin as Adam and Eve once were. Instead we are constantly vulnerable to the devil. Constantly vulnerable to attack. Only those who are truly prepared to fight the devil on all fronts, to fill themselves with the Spirit – only those people will be saved. Remember the mark placed on one of us, as a reminder for *all* of us.'

Moses put his hand to his face, feeling the bad side burn. But nobody turned towards him, because they were still staring at the prophet.

'Do not give the devil a way in,' the prophet said. 'When you struggle, turn to the prayers I've given you, your spiritual armour.' Suddenly, he shouted. '*No, Satan, I refuse you!*'

Moses felt a jolt go through him. He tried to hold himself still.

'Repeat it, Judith,' the prophet said. When she didn't speak, he said again, '*Repeat it*. Or you'll never be forgiven.'

'Judith,' her mother said. 'Please say it.'

Still Judith didn't speak. Moses thought if she were hit he would feel the pain in his own face. He kept his eyes on Judith's face, willing her to look at him.

Then she did glance up and their eyes met. He knew he must look desperate. Hoping no one else could see, he gave her the smallest of nods. No response registered on

Judith's face. She closed her eyes for a moment. Then he noticed her lips were moving.

'Speak up,' Ruth said.

Judith said softly, 'Satan, I refuse you.'

The prophet seemed to grow taller. 'Again.'

'Satan, I refuse you.'

'Again.'

'Satan, I refuse you.'

Judith's voice grew stronger each time. By the tenth time, she was close to shouting. Finally, the prophet seemed satisfied. He said, 'Remember how kindly you've been dealt with this time. Don't make the same mistake again. Next time, Judith, you'll be mercilessly corrected.'

A nod from the prophet, and with a burst of relief they realized the session was over. The air seemed to change in the barn. People were shaking themselves, as though they'd woken from sleep, and smiling at one another as if to say, Good morning. Moses watched the others moving around him and thought for the first time how strange it was they could be still and terrified one moment, and then seem to forget it all the next. Everyone had begun to file out of the barn, but Moses stayed where he was. Judith hadn't moved from the chair. She was staring down at her lap again.

Judith's mother went up to her. 'See, love?' she said. 'It feels better now, doesn't it?'

Judith wouldn't reply, nor even look at her.

The prophet gestured towards Judith's mother and she placed her hand quickly on Judith's shoulder, then took it away again and followed him out of the barn.

Moses bent down and pretended to tie his shoelace in case anyone asked him why he was waiting around. Most of the others were gone now. Peter paused next to him.

'Coming to play Jericho?' he said.

It was a rare thing for him to ask. He was usually nicer to Moses after a session. But Moses shook his head.

'Don't feel like it.'

'You should leave her alone,' Peter said. Peter, the mind-reader.

Moses did a Judith-shrug.

At last, he and Judith were by themselves. He wasn't sure how long she was going to sit in the chair without saying anything, so he sat down where he was on the floor and waited.

Eventually, Judith raised her head. She said, 'Don't you want to run off like the others? I'm wicked, aren't I?'

'You're not wicked,' Moses said. 'You're my friend.'

Judith got to her feet and headed for the door. He wondered if she was going to go off and leave him there, sitting cross-legged in the dirt, but at the last moment she paused, and turned around.

'Coming?'

He sprang up and followed her.

By unspoken agreement, they went to the forest, bending down to push through the branches at the edge, and not pausing until they'd reached their usual clearing.

Standing with her hands in the pockets of her dress, Judith said, 'I only said what he wanted me to say because of you. I didn't mean it.'

'You probably did really.'

'I didn't. You made me say it.'

'Sorry,' he said. 'I didn't want you to be hit.'

'I'd rather have been hit,' she said fiercely. 'Rather have been hit. At least then all the nastiness is on the outside, not hidden away in *words*.'

He couldn't follow what she was saying. 'It was to save you,' he said. 'The words. To keep the devil away.'

She glared at him for a few moments, then her legs seemed to go from under her. She sat down on a tree stump and began to cry.

Moses hovered, unsure how to comfort her.

She rubbed her hands roughly into her eyes. 'Stop watching me,' she said in a small, jerky voice. 'It's weird how you're always watching me.'

'Sorry,' Moses said. He tried to look away. 'Don't cry. God loves you,' he added in a burst of inspiration. 'One day we'll be in heaven together.'

'Shut up,' she said through her tears.

'We will.'

'If *he's* there,' she said, 'then I'm not going anywhere near it.'

He wasn't sure what to say to this. He wanted to tell her he wouldn't go without her, but he didn't think you got to choose. But perhaps he wouldn't be welcome there anyway.

Judith said, 'One day, I really will escape. I'll make it to the town, and I'll go and live with Megan and her mum and dad. And my mum will come and beg me to talk to her, but I won't. I'll ignore her. I'll never speak to her again as long as I live.'

She was crying harder now. Moses sat down on the ground beside her. He said again, 'Don't cry.'

She ignored him.

He said, 'If you stop crying, I'll tell you why my face is like this.'

She gulped and took some deep breaths. 'Is it a good story?'

'It's a sad one.'

She put her palms to her face and spread out her fingers, stroking her eyebrows as if to calm herself. After a few moments, she said shakily, 'Alright. I've stopped.'

He took a breath, wondered where to begin. 'Everyone knows the story of my birth,' he said. 'It gets told as a warning. If my mother strays from God's path, she's reminded of it. It makes her cry. It's not just important for her, though. It's important for everyone, because nobody is safe from the devil.' He stopped, and Judith leaned forward a little.

'So? What happened?'

Moses said, 'My brother Peter was the first baby born in the Ark. It was a blessing, but we have to pass through fire to be purified. It was a difficult birth. It went on a long time and there was a lot of blood. They thought my mother might die, but she didn't, and nor did my brother Peter.'

'I know what he's called,' Judith said. 'And I know he's your brother. You don't have to keep saying it.'

Moses decided to ignore this. 'So when more than a year had passed and my mother found out she was going to have another baby – that was me – she became afraid. And the fear made her stumble from God's path. She lost faith, and she looked to the devil for help. She begged my father to take her out into Gehenna, to a hospital, which is where the sinners try to look after each other.'

'I know what a hospital is.'

'She told my father that otherwise the baby might die, or she might die. My father was worried, and he went to the prophet. The prophet said he wouldn't stop my father from taking my mother to a hospital in Gehenna, but if he did, neither of them could ever return. And they would no longer be saved, and they wouldn't be taken up to heaven when the end times came. So then my father faced a terrible decision, because he loved my mother, but my mother wanted to leave.' He paused. He was relieved Judith had stopped crying, but the story was making the dread creep up from his stomach and settle high in his chest.

Judith said, 'So why did they stay?'

He made himself go on. 'They took too long to decide, and then the baby – me – came early and there was no time to go to Gehenna. And it was shown that it was just the devil whispering to my mother all along, because she didn't die, and neither did I. But as punishment for my mother's lack of faith, I was born with this mark on my face. And I will always be more vulnerable to the devil, because God let the devil mark me the day I was born, as a reminder of what happens if you turn away from God.'

A long silence after he'd finished. Moses was beginning to regret telling her, because now she would be scared of his mark like all the others.

Then Judith said, 'I think that's a stupid story.'

'What?'

'It's only a birthmark on your face. Surely if the devil wanted to mark you he would have given you something way worse. Like – an extra arm, or horns coming out of your head.'

Moses paused briefly to consider this. 'You mustn't question.'

'I'm just saying. If it's meant to be a curse, it's not that bad.'

'It's not about what it is. It's about what it stands for.' But she didn't seem frightened. And now he'd told her, he thought, they really were friends.

Abruptly, Judith said, 'What shall we play? David and Goliath?'

'Alright.'

'I'll be Goliath.'

'But you never die when you're supposed to,' Moses said. 'You always end up killing David.'

Judith shrugged. Moses sighed and resigned himself to a bloody end.

After

She was horribly at home in prisons these days, Judith thought; the officers had come to feel like old friends. Not that they seemed to view it this way. Today, she flashed the woman conducting the search her most winning smile. 'We must stop meeting like this.'

The officer paused, a pained expression on her face, then continued as if Judith hadn't spoken.

Judith said, 'I didn't bring you a snack this time. You'll have to wait till lunch.'

The officer ignored her.

Oh God, Judith thought. She'd been responsible this time, had taken nothing on the train except an aspirin for her headache. But now it occurred to her that an *unmedi-cated* Judith might actually be worse.

She wondered if Moses ever visited prison. He'd never mentioned it.

Sitting across from her mother once more, she struggled to think of some words she could say, any words, to fill the empty space before she could leave.

'I watched *Brief Encounter* a couple of nights ago,' she tried. Seeing Stephanie's surprise, she added, 'Gran's choice. To get me back for *Cloud Atlas*.'

'I remember watching that with her as well when I was young.'

'I think it's her favourite film,' Judith said. 'Or possibly the only film she's ever liked. She says it's good to see people on film who still have some sense of duty.'

'I never liked the ending much,' her mother said.

'They did the right thing,' Judith said.

'But they would have been happier if they didn't.'

'That's not the point, though, is it?'

There was a brief pause, then her mother said, 'You know, she'll be making you watch *Casablanca* next.'

'That's scheduled for next week.'

They smiled at each other; a moment that warmed and then unsettled Judith.

Her mother said, 'How's your job going?'

Judith had told her once – inexplicably – that she was working in a library. 'Oh – well, I've decided to move on. Try something new.'

'You could do anything,' Stephanie said. 'You're so bright.'

Judith didn't respond to this.

'You have a *degree*,' her mother added.

To her mother, a degree was a golden ticket. For Judith, this hadn't turned out to be the case. Her life had become an exercise in muddling through. She had started out studying Psychology at university, thinking that now, at last, the past might spill its secrets. But the course had been a huge disappointment. Within a term, she had switched to Social Anthropology. She wrote her third-year dissertation on the group mentality of Jeffrey

Lundgren's Kirtland Temple cult. It was interesting, but it didn't help, not in the long run. She'd been lost in a haze most of the time, in any case: black coffee in the mornings, ketamine in the evenings; bright enough to get a 2:1 without breaking much of a sweat, arrogant enough to know it.

At her graduation, her grandmother had wept, which Judith counted a stranger sight than all the wonders she'd seen in the Ark put together. Not crying like a normal person, obviously. Just a little quiet leaking around the eyes.

'You've done so well,' her gran had said, standing outside the hall clutching a glass of cheap prosecco and a soggy smoked salmon sandwich; her gran, who never drank, who had never once said 'I love you.' 'You've come through it all. I knew you would.'

And Judith had gone on smiling stiffly as she stood in her graduation gown, already damp from the rain, while her gran laboriously went about the task of immortalizing the moment on her ancient camera; and she had thought, 'What the hell do I do now?'

Difficult to make her mother see how her options had narrowed rather than expanded. Judith felt the bitterness returning.

She said, 'I got doorstepped by a journalist after seeing you last time.'

Stephanie's head came up quickly, but she didn't speak.

'She wanted to know about you,' Judith said. 'How you're getting on.'

'I'm fine,' her mother said weakly, as though being interviewed by the journalist there and then. Then, seeming to rally, she said, 'You shouldn't talk to them.'

'I didn't.'

'They twist everything.'

As far as Judith could see, it didn't need much twisting. She looked down at her fingernails, bitten to stubs, and didn't speak.

'We watched *500 Days of Summer* last week,' her mother offered.

'Oh.'

'I didn't like the ending much.'

'You never like the endings.'

Her mother leaned forward. 'Do you remember when I took you to see *The Parent Trap* at the cinema when you were little?'

'Yeah.'

'You decided you wanted a twin, so you invented one. You kept it up for weeks. I had to alternate between calling you Judith and calling you Suzie, and when you were Suzie you'd put on that strange American accent.'

Reluctantly, Judith smiled. 'I remember.'

'You were only interested in the twin part, though. You never tried to get me and your dad back together.'

'I barely knew him.'

'No,' Stephanie said. 'But you know, we were just kids. He might be different now.'

'Not interested,' Judith said. A pause, then she added, almost too softly for her mother to hear, 'I was happy just with you.'

Stephanie did hear. Judith knew, because she saw her mother's face close.

Afterwards, Judith leaned against the wall outside the prison gates and cried. It hadn't been a particularly awful visit, no worse than any of the others. But she knew she was reaching a tipping point.

It made no sense, she thought, how the idea of family still exerted such a pull. Surely her time in the Ark had taught her what nonsense that was, how foolish to expect anything more from your mother than you would from a stranger in the street, as though shared genes and a bit of shared history actually translated into things like loyalty and trust and love. Blood counted for nothing. They owed each other nothing. Judith was stupid to be disappointed by Stephanie back then, just as she was stupid to keep visiting her now.

Some of the other visitors were trailing out now, heading for the shuttle bus. Judith wiped her face on her sleeve and went over to join them.

IV

Falling

1

Two days had passed since the session before Stephanie was able to get Judith on her own.

'I wanted to do what was best for you,' she said when she'd finally tracked her daughter down outside the barn. 'They were just trying to help you. Do you understand that?' She was almost in tears, and knew she must get herself under control, especially as Judith was so calm. Stephanie had expected rage and accusations, but this was worse.

Judith simply shrugged, as if the whole subject bored her.

'He promised me he wouldn't hurt you,' Stephanie said. 'He *promised*. And he didn't, did he? I told him he mustn't.'

'Oh,' Judith said. 'Thanks *very* much.'

'Judith, please.'

But her daughter turned away from her. 'I have to go and find Moses,' she said.

'Judith, listen,' Stephanie said, catching her arm. 'This is good for us. This is a better life. And there may be difficulties along the way, but you have to trust me – this is all for the best.'

'I have to find Moses,' Judith said again. And she turned and walked away.

Stephanie watched her go. 'Being a good mother requires great courage,' Nathaniel had said to her. 'There may be times when you have to let your child pass through fire so they can be purified, however painful it feels. You're a courageous woman, and a wonderful mother.'

Stephanie thought again of the scene in the barn, Judith sitting on the chair in the middle, looking far younger than usual, not understanding what was happening, not understanding it was all done to save her.

But none of us knew what was best for us when we were young. And if Stephanie had suffered an agony alongside Judith, if she felt a pain in her stomach and then an ache in that secret low part that must be her womb – well, it was her own weakness, and she must overcome it.

Nathaniel came to her room that night after the evening prayer meeting.

'Here,' he said. 'I have something for you.'

From behind his back, he produced a bottle of red wine.

'Probably best not to mention it to the others,' he said. 'But you've had a tough few days, and I don't see the harm in this as a one-off treat. What do you think? Can we be trusted?'

His excitement was catching; she felt her lips curving up in response to his. It was just like one of their early dates: that heady, precipice thrill, that sense that things were moving beyond her control, but so smoothly, so beautifully.

He fetched her water glass from the bedside table.

'Finish it up,' he said, and although it was left over from the night before and she could see specks of dust on the surface, she drank it down quickly.

Then he unscrewed the bottle cap and poured wine into the glass. He held it to her mouth, pushing her hands away when she tried to take the glass from him.

'Drink.'

She sipped, and smiled at him when he moved the glass away. He drank some too, his eyes staying on her face.

'Do you know how happy you've made me over the past few months?' he said, and she saw him clearly again for a moment, this earlier Nathaniel who was sweet and a little unsure of himself.

'You've made me so happy too,' she said. But she was worn out tonight and it was harder to read him properly; the different Nathaniels were blurring together too quickly, so she didn't know what to give him in return, how to avoid disappointing him.

They finished the bottle between them, sitting side by side on the mattress, his hand straying sometimes to her hair, then drifting down her back. Gradually, she began to relax. She remembered how much she'd loved being drunk once, those ragged nights in her early twenties, Judith left with her mother, the third vodka tonic softening and disjointing everything; the men she'd fallen in love with – just for an hour or two; how fearless and free she felt when she went home with them. When the moment swelled and spread and was made only of itself, not at all of before and after.

Then Nathaniel was pressing against her, laying her back on the mattress.

I could never love anybody more, she thought.

It was only when he was already pushing his way into her that she realized he hadn't paused to put on a condom. Had he simply forgotten? She wrestled with the matter for a few moments.

'Relax,' he said. 'You're tensing up.'

'Nathaniel,' she whispered. 'You're not – we don't have any protection.'

He seemed not to know what she meant, continuing as if she hadn't spoken. She put her hands on his shoulders to slow him and tried to look in his face.

'Nathaniel, I don't think – I don't think you put one on. A condom.'

He shook his head. 'No, I didn't.'

'But I could get pregnant.'

'That's the idea.'

Dismay. 'But – I'm not ready for that. We haven't talked about it or – anything. I—'

'Be quiet,' he said sharply and she fell silent, wondering what she could say next, what wouldn't make him angry.

After a few moments, she said, as calmly as she could, 'Nathaniel, could we just stop for a moment? I'm sorry, I just—'

'Be *quiet*,' he said again. 'You're putting me off.'

His movements grew suddenly fast and brutal, and the

shock and pain of it prevented her from speaking any more.

And then it was over. Nathaniel shuddered and collapsed on top of her. She could feel the film of sweat on his chest and neck making her own skin damp, and then a wetness between her legs, a creeping stickiness. She was finding it difficult to understand what had just happened. She wondered if perhaps a whole conversation had taken place that she'd missed entirely.

There was a long silence, then Nathaniel murmured, 'You made it difficult for me.'

'I'm sorry,' she said. 'I was – surprised.'

'I told you to be quiet.'

'But I don't want another baby, Nathaniel. We haven't talked about it.' Her voice came out shrill. 'You have to talk about these things first!'

He pulled away from her and sat up abruptly. Then, without warning, he turned back to her and slapped her across the face.

The blow was not hard, but it was so unexpected she bit her tongue, and whimpered at the pain.

'Don't be silly,' he said. 'That can't have hurt. It hurts me far more to have to do that to you. Why are you being like this?'

'Like what?' she said, but her voice was a whisper and she wasn't sure if he'd heard. She put her hand to her face where he'd hit her.

'You know better than this,' he said. 'Stop challenging me. I thought you'd made so much progress but now look at you. Rebelling against everything.'

'I'm not rebelling,' she said, her tongue feeling swollen in her mouth. 'I didn't know we'd decided this, that's all. I didn't know.' Pitifully, she began to cry.

Nathaniel seemed to soften a little. 'Come on,' he said. 'You must have known. What do you think a woman's purpose is?'

She looked up at him, stricken.

He said, 'I allowed you a period of grace, Sarah, a period of adjustment. It's over now. You need to do your duty as a woman.'

She saw how stupid she'd been. All the women here had borne children in the Ark, all except Esther who, as she knew so well, could not. The prophet had only one child so far, the sour-faced Ezra who seemed to grow more like his mother every day – and there seemed no question of Nathaniel paying Ruth any night-time visits. Was it surprising that he wanted another child? And what kind of woman was she, to baulk at bearing it for him? Every one of her instincts was wicked. She deserved the punishment he had given her. Perhaps she deserved worse.

'You're afraid,' Nathaniel said. 'I can see that.'

He always knew her thoughts. He could look into people's eyes and see the ebb and flow of their soul.

She said, 'If I am, it's only because I'm weak.'

'You still have some of the world in you. The world's selfishness. The world's fear.'

She bowed her head.

He said, 'When you bear this child, you will be made clean.'

2

Thomas had a bottle of whisky in the desk drawer of his office at the back of the supermarket. The bottle was unopened, but he had pictured himself, many times, unscrewing the cap and pouring a slug into a glass, taking a sip. He had chewing gum in the drawer too, to mask the smell. Sooner or later, he would take a drink. It would, he supposed, be an experiment of sorts.

The session, rather than cleansing him of sin, seemed to have shaken something loose. His thoughts were roaming at will and latching onto anything that was forbidden. He couldn't stop thinking about his colleagues' lives, for instance. He'd felt no interest before, but now he pictured his assistant manager Jas going home to her husband in the evenings, some kind of small house where they lived alone, eating together at the kitchen table, going upstairs to bed. The new kid, Kieran, meeting his friends after work, their easy laughter, their silliness.

Thomas knew they must wonder about his own life, too, though they had long ago given up trying to persuade him out to socialize. He had heard Jas outside the storeroom once, whispering to one of the others about his 'sick wife'. He was glad of the misunderstanding, even whilst it unsettled him.

What if it was just Esther he was going home to? No one else claiming her, no one coming between them?

Satan, I refuse you, he thought, but the words didn't have the effect they should, were irritating rather than soothing.

And where was Jesus these days, anyway? God was everywhere, relentless and disapproving, but when Thomas looked for Jesus, he found no trace. He had known the Gospels virtually by heart once, and parts returned to him now, the long-submerged words rising gently to the surface.

Thomas saith unto him, Lord, we know not whither thou goest; and how can we know the way? Jesus saith unto him, I am the way, the truth, and the life: no man cometh unto the Father, but by me.

But at some point, it seemed, Nathaniel had discovered Jesus was superfluous. They almost never read the New Testament now, only the Old, and that was read to them, not by them. How long was it since they'd given up their Bibles? Thomas couldn't remember, which must mean it had been a long time. He'd had his almost from birth; it was a christening gift from his godfather, a pocket King James, bound in an unusual rich blue leather. But he'd handed it over gladly to Nathaniel when the time came. The prophet said, The devil sits between you and the Word of God. Your sinful eyes colour the meaning.

'Do you think it's strange,' he said to Esther as they lay together that night, 'that Sarah doesn't know anything about the Bible?'

'She wasn't religious before she was saved,' Esther said. 'But she was still saved.'

'I know. But it's so different to how we came to it.' He thought back to those late nights in London, all of them sitting round Nathaniel's cramped bedsit as Nathaniel drew their attention to passage after passage of the Bible, extemporized on the true meaning of the words. Thomas was amazed to discover how much he himself had missed, despite his diligent attendance at Bible study sessions throughout school and university. No one knew the scriptures better than Nathaniel, and particularly the Gospels; no one could quote them more promptly or comprehensively. Thomas had been stunned at his good fortune in finding such a teacher.

But when did merciful, loving Jesus get pushed out of the picture? Now there was only the wrath of God and the tricks of Satan.

Beside him, Esther was silent.

'Do you ever imagine a different life?' he said.

'*Thomas!* Of course not.'

'Do you ever wonder if there's more than one way to be saved, more than one way to serve God?'

'No. We've been shown the way,' Esther said. 'The prophet showed us.' She raised her head from his chest so she could look at him properly. 'Thomas, what's got into you?'

'I don't know,' he said. 'I'm sorry. Just tired.'

He asked himself if she would report him; already knew she would not. She would chastise herself for being weak and sinful, but she would protect him from another session. He tightened his arms around her. He wanted to say, Sometimes when we're alone I imagine we're on an island, or in a house surrounded by fields, and nobody can reach us. Sometimes I imagine there are only the two of us left in the world.

Once, he would have approached Nathaniel for help. He couldn't now. He had no idea what he was asking for, no idea if he was fighting towards the truth or away from it. It seemed impossible to untangle the mess in his head, to sift what made sense from what didn't. His mind didn't work the way it used to.

Satan, I refuse you.

And he saw it again. Nathaniel beside him in the rain outside the town hall, Nathaniel giving him that wolfish grin, saying, 'Let's go back to my flat so we can talk more.'

And Nathaniel grasping his hand across the table – Thomas taken aback, but not pulling away – saying, 'God sent you to me.'

Thomas too surprised to speak.

Nathaniel saying, 'You dreamed of heaven last night.'

Thomas had. And told no one.

'God spoke to you. But you're still not sure of the message.'

Thomas still saying nothing, his hand still being held. But the intensity of Nathaniel's gaze – he'd never seen anything like it. Those clear green eyes. They fixed you in one place, held you still whilst he examined every inch of your soul. It felt like a violation – and yet you welcomed it, *wanted it*. You found yourself bereft when he finally looked away.

'You've been praying for years, asking God to show you what He needs from you,' Nathaniel said.

Now Thomas was nodding, because yes, he had. For *years*. They all said, all of them in the Youth Church, that if you prayed for it then God would tell you. But He'd never told Thomas. Told the others, apparently, but passed over Thomas.

'Thomas,' Nathaniel said. 'He's telling you now. This is the beginning.'

And, later in the evening, 'Do you feel it? If you don't feel it, then there's no point carrying on. If you don't feel it now, you never will. Can you feel the Spirit moving within you?'

For a moment Thomas had been afraid. He felt nothing. There had been a mistake. Then a flicker in his stomach, an explosion like butterflies, pleasurable and unbearable, and heat and light rising up through his body.

'Yes, I feel it!'

Nathaniel – Nathaniel, the fisher of men – had put his hand on Thomas's chest and then (had he imagined this, or had it really happened?) Nathaniel had leaned forward and kissed him on the mouth.

'As Jesus chose his disciples,' Nathaniel said, 'his chosen followers, so I choose you.'

The memory brought heat to Thomas's face, and a weakness to his limbs. It ought to be reassuring, but something was amiss. He closed his eyes. Nathaniel was all edges and angles now. You could see the movement at the surface, but you couldn't see beyond it.

Haven't I fought this? he thought. Haven't I tried? But

this was an immovable enemy. It was different from the doubts he'd battled in the past, those niggling worries Nathaniel said were sent by Satan. It was an absence rather than an intrusion, a hollowness at his core that left him short of breath. It was impossible to articulate his thoughts any more clearly than this, but he knew that something was off balance. What had once appeared pure and good was now seen through a glass, darkly.

3

Esther was upstairs in the big house, changing the beds with Ruth. Better to be active than to sit downstairs sewing, trying not to worry about Thomas. The old sheets were bundled into a heap in the corner of the room; they smelt fetid and sweet, of damp skin and secret flesh. Sometimes a picture came into Esther's mind of Rachael and Seth together, or Deborah and Joshua. The women's nightgowns pushed up, the men labouring solemnly, faces averted. Did Ruth lie awake in the next room and listen?

These were the devil's thoughts. Esther looked across at Ruth to steady herself. No one like Ruth for putting the fear of God into you.

Together they stretched the fresh sheets taut over the beds. Esther tucked in the corners at her end quickly and neatly, taking private satisfaction in her efficiency, in the sharp edges and crisp finish. She paused whilst Ruth finished her side, trying not to feel smug.

'Do the pillows and duvet,' Ruth said. 'I'll go and make a start next door.'

Do the pillows and duvet *please*, Esther thought as Ruth disappeared. She fetched the pillowcases from the chair and began to swaddle the pillows, before turning her attention to the duvet. Ruth always struggled with this, which was probably why she'd made herself scarce. Ruth didn't like to be seen to struggle. Sometimes Esther suspected her of being prideful.

A slight shuffling noise, an almost imperceptible rustle, and she froze for a moment. The devil? Not the devil, Esther.

She crouched down and made herself peer under the bed, then jolted at the sight of two shadowy, hunched forms. She sighed.

'You'd better come out,' she said. 'The game's up.'

They crawled out shamefaced, Moses and Judith, and stood awkwardly in front of her. Children were so odd sometimes, Esther thought. Would she understand them better if she had some of her own? She tried to be stern; tried to channel Ruth. 'What do you think you're doing?'

'We're the spies in Jericho,' Moses said. He looked sorrowful. 'We were hiding in Rahab's house.'

'We didn't know you'd be coming in here this morning,' Judith said. 'Sorry,' she added belatedly.

'You shouldn't be in here at all,' Esther said.

'It was my idea,' Judith said. 'It wasn't Moses' fault. Don't report him.'

'Moses has a mind of his own, doesn't he?' Esther said.

'I do,' he answered, clearly irritated. 'And in any case, the actual *game* was my idea. So if anyone should be reported, it's me.'

'You need to be more sensible in your choice of game,' Esther said.

'The Bible is full of possibilities,' Judith said.

'Right, well, explore its possibilities elsewhere.' Esther

paused, weighing it up. 'We'll say this is your warning, alright?'

'Thank you, Esther.' They went towards the door.

'And go quietly,' she added, remembering Ruth's presence along the corridor.

They tiptoed theatrically out, Moses giving her a quick, grateful wave as they disappeared.

Esther returned to the duvet. She decided that if Ruth had heard anything, she would have already appeared, full of fury. As she turned the cover inside out and pushed her hands into the far corners, she carried out a quick examination of her conscience. But there didn't seem any need to report them, especially as Judith was on her last warning with Nathaniel. She remembered Thomas saying after the session, 'I thought they were hard on Judith. She's just a child, and she hasn't been here long.' Esther had been amazed by the comment and hadn't replied.

She took hold of the duvet corners and expertly flipped the cover over it, shaking it out. (She had learnt this trick from her mother, long ago. I may not be able to bear children, she thought, but look what I can do with a duvet cover.) She did up the buttons and laid it on the bed, then went next door to join Ruth.

The cold gaze was turned upon her as she entered the room.

'You took your time.'

Esther said nothing, unwilling to incriminate herself further.

'Fetch the sheet, then,' Ruth said.

Esther did as she was told. As they stretched it out

across the bed, she watched Ruth's face, those thin lips, the lined forehead, and wondered what she would have thought of her if they'd met in the outside world. Would they have been friends? She considered voicing this question, and the thought of Ruth's reaction made her choke back a laugh. Would she have been friends with *any* of them, come to think of it? Rachael and Deborah, she suspected, she would have placed in the category of *dull*, or, more damning still, *too nice*. But of course, her younger self had been stupid and sinful and wrong. Perhaps if she'd met Thomas in Gehenna, she would never have fallen in love with him. The idea made her lonely.

He'd said after the session that he didn't blame her for acting as the rod – she'd simply done as she was told. But then why was there this distance between them? Where was his usual warmth, his steadiness?

'Hurry up,' Ruth said, and Esther realized that her hands had stilled where they held the sheet. Briskly, she tucked the corners in at her end.

'Done,' she said.

She was almost relieved when the prophet requested her presence that night. For the first time in years, she found she was looking forward to a night away from her husband. It was impossible to be with him without feeling his unhappiness as though it were her own. And in fact, it had become her own. Esther hadn't known, before she married him, that she would come to feel the truth of the ancient words: *This is now bone of my bones, and flesh of my flesh.*

Watching Thomas sometimes when he was unaware, she saw that shadowed, preoccupied expression on his face and it hurt her. Nothing she said could soften it.

Nathaniel was languid and gentle with her tonight. He made it last a long time, but although she was tired, Esther didn't mind. Nathaniel absorbed all her attention – demanded it – and it was a relief. This part of her life, at least, was clear. She would do as God instructed, as she always had, and that was the way you kept yourself safe.

Afterwards, Nathaniel pulled her to him. He said, 'I love you.'

'I love you too.' It came out automatically, not carrying the rush it once had. But everything felt strange at the moment, so perhaps that was no surprise.

'You're very beautiful,' he said.

Esther didn't reply.

He said, 'I couldn't guide the others, I couldn't serve God fully, without your support. I hope you know how much I rely on you.'

Knowing he needed a response from her now, Esther said, 'I love being with you, Nathaniel.'

He stroked her hair. 'You must prepare yourself.'

She raised her head.

'Something's on the horizon,' he said.

'What?'

'Trust God. It won't be easy for you at first. Remember how much I love you.'

Esther wasn't exactly sure what he meant, but she had an idea. Sarah would succeed where Esther herself had failed. Suddenly, desperately, she wanted Thomas.

Alongside her, Nathaniel was still speaking. Reciting. She tried to make herself listen.

'Behold, I show you a mystery,' he said. 'We shall not all sleep; but we shall all be changed.'

After

On the nights when she couldn't sleep, Judith often wondered how other people managed it. The temazepam no longer had the effect it used to; she had to take two or three pills now even to make a dent, and that tended to wipe her out for most of the next day. Plus it was dangerous on top of whatever else she might have taken. Once or twice, in the early hours of the morning, she'd allowed herself to follow this thought to its natural conclusion. But that would be pretty horrible for her gran. And she didn't really want to be dead; in her more lucid moments, she recognized that she had no right to that kind of despair.

(*Did I tell you we keep chickens?* Moses wrote. *Every morning I collect the eggs.*)

Judith lay stiffly each night in her narrow single bed, the darkness slopped with queasy orange from the street lamp outside the window. She willed herself to fall asleep as two o'clock became three, and three o'clock became four. But instead there was just this tension, this sense that she must be ready for flight. Insomnia was murderous: it marooned you for too long with your own thoughts. And it was weird how tenaciously it had taken hold of her. Even after however many nights of this, nothing but a little fitful dozing before dawn, Judith never felt sleepy in the daytime, though her exhaustion was bone deep.

Her gran said she looked pale, and tried to feed her cod liver oil. People died of insomnia, Judith thought. You couldn't medicate it forever. Even temazepam betrayed you in the end. Everything did.

'Do you think you're evil?' she had asked her mother once, many years back, when she was still too frightened and angry to keep the words silent.

Stephanie hadn't answered directly – but how could she have done? She had cried, as she often did during those early visits. Judith had cried too. Then Stephanie had said something along the lines of, 'I wasn't myself.' A meaningless statement.

It didn't matter, anyway, what she had said. Judith knew her mother avoided dwelling on questions like this. Stephanie would prefer to fall back on the words of the psychologist at her trial: that many people, when subject to the same pressures, would have behaved in a similar way. But where was the defence in that?

It was on sleepless nights like this that Judith found herself in the Ark again. It was not simply the violence and terror of the end she remembered, but quieter moments too, roaming across the moors with Moses, or playing one of their stupid games in the forest. It was funny how difficult she had found it as a child to remain miserable for long. Somehow her mind always readjusted itself and cheerfulness crept in again. You seemed to lose that knack as you grew older.

The others had more of a right to fall apart, she thought,

because they'd actually believed, whereas she never had. Moses had so much more to lose.

In a shoebox at the bottom of her wardrobe were his letters. She knew she should have written back to stop him, but she'd said nothing, and the letters kept arriving. Some strange hopeful part of her had assumed they'd go on forever. But he'd been silent for nearly two years now.

The temping agency had got back to her at last with an admin role that proved as depressing as it sounded. Day after day, she went and sat in a hot little room at the back of the FE college and punched attendance figures into a database. None of the permanent workers spoke to her – temps, it seemed, were universally despised – but this suited Judith fine. She took her sandwiches out at lunchtime and ate them on a bench in the cold wind, looking onto the concrete yard of a warehouse. Sometimes she took a little something with her to ease her progress through the day, and sometimes she managed not to, finding a perverse enjoyment in the raw blaze of desolation an unmedicated day brought with it.

'Time you sorted yourself out,' her gran said. 'Found a proper job.'

'I'm trying,' Judith said.

'No, you're not.'

Judith was going to protest, but her gran had already turned her back to clatter about with the plates in the sink. Judith slunk up to her bedroom.

Sometimes, without being able to help it, she thought

of Nathaniel. He stalked down her attention and pushed his way to its forefront, a pure throb of malice. She'd actually considered going to visit him a few years ago, when she thought she was going mad with fury, to say all the things she'd never been able to say as a child. She'd even got as far as getting the visiting order, surprised and disturbed that he agreed so readily to see her. But she hadn't gone in the end, and now she was glad. He would have enjoyed it too much. Better to let him fade away, unnourished by attention.

She would never know now what it had been, what hunger there was in him to dominate and destroy, or whether he'd truly believed he could save them. But she never would have known anyway, she thought. Especially not if she'd asked him.

Nathaniel sent us a letter, Moses wrote. *But I don't know what it said. Peter put it on the fire before Mum could see it. I don't think I wanted to read it anyway. His words are dangerous.*

4

When he tried to explain to Esther what was wrong, alone in their bedroom after supper, Thomas found that however much you'd planned, it didn't help.

He said, 'I've been struggling recently.' But she knew this already, he thought; she was willing him not to say it out loud.

When she stayed silent, he searched for the words he'd rehearsed, but they'd turned to liquid and wouldn't keep their shape. He said, 'I don't understand it any more. This life. My place in it.'

He saw the shock rise in her – then saw her force it back down, and present him again with that smooth, clear surface; it always looked natural on Rachael or Deborah's face, but not on Esther's.

'You need to ask the prophet to pray for you,' she said.

'And have another session?'

Her forehead creased for a moment, then cleared. 'If that's what's necessary.'

'It won't help.'

'You have to try, Thomas.'

'I have.'

'We all have our faith tested sometimes. It makes it stronger.'

'This isn't about that,' he said. 'It's about this life. It's about Nathaniel.'

'Nathaniel?'

'I don't—' He stopped, feeling himself at the edge of a precipice. 'I don't trust him.' He'd thought he was going to soften these words with 'the way I used to', but he didn't.

'You don't mean that.'

'I do. Everything feels different now. I'm seeing things differently.'

'You're frightening me,' Esther said, plaintive.

'I know. I'm sorry.'

'Stop this,' she said. 'Let's just go to bed. You'll feel better tomorrow.'

'I won't,' he said. 'I'll feel the same.'

'You're giving in to weakness.'

'I can't help it,' Thomas said. 'I have to say it.'

'*Why?*' she said. 'Why do you have to say everything that comes into your head, whether or not it's right, whether or not it's helpful? Don't we all know better than that? You're not even trying to fight it.' She began to cry, and she raised her hand as if she might hit him, but instead she laid it gently, palm flat, across his chest. 'How can you just give up?' she said.

He tried to put his arms around her, but she stepped away. He felt the place where her hand had left his chest like a chill spreading.

'I'm trying to explain,' he said. 'This doesn't feel pure any more. It feels wrong.'

'But how can you tell?' she said with sudden hope. 'All your instincts are wicked. Remember what God says in

186

Jeremiah: *the heart is deceitful above all things.* We have to put our trust elsewhere, give ourselves up to God.'

'But is that what we've done, Esther?' Thomas said, with a bitterness that surprised even himself. 'Haven't we just given ourselves up to Nathaniel?'

'Stop it.' She put her hands over her ears like a child.

'I'm sorry.' He reached for her again and this time she let herself be pulled against him. 'I'm sorry,' he said again, mouth against her hair. He could feel her trembling. It came to him that if it were within his power to *make* himself believe again, he would do it; anything to avoid distressing her so much. But faith wasn't dependent on will alone.

He steered her towards the bed and they lay down together without getting undressed. They'd exhausted themselves. The only thing left was to go to sleep, and Esther obeyed when he stroked her hair and told her to close her eyes. But Thomas lay awake for a long time, his hand resting on her hip, listening to her breaths as they slowed.

She has to report me now, he thought. She'll realize that tomorrow.

And – I can't live without her. I can't leave without her.

But a couple of days passed without any summons from Nathaniel. Thomas told himself he was surprised, but perhaps he wasn't, perhaps he'd already understood how much she loved him. He could feel her confusion and suffered with her.

Nathaniel called Esther to spend the next night with him, so Thomas had to sleep alone. But the following evening, she slipped up to his room after supper.

'I'm with you tonight,' she said, stopping in the doorway.

He held out his arms and she came towards him. He thought of all the moments in the past when he'd waited to see if she'd come, his disappointment or joy entirely dependent on hearing her light step on the stairs.

Without another word they made their way to the bed, and Thomas forgot for a while his feeling of dread. But afterwards it was back, even stronger than before. As they lay curled together, he said, 'It could be like this every night. Imagine if we never had to be parted.'

Esther didn't reply.

He'd had time to think about it further, but still nothing was clear. It seemed best to use the simplest words, to stick to the simplest truth. He said, with more firmness than he felt, 'We can't stay here.'

'We can't *leave*,' Esther said.

'We can't stay.'

'Thomas, don't start this again. I thought you were feeling better.'

He shook his head. 'I can't go on.'

'You're not making sense.'

'That's because I don't know how. None of us knows how any more.' He had to do better. He had to make his brain work again and his thoughts flow clearly, so he could persuade her, so she would see they couldn't stay.

'It's all wrong,' he said. 'It's not what we wanted in the

beginning. It changed, and none of us noticed it changing. We thought we were moving closer to God, but I think we were leaving God behind.'

'That's not true.' Esther twisted round to face him. She was shaking her head as though she had water in her ears.

'There's another way for us to live,' Thomas said. When she didn't speak, he rushed on. 'We could leave here, go south. There's a job down there for me. I already asked them about transferring. There's a store in Southampton I could manage. I'd find us somewhere to live, I'd take care of everything. We could be happy. Think of it, Esther, being by the sea. And there would be no one but the two of us, and nothing to be afraid of.'

'Nothing to be afraid of?' she said softly. 'What about Gehenna? What about hell?'

'I know how frightening it is for you,' he said. 'You haven't left the Ark for so long. But it's OK out there, I promise. It's the same as it always was. Good and bad. I'd look after you. I'd never leave you.'

'Turn away from this wickedness,' she said. She put her hands to his face. 'Please, Thomas. Let me ask Nathaniel to pray for you.'

She would never come with him, Thomas thought. And he couldn't stay. The two realizations came together in his mind and took on a nightmare quality, a trickle of horror that ran the full length of his body and turned him cold.

He said, 'You have to come.' But he was warding off the truth with his useless words. He was causing her agony every time he raised the subject, could see how she was torn between the knowledge that she should report him and her need to protect him. He was making her suffer. It hurt him, right in the centre of his chest, and he understood now why people talked about the heart breaking.

He put his arms around her again, because there was nothing more to be done, and nothing more to be said. He felt her body against him, familiar and strange. He'd loved her so long, but still she was unknowable. This life had made her unknowable.

Whatever impulse had started all this would carry him on. He himself was worn out; he could do nothing further. In rare moments he allowed himself to wonder if it was the true God returning, the God of his childhood, come to save him; Jesus, endlessly loving, endlessly forgiving. The idea made him tearful but it never stayed long. Mostly there was just numbness and panic taking turns with one another, and always, always this sensation of falling.

5

Stephanie should have known better than to be surprised at how quickly she became pregnant. Within a couple of weeks, she found she'd missed her period. Of course Nathaniel had succeeded. He had gone about it with an almost frightening determination. Once every few days turned into twice a night, pragmatic and without prelude. How could she help getting pregnant unless her body deliberately resisted him?

And of course she was delighted. She carried the news to him proudly, a little shyly.

'I'm almost certain,' she said.

If she had expected praise, she was disappointed. She received a small nod of his head, and a satisfied 'Right.'

But after they'd waited another few weeks to be absolutely sure, there was a celebration dinner, and Stephanie felt herself basking in the joy and congratulations of the others. This was what Nathaniel had wanted for her, she thought. The kind of satisfaction that comes from accepting a will greater than your own; fulfilling your true purpose.

('You feel God at last, don't you?' he'd said to her. 'Finally, you've let Him in. Well done, little one.')

Pregnancy was easier this time round. With Judith,

Stephanie had piled on weight, she'd felt sick all the time, her whole body was sore and stretched; Judith had kicked and fought inside her. Now, though, she experienced almost no nausea, and no cramps. There was just a little blood, as there had been whilst she was carrying Judith. It must be so straightforward, Stephanie thought, because this time Nathaniel was looking after her – and God as well.

But still, the process felt strangely detached from her. She remembered that there had been a pleasure in carrying Judith, despite her discomfort. The baby had been part of her, a fat, hot, growing thing. It had been at the centre of her. This time, she occasionally had to remind herself that she was pregnant. It felt almost as though she'd been entrusted with something that didn't belong to her, and must hold it carefully until its true owner came back.

She'd been wary about telling Judith – their relationship was so precarious these days – but Judith had taken the news calmly.

'Oh,' was all she had said, and Stephanie was reminded dispiritingly of Nathaniel's reaction.

'A little brother for you,' she said. 'Won't that be great?'

'I'm not very interested in babies,' Judith said. Then, 'How do you know it's a boy?'

'Nathaniel said so.'

'Right.'

'Aren't you excited?'

'Not really,' Judith said, wandering off again.

This new composure on Judith's part troubled Stephanie. It appeared to be a stage beyond her original anger, and

Stephanie had a vague, saddening impression that there could be no going back. Judith had wanted things from her once. Now she wanted nothing.

Unexpectedly, she found herself thinking more and more about her own mother. Perhaps it was the hormones. She remembered how she'd clung to her mum during her pregnancy with Judith, once the initial stage of wonder and proud independence had passed. It had been super-seded by terror, and Stephanie had looked to her mum for reassurance as she hadn't done since she was small. Her mum had been brisk and practical each time Stephanie grew hysterical; a woman who came into her own in a crisis.

Now, Stephanie was surprised to find she missed her, though they hadn't had a satisfactory conversation for years. She and her mum had so little in common; they'd been fatally mismatched as mother and daughter. But per-haps she loved her mum after all. And probably her mum loved her, even if she wasn't the kind of woman to say it.

'It's funny,' she said to Nathaniel that night. He rarely visited her room these days, saying it would disturb the growing baby, and relief at seeing him made her unusually talkative.

'What's funny?' he said.

'My mother will never see this baby.'

'What's funny about that?' he said, and she was relieved his smile was in place.

'I mean, he'll be her grandchild. And she'll never know anything about him.'

'And why should she?' Nathaniel said, and she recognized it instantly, the change in his voice.

'It just seems – a shame. In a way,' she said.

'Would you like to go back and see her?'

'No, I don't want that.'

'Perhaps you'd like to visit, to show her the baby?'

'I wasn't thinking about that. Honestly, I wasn't. I just thought it was sad. Just in one sense.' She tried to smile at him. 'Mostly, it's wonderful.'

She thought he would have hit her again, were it not for the baby.

He said, 'You choose now of all times, *now of all times*, to turn your face back to Gehenna? You wait until you're carrying my child to turn back to the world?'

'No! I didn't mean it. Sorry.'

'The time for stumbling is long gone,' he said. 'You had your chance. Now if you stumble, you bring down not only yourself but the whole Ark.'

She allowed herself to cry, because she had seen that sometimes it softened him. After some hesitation, he put his arms around her.

'You're not yourself,' he said. 'Pregnancy makes women fearful. You're very vulnerable.' He stroked her hair. 'Let me protect you, little one.' She relaxed against him. After a moment, he pulled back to look at her. 'But make no mistake, Sarah. If you give the devil a way in, you will be punished, even if I have to wait until after the birth.'

She nodded, barely afraid. She would give him no reason to punish her.

6

It would be kinder, Thomas realized in the end, not to say goodbye. What right did he have to stir up her doubts and fears, to make her choose between him and God, him and Nathaniel?

He had imagined one final evening with Esther, when he would cling to her and memorize every part of her, every gesture and expression, every word she said, the sound of her voice and the smell of her skin. But Nathaniel took her on that last night, and in the end Thomas was grateful. It would have been too much to bear, knowing it was the last time.

When he kissed her goodbye in the morning and she said 'See you later,' he felt himself coming loose from the world. He said, 'I love you so much,' and she smiled up at him because it wasn't the kind of thing he usually said out loud.

It was Seth's turn to drive, so Thomas got in the back of the car. It wasn't one of Nathaniel's days for going to the town, but he came forward and tapped on Thomas's window. Thomas wound it down.

'You look rough,' Nathaniel said. 'Are you alright?'

How did he always know? He had always known everything. 'Getting ill, I think,' Thomas said.

'Are you well enough to go to work?'

'Yes,' Thomas said. 'Thanks.'

Nathaniel kept his eyes on him a moment longer. Thomas felt sick; it was possible that Esther had reported him after all. He wouldn't blame her.

Then Nathaniel stepped back. 'Drink plenty of water today,' he said at last. 'We need you well, Thomas.'

Thomas nodded. He would never see Nathaniel again. It seemed impossible. 'Yes, prophet,' he said.

'Right,' said Seth. 'Off we go.'

He turned the engine on and the car moved away. Thomas twisted his neck to look through the back window, squinting against the morning sun. Nathaniel was a dark shape against the wall of the big house. Thomas focused on Esther instead. The light had turned her hair to gold. She stretched her hand to the sky and held it there. He saw her growing smaller, and the two houses growing smaller behind her, until the road dipped and everything disappeared from view.

7

It was cold but they were used to the cold. Moses and Judith had tramped a long way across the moors and descended into a hollow they sometimes visited, a place where the ground fell away and turf walls rose up on all sides, lined with heather and bracken. They had discovered today that it was possible to push your way behind the bracken into a dip in the side of the wall, and let the overgrowth fall back in front of you like a curtain.

Moses watched Judith disappear.

'I could hide here,' she said, 'and never be found. Nobody would ever see me again.'

'God would see you,' Moses said.

There was a pause, then her voice from behind the curtain said, 'Is your God a good God?'

It was strange hearing this question from a disembodied voice. He'd often imagined this was how the devil would address him when the time for his temptation came; only the devil wouldn't speak in Judith's voice.

'Of course,' he said. Then, so there was no confusion, 'He's your God, too.'

'If God's so good,' Judith said, 'why are you scared of Him?'

Moses was beginning to see the danger of the curtain.

It had freed Judith to say whatever was in her mind. 'Because of all my wickedness,' he answered.

'I don't think you're wicked.'

'That's because you're wicked too.' There was silence for a while, and he was afraid he'd hurt her feelings, so he added, 'I like you, though.'

'I know.'

'We're *all* wicked.'

'Especially Ezra.' She emerged, dishevelled, with sprigs of heather in her hair. 'You try it.'

'What?'

'Hiding.'

He did as he was told, pushing his way through and making himself as small as possible. Judith rearranged the bracken and heather overhang in front of him.

'It's amazing,' she said. 'I can't see you at all.'

'I can see you.' He could, through the tiny gaps in the heather, see a Judith who was bright in the winter sun and fractured into a thousand pieces.

'We could play hide and seek here with the others,' she said. 'They'd never find us. We'd win every time.'

'We'd have to take it in turns to use the hiding place,' Moses said. He pushed his way out so they were face to face again.

'I don't want to play with them anyway,' Judith said. She looked around, swung her arms out a few times restlessly. Her mood was changing, Moses saw, the way it sometimes did, switching in an instant like the weather on the moors, when the sky darkened and the wind rose out of nowhere. He'd spent a lifetime trying to gauge the mood of the moors but they were impossible to predict. You'd be playing in bright sunshine one moment, then shivering and wet the next, the only warning before the rain fell that sudden chill in the air, that stillness and pause that never gave you time to run for shelter.

'What shall we do?' Judith said, and there was already a bite in her voice, the undercurrent of impatience he could always detect. Her temper had got worse, he thought, in the month since they'd made the announcement about the baby. In a moment she'd be talking angrily about her friend Megan, or her Game Boy, or McDonald's, or any other subject from the list of forbidden, mysterious things that had been taken from her. He always found himself wanting to listen and wanting to run away at the same time.

'Let's play Saul on the Road to Damascus,' he said.

'No. That's boring.'

'Or Casting out Demons?'

'I don't want to play any of your games,' Judith said. 'I'm fed up with them. There's nothing to *do* here.'

'There's loads,' he protested. 'The moors, the forest, the river.'

'You're not suggesting activities,' she snapped, 'you're just *listing* bits of landscape. There's nothing to *do* with any of them.'

He frowned at her. 'You said you liked the forest. Remember when you were Samson, bringing the pillars down? And when we were Absalom and Joab? The battle of Ephraim's Wood?'

'Those games are stupid,' she said. Then, bafflingly, 'I want to go to Laser Quest.'

He forced himself not to ask what Laser Quest was. Searching for some way to impress her, he said, 'We tried to build a bridge across the river once. It was exciting and dangerous.' Seeing he had at least a sliver of her attention, he went on, 'We used a fallen tree trunk. We all had to hold it just to lift it. Even Abigail and Mary.' He reflected happily for a moment – he'd been invited specially to help by Peter and Jonathan. 'We lifted it right up together, then dropped it across the river like a bridge.'

'So what went wrong?' Judith said. 'Did it fall off the edge?'

'No. It worked fine.'

'You said you *tried* to make a bridge. So something must have gone wrong.'

Once again, he marvelled at the sharpness of her mind. Nothing got past her. (This was also what the prophet said about the devil.)

'We had it all ready,' he said. 'But when it was finished, no one wanted to go across it.'

'Were you afraid of falling in?'

'Yes. But mainly of crossing into Gehenna.'

'That's stupid.'

'The river marks where the Ark stops and Gehenna begins.'

'So if you'd crossed it,' Judith said, 'would the devil have suddenly grabbed you?'

Moses didn't like the way she said it. 'I don't know what would have happened.'

'What became of your bridge, then?'

'We pushed it off the edge into the river.' He paused. 'I suppose it wasn't really a bridge.'

'Why not?'

'You can't call something a bridge if it can't be used to go across anything,' Moses said. 'It was just a tree trunk. It never changed into a bridge.'

Judith narrowed her eyes at him, but he felt pleased to have beaten her at her own game. He had, he felt, regained her respect.

'We'd better be getting back,' she said.

They scrambled out of the hollow, and as they headed back towards the houses, she said, 'If you want, we can play Twelve Spies on the way.'

'Alright.' He tried to conceal his pleasure. 'I'll be Igal, son of Joseph, from the tribe of Issachar. Who will you be?'

'I'll be Sethur, son of Michael, from the tribe of Asher.'

They crouched down low and began to creep over the moorland, pausing sometimes to duck behind rocks and hillocks and survey the enemy territory.

It was Judith who noticed it as they drew closer to the houses.

'The car's there,' she said.

Moses was a little way away from her, scouting the regions to the east, so he had to shout at her to repeat it.

'I said, the car's there.'

He came over to join her. 'It's too early for them to be back.' Already, he felt the first shiver of unease. 'Why would they be back now?'

'Perhaps one of them's ill,' Judith said. 'I was ill at school once, my throat was so sore I couldn't talk, and they called Mum to take me home. She had to leave work and she was annoyed at first, but then she saw I was really ill and we both put on our pyjamas and got the duvet from her bed and watched TV all day, and she made me hot chocolate for my throat.' She was smiling at the memory, but then the smile was gone. 'I hate her,' she said, but softly, almost to herself.

Moses didn't reply. He had stopped being a spy and was walking towards the big house as fast as he could.

'It won't be anything bad,' Judith said, quickening her pace alongside him.

But Moses knew it was, although he couldn't say how he knew.

They went through the door of the big house and along the corridor. The kitchen door was closed, but they could hear muffled voices. Moses hesitated, but Judith pushed the door open and went straight in. He followed her, because he always did.

All the women except Ruth were in there, and so were Moses' father and Joshua. Moses looked at his parents. His mother was crying, and she had her arm round Esther, who wasn't crying, but who was almost doubled over. Moses wondered if she were the one who was ill. His father was holding onto the back of a chair, looking down at his hands where they held the chair.

'He can't have meant it—' Deborah was saying when Moses and Judith came in.

'He did,' Moses' father said without looking up. Then, as if he'd been asked a question no one else had heard, he said, 'I couldn't have stopped him. How could I have stopped him?'

Then they all seemed to notice Moses and Judith.

'Go away and play, Judith,' Judith's mother said. 'We're busy here.'

'What's going on?' Judith said.

'Nothing's going on.'

Moses' mother said, 'Go on, Moses. Take Judith outside. You can't be in here now.'

But as they were going out, Judith muttering under her breath, there was the sound of feet in the corridor. The prophet burst in, followed by Ruth, who seemed unusually flustered and out of breath.

Moses and Judith had been forced to jump aside as the prophet came in, and now they shrank back against the wall, unwilling to draw attention to themselves by making their escape.

'Tell me it's not true,' the prophet said.

Moses saw his father's grip tighten on the back of the chair.

There was a long pause, then Joshua said, 'It is.'

'Which of you knew?' the prophet said.

'None of us,' Joshua said. 'We swear. We didn't know anything until today.'

'Liar,' the prophet said. His voice was quiet.

Moses' nerves felt raw, as though someone had peeled away his skin.

'Are you all so blind?' the prophet said. 'I told you to

be vigilant. Have you deliberately ignored me, or are you so forgetful you'd let the devil slip in whilst you sleep?' Anyone else, Moses thought, would be shouting. But the prophet spoke as carefully and delicately as he always did.

'Forgive us,' Joshua murmured. The prophet's fist flew out and connected with his jaw. It wasn't a forceful blow, and it wasn't well placed. But it was unexpected, and Joshua staggered on the spot. There was an intake of breath around the room.

'Be quiet,' the prophet said. 'Forgive you? As though this can be wiped out. The devil is amongst us,' he said, and his voice began to grow louder now. 'The devil is amongst us.' Then he turned, very slowly. 'Esther,' he said. 'Will you tell me you didn't know?'

She shook her head.

Perhaps he would have hit her, if Moses' father hadn't spoken up.

'Prophet, Thomas said so himself when he came to my office. That was all he *would* say – that he was going, but Esther had no idea. I tried to talk him out of it, but he wouldn't listen. He asked me to tell Esther he was sorry.'

'Can we trust his word?' the prophet said. 'The word of a sinner?'

Esther whispered, 'I didn't know.' Her eyes were on the floor. She seemed to be swaying gently.

As the prophet took a step towards her, she slumped forward, falling to her knees, and then onto her side. It took Moses a few moments to realize she had fainted.

In the confusion that followed, he felt Judith take his

hand. When he still didn't move, she tugged at his arm harder, and practically pulled him out of the room.

They went along the corridor and out of the front door, breaking into a run once they were outside and not stopping until they were hidden from sight behind the barn.

Moses leaned against the wall, trying to catch his breath.

'This is big,' Judith said.

'But what's *happened*?' Moses said.

'Isn't it obvious? Thomas has done a runner.'

'A what?'

'A runner. He's left.'

'That's not possible,' Moses said.

'Why not?'

'Nobody leaves. Nobody's ever left.'

'Well,' Judith said. 'There's a first time for everything.'

Then she was quiet for a while. Moses wondered what she was thinking. He himself was finding it difficult to think anything at all. His head felt too full, or too empty, or something—

'Are you alright?' Judith said.

Moses nodded and tried to take some deep breaths. He thought of Thomas, out in Gehenna, walking away from God.

The door at the side of the barn opened then, and Ezra, Peter and Jonathan emerged, Peter idly throwing a ball up in the air and catching it one-handed.

'What's wrong with you?' Jonathan said to Moses. 'Has Judith said she won't marry you?'

'Shut up,' Moses said savagely, and Jonathan looked surprised, though not nearly as surprised as Moses himself.

'It's Thomas,' Judith said.

There was no supper that night. The adults remained shut away in the prayer room for hours, except for Esther, who'd been put to bed.

The children sat huddled together on the stairs: Moses and Judith, Jonathan, Peter and Ezra, Abigail and Mary. For long periods of time, they didn't talk at all. But there was no one to tell them to go to bed, so they stayed.

'They've been quiet for a while,' Peter said eventually. 'Perhaps it's over.'

Then they heard the distant sound of the prophet's voice starting up again.

'I think it'll go on a while yet,' Jonathan said.

'Will Thomas come back?' Mary asked.

Nobody answered.

Moses was next to Judith, a couple of steps above the others. Their knees touched. She whispered, 'This is going to be bad, isn't it?'

Moses thought for a moment. Then he nodded.

After

If you're doing data entry, don't do it sober. Judith had found that taking a water bottle full of vodka with her had transformed a soul-destroying task into something pleasantly restful. There was a beautiful, rhythmic simplicity to data entry. You had a system and you stuck to it, just like the Romans with their lovely straight roads. *P* for Part-time. *F* for Full-time. A single number for Hours Attended.

After a while, she ceased even pretending to look at the list in front of her and entered whatever figures she felt like, depending on her reaction to each student's name. (Luke Baker: you sound like a full-timer, she thought, pressing the F key with a flourish.) She was careful not to sip from the bottle too often, and not to do it when anyone was looking, for fear of betraying herself with even the most infinitesimal shudder.

The voices of her colleagues drifted gently across the room, though never actually speaking *to* her, of course. They were discussing last night's television: *Silent Witness*, by the sound of it. Judith had actually watched this with her gran. I could join in, she thought in surprise, but then it seemed too much effort to formulate a coherent sentence that wouldn't give away the fact that she was smashed.

God, I love databases, she thought instead, punching in another *F* in triumph.

It was overkill, she knew, but at lunchtime she took half an oxycodone, and then, when she didn't feel any different by the end of her break, the other half as well. But the pill proved a mistake, and sitting at her desk that afternoon she felt increasingly dizzy and sick. A cold sweat had broken out on her forehead and under her arms. Was she going to die, right here, in the poky back office of a second-rate FE college? Forgetting for a moment that it wasn't actual water in the bottle, Judith took a large swig and then spluttered it out all over the keyboard.

'Are you OK?' large Kathy asked with evident disdain.

Judith nodded wildly, still trying to catch her breath. 'Went down the wrong way,' she managed to wheeze.

'You don't look well,' mousy Jeanette said. 'You ill?'

'Yeah,' she said. 'Maybe.'

Soon enough, she'd been packed off home, still sweating and shivering, wondering if she'd even survive the journey. But at least I won't die in the office, she thought. At least I'll die free, with the wind on my face.

Too nauseous to risk getting the bus, she walked a little way, and then, when her headache grew so pounding and insistent that even her steps seemed to be making it worse, she sat down shakily on a low wall by the side of the road and got out her phone to distract herself. Another missed call from Nick, but she knew he'd give up in the end.

She got herself home eventually, and found her gran in the sitting room by the electric fire, reading Proust. It was such an unlikely sight that Judith almost started sniggering, and had to turn away and cough a few times to mask it.

Her gran took one look at her and put her to bed with a hot-water bottle.

'This isn't acceptable, Judith,' she said once she'd brought her a cup of hot water with lemon and honey. 'This is disgraceful.' Her eyes moved over the heaps of dirty clothes on the floor, the old mugs of half-drunk tea, globs of sour milk pooling on the surface. 'And look at the state of this room.'

Judith was glad she hadn't left her drawer of pills open. She'd become careless recently, emboldened by the knowledge that her gran never came into her room whilst she was absent. Quailing under that severe gaze, she could see there was no point in protesting that she was ill. 'Just overdid it a bit,' she said, and tried giving her gran what she hoped was a disarming smile. She had a suspicion it came out wrong, since her gran did not look appeased.

'We'll talk about this tomorrow,' her gran said, turning to leave the room.

'Can I borrow *Swann's Way* when you've finished with it?' Judith asked, and then laughed so hard she almost threw up.

The temping agency rang at the end of the week to say her services were no longer required at the college. It wasn't clear to Judith whether the job was finished or if she was being fired, which probably just meant that the person at the other end of the phone was a coward.

'I'll find something else,' she said to her gran, without any clear idea whether this was true. She had a suspicion the agency wouldn't be forthcoming with any more work, and she couldn't go back to the pub because Nick worked there; it was he who'd got her the job in the first place.

'Why not take it as an opportunity to look for something better?' her gran said. 'Use that degree of yours.'

Judith had a feeling that since the coming-home-drunk incident, her gran was being stiff with her, but since this was her gran's natural state anyway it was rather difficult to tell.

She said delicately, 'Sorry again about Wednesday—'

But her gran held up her hand to silence her. 'The less said about that, the better.' Judith was about to breathe a sigh of relief when her gran went on, 'But let me tell you, Judith, if this goes on, you won't have a home here. Do you understand that? Get yourself together, or you won't be living under my roof any longer. Is that clear?'

Judith managed to nod.

Her gran seemed to relent a little. 'It's for your own sake, Judith. Do you see that? I sometimes think if I'd been stricter with your mother—' But she apparently decided against pursuing this line of thought and said instead, 'I want you to have a good life. That's all.'

Judith went up to her room and lay down on the bed. Maybe this time she really would sort herself out, she thought. Perhaps she would get a proper job and settle down and be happy. And then at last she'd write Moses a letter. Even though he'd have given up waiting by then, she'd write one anyway, because finally she'd have something good to tell him.

She let herself think about this for a while, feeling it soothe her. Then she let it go.

V

Deluge

1

'The baby's a symbol of hope, isn't it?' Stephanie said to Nathaniel. Always these days she was looking for ways to comfort him, even if it was only repeating his own words back to him.

'It's not enough,' he said. He didn't turn towards her, and when she tried to put her arm around his shoulder, he moved away from her to the edge of the mattress.

'I should go back to my room,' he said.

'Stay a little longer.'

'Don't tell me what to do.'

'Sorry.'

'He was my right hand,' Nathaniel said, as he often had over the past couple of weeks.

Stephanie remained silent.

'I gave him everything,' Nathaniel said. 'I raised him up from nothing to look on the face of God. How could he do this?'

Stephanie reached out and laid her hand on his back. This time he didn't shake her off. She'd seen him weep for the first time in the days after Thomas left, though not in front of the others – only her. It touched her, that he would trust her with his unhappiness.

'Soon the baby will start to move,' she said. She sometimes thought she could feel it already, coiled and pulsing inside her, though it was only about seven weeks old.

'It's a blessing,' Nathaniel said, but his voice was distant. After a pause, he added, 'I understand now why God never let Esther carry a child. I always wondered. He knew her wickedness all along.'

'But Thomas told Seth she didn't know anything,' Stephanie said.

For a moment, from the way he froze, she thought he might hit her again. But he seemed to hold himself back. He said, 'Are you really so naive?'

Perhaps she was. Nathaniel said Esther was bad, so Stephanie supposed she must be. This was the triumph and vindication she'd been waiting for; but it brought her no joy. She'd watched Esther since Thomas had left. They all had, couldn't help it, even as Esther turned away from them. Without Thomas, Esther became clumsy. She broke plates in the kitchen. Her sewing was awkward and uneven. The others said she would improve in time, but time passed, and Esther became clumsier still. Stephanie pitied her, which must be another sign of her own weakness.

None of them mentioned Thomas as they went about their work tasks, though he was in every silence between them. They adjusted the laying of the table so there wouldn't be an empty place at supper. Rachael and Deborah were jittery and awkward, Ruth fierce in her efficiency.

For a week after Thomas had gone, Seth and Joshua

went straight into the prayer room with the prophet after work, and stayed shut in there for an hour or more, although nobody knew what they were discussing. Perhaps the other men had been searching for him in the town, though Stephanie didn't think there was much point in this. Thomas would be far away by now.

'I've been a fool,' Nathaniel said as she stroked his back. 'I didn't see what was right in front of my face.'

'You're not a fool,' Stephanie said.

'I've been blind,' he said. 'But I won't be blind any longer. Thomas and Esther tricked us all. I should have known better. But Esther can be—' He broke off, so Stephanie never found out what Esther could be. Nathaniel said instead, 'She was so unhappy when I met her.' He paused again for a moment, then said briskly, 'Her brother was murdered. Did you know that? Stabbed to death outside a pub. They never found out who did it, or why.'

Stephanie hadn't known this – it was horrible. It seemed strange that she was being given the information she'd craved about Esther's early life only when it was too late to be of any use.

'Now I think I misread the signs,' Nathaniel said. 'God wasn't telling me to save her from all that misery. He was telling me her family was marked, that she was marked. I thought I could help her. She was so young. And I was weak. But I was wrong. I believed what I wanted to believe.'

'No,' Stephanie said. 'You were kind and good. This isn't your fault.'

*

That night she dreamed of Esther's brother, faceless and indistinct as he was, felt the terror of his final moments as though they were her own.

When she woke she was being stabbed in the gut. She clutched her stomach and strained to see through the dark. Nathaniel, holding the knife above her. That brilliant smile.

Then she woke again and there was no blade. But there was still the pain, and a sticky wetness beneath her that turned out to be a mess of blood. There was no woman to scream for now Esther had been moved to the big house to sleep in Thomas's old room, but Stephanie screamed anyway and after what seemed a very long time Nathaniel came. He stood in the doorway and she wondered why he wasn't coming closer, why he wasn't coming to help her. Then he disappeared, just turned and went away. She tried to call after him, to plead, *don't leave me*, but another slice of pain doubled her up. She clutched herself, smearing her hands with the blood that soaked her nightdress.

It was dawning on her now, what was happening. But it's much too early, she thought. It's coming much too early. And then – oh.

She would die with the baby. No doctors here, nothing but the wild moors. At first, as another cramp convulsed her, and she thought of how Nathaniel had come and looked at her and left again, she found she didn't much mind the idea of death. But Judith, what about Judith? From the depths of pain, Stephanie pulled a single clear thought: leaving Judith in the others' care wasn't good enough. The realization shocked her, and it was this that made her unfurl herself and cry, 'Help! Please, help.'

It began as a scream and ended as a whisper, but then Ruth was there, kneeling beside her, feeling Stephanie's forehead with her hand. Over her shoulder, Stephanie saw Nathaniel and realized that of course he hadn't left her – he had simply gone to get a woman, because a woman would know what to do.

Ruth was already lifting Stephanie up and calling for Rachael to get some towels.

Stephanie let them do what they wanted. Dimly she was aware of someone bringing a bowl of water and beginning to clean her, someone else peeling off her nightgown and pressing a towel between her legs. Another cramp made her whimper and curl up on her side. Someone pushed the damp hair off her face and murmured, 'Shhh, it's alright.'

The pain was coming in waves now, starting each time as a dull ache and becoming a blaze of agony. She felt something give within her, something come loose, and wondered if this was what death felt like: if you actually felt the moment your soul was pulled from you.

She heard someone say, 'Don't let her look,' but the voice seemed to come from a great distance and she wasn't sure if they were talking about her or someone else. And now something was being bundled up in a towel. Stephanie craned her neck, but Ruth was already on her feet and moving towards the door with the bundle of towels in her arms.

'Is that—' Stephanie tried to say, but Deborah cut in.

'It's not a baby, darling. It hadn't grown properly. It wasn't a baby yet. I'm so sorry.'

Arms around her. Stephanie closed her eyes. She felt herself being lowered back down onto the mattress.

'You need to sleep now, Sarah.' Nathaniel's voice.

She closed her eyes and did her best to obey him. It wasn't a struggle in the end.

She knew she was awake at times over the next few days, but she felt as though she had been wrapped in thick material. The world had taken on a strangely muted quality; sights blurred, noises muffled. They washed her again, Rachael and Deborah, and put her in the chair by the window, wrapped in blankets, whilst they changed the sheets on her bed. They brought her soup, and when she stared at it, unsure what to do, unsure if she'd ever seen soup before, Rachael brought the spoon to her mouth for her, coaxed her into swallowing. They talked to her soothingly, and told her it would be alright. (What would? she thought.)

The first time she woke properly, it was to hear her daughter's voice. Perhaps this was what brought her back: that familiar, strident tone. Because of course Judith was arguing. She'd been born arguing.

'She's my mum,' Judith was saying. 'Just let me see her.'

'Do as you're told and go away.' Ruth's voice. Stephanie

had opened her eyes now, but there was no one in the room with her; they must be just outside the door.

'She's my *mum*,' Judith said again.

'Please, Ruth.' A more timid voice backing up Judith's. Moses, of course.

Stephanie wanted to intervene, but felt too tired to call out. She was relieved when she heard footsteps, and then Rachael's voice joining in.

'Perhaps just for a minute, Ruth? Judith's been very frightened.'

And then a moment later, Judith was in the room, and Stephanie was trying to sit up so she could hug her.

'It's OK, Mum,' Judith said. 'Lie down. You need to rest.'

Stephanie did as she was told.

'I was worried about you,' Judith said. She sounded accusing, but Stephanie knew her daughter too well not to see she was holding back tears.

'I was spared,' Stephanie managed to say. But this reminded her who hadn't been spared, and she couldn't breathe for a moment.

'Are you feeling better?' Judith said.

'A bit.'

Judith reached down and awkwardly, a little too heavy-handedly, stroked Stephanie's hair, the way Stephanie had used to do for Judith herself when she was very little. Stephanie closed her eyes at the touch.

Judith said softly, 'Mum? I'm sorry about the baby.'

Stephanie nodded, tears leaking from her eyes. 'It

wasn't meant to be,' she tried to say, but only the first two words came out.

Ruth appeared in the doorway. 'Time's up,' she said.

*

Nathaniel didn't come. It was clear to Stephanie now that she had been unworthy of carrying the child. It had been taken away.

She drifted in and out of sleep, but sleep was no longer a safe place. Often it rose up before her, the dead child, crying for her. Later she remembered Deborah's words – 'It's not a baby. It hadn't grown properly' – and the child was reduced to an ugly clot of blood.

Forgive me, she tried to ask, but when God spoke to her, all He said was this: The wages of sin is death.

By the time Nathaniel did come, she was hysterical. She had woken from another nightmare to find him kneeling beside her.

'I'm sorry!' she said. 'I'm sorry I'm sorry I'm sorry.' The words became distorted as she sobbed.

He let her cry, watching her steadily. She wished he would shout. She longed for him to shout, to punish and finally absolve her.

'Forgive me, Nathaniel. Will you send me away? Send me anywhere if it's better for the Ark. I don't deserve to be here.'

She felt his arms go round her.

222

'Hush, little one,' he said. 'Calm down first, then we'll talk.' He rocked her gently as her sobs became quieter and eventually she rested her head against his chest, exhausted and silent.

'Where is he?' she whispered.

'Who?'

'The baby.'

'We buried him in the woods,' Nathaniel said. 'He's with God now.'

'What was his name?'

'What?'

'His name.'

'He didn't have a name. He was taken from us too soon.'

'He must have a name!' The panic was returning. 'He can't be buried there on his own, all on his own, with no name.' She began to cry again.

'It wasn't God's will,' Nathaniel said. 'God didn't send me a name for him. We weren't allowed to make him one of us.'

When her sobs became wails, he seemed to relent.

'God knows his name, Sarah. Let that be enough for you. In heaven, God calls him by his name.'

She rubbed her hands into her eyes.

'Sarah,' Nathaniel said, 'this wasn't your fault.'

'It was.'

'No, my poor darling. Other people did this. Infected the Ark with their sin, turned us rotten from the inside. Brought punishment down on us.'

A prickling in her flesh. 'Who?'

'You already know.'

She would save it for another time, thinking about Esther and Thomas, and what they'd done. She wasn't strong enough yet. For now, she couldn't look beyond the out-come to the cause. The outcome was death: not just the baby's, she began to see, but her own. A kind of death that took you apart, and then sent you back, bloodied and broken, forced you to live on in the mess of your own defeat. Men, she was certain, couldn't understand this kind of death. Perhaps women weren't as weak as people thought. Men held the power, of course, and that was how it should be. But didn't women deserve some recognition too, for their endurance? Men were made for war and heroics, to fight and conquer for God. But women were made to suffer. And suffer they did, because the blood and the battle were within themselves, always within them-selves.

2

A few days after they buried the baby, or whatever the thing was staining the bundle of towels with blood, it began to rain.

They'd never seen rain like this before. It came down in wide slices with no gaps in between, no pause for you to get your breath. The drops were heavy and fell hard. A wall of water.

Moses and Judith fled to the barn because it no longer felt safe in the big house. People were becoming unpredictable. Moses' mother had snapped at them when they interrupted her and his father talking softly in the kitchen. Rachael never snapped.

'Let's go to the forest,' Judith said, seeing his face.

But they were soaked before they'd gone a few steps, hair plastered to their foreheads and clothes sticking to them. The barn was closer. The roof leaked, but only in some places. Sitting with their backs to the wall, pulling at their wet clothes, they shivered and listened to the rain on the roof. It sounded like a rattle.

You must wash yourselves clean, the prophet said. You are filthy with sin.

The moors were waterlogged, and they'd been banned from walking on them. Flooding and bogs. The Ark had shrunk around them. The rain came down so hard you could barely see in front of your face.

A few more days of this and even the forest floor would be spongy and sodden, the rain sliding in amongst the dense branches and the water level rising. Moses pictured it: rising and rising until it lapped at the tops of the trees, finally swallowing everything. Then perhaps God would be satisfied. All that remained would be a pure, still surface of water.

'How long do you think it will last?' he said to Judith.

She shrugged. 'As long as God decides.'

He was surprised; it wasn't like her to talk about God.

He thought of the rain churning up the fresh earth on the grave, uncovering the dead thing. They'd said a prayer together as they put it in the ground. Strange to remember what it was like to stand there in the dry air, the wind lifting their hair, no warning of the rain to come, except perhaps for the slightest chill – or was he only adding that now? Judith's mother had been too ill to get up, but every-one else came to the burial, except for Esther. She had been told to stay away. She was tainted now. Moses won-dered if this meant she would get a stain on her face like his. But perhaps that only came if you were marked from the start.

The prophet said to them as they stood around the grave, 'Sin will destroy us. You allowed it into the Ark. That's why God took the child.'

In the barn, Moses said to Judith, 'The only way to stop it is to cast sin out of the Ark. Otherwise we'll all be drowned.'

'Do you really think this is Esther's fault?' Judith said.

He knew it wasn't a proper question, but he still tried to consider it carefully, the way Judith always did. 'I don't know.' Then, 'The prophet says so.'

'So,' Judith said, which seemed to mean nothing and mean a lot at the same time.

And Moses felt something strange happening, as though he could stand outside the prophet's words and look at them instead of living in a world made of the words. 'He says so,' he said again, to make the feeling go away, to put himself back on the inside of the words where things were less frightening.

The rain came down like a rattle.

They began to get used to it, the sound of rain accompanying everything they did. There were leaks all over the big house and the small house. They kept buckets and pans under the drips but they were running out of containers. During lessons, it was difficult to hear Ruth speaking over the hammering on the roof and the steady *drip-drip* into the pans on the floor.

Moses wasn't sure what the adults were waiting for, why they were so tense and quiet, but he thought that like him they must be afraid the rain would never stop. It became more unsettling the longer it went on. No weather should last so many days without a break. Even the wind rested occasionally. Where was it now? It didn't have the energy to compete with the rain, not even the raging moor wind that at other times could lift you off your feet. Still the water fell in straight sheets.

Judith's mother came back downstairs after a week, but she looked pale and she often seemed to be crying. It was unsettling, coming into the workroom to find all the women in there but nobody speaking. Moses hadn't realized until now how it had set the rhythm of his days, the chatter of his mother and the others in the background, a soft swell of sound. Now it was gone and below the silence was a low beat of fear.

God said, *I will cause it to rain upon the earth forty days and forty nights.* Moses knew a thing or two about punishment. Plagues, curses, scourges. After ten days, he began to think this had been coming, always coming, rolling towards him since the day he was born with the mark on his face like he was bleeding beneath his skin. Nobody was forgiven because nobody had earned it. With the rain coming down – was it getting stronger every moment? – it was difficult to think at all.

And what would God send them next? Darkness or locusts? A hail of fire and brimstone?

What could follow death, which had already come?

On the eleventh day, the prophet called them back to the prayer room. It was a Saturday, but the children had been kept in the schoolroom all morning, writing out Bible verses under Ruth's watchful eye. We must show the Lord we are sorry, she said.

The harvest is past, Moses wrote, *the summer is ended, and we are not saved.*

He looked over Judith's shoulder to see which verse she'd been given.

Thou hast forsaken me, saith the Lord. Thou art gone backward: therefore will I stretch out my hand against thee, and destroy thee; I am weary with repenting.

His own father appeared in the doorway.

'The prophet wants us in the prayer room,' he said to Ruth.

'Even the children?'

'Even them,' Seth said.

They were all gathered, every member of the Ark, including Esther. Perhaps this was a session, Moses thought. They'd all felt it over the past few days: Esther's session, hanging in the air. She would be made to suffer for Thomas, to endure his punishment, long overdue, for betrayal, as well as her own for not preventing it.

But the prophet stood alone in the middle of the room, and didn't lead them to the barn. Instead, he addressed them.

'For eleven days, God has made it rain. For eleven days, we have seen His disappointment and fury. This is our second punishment. Peter, what was our first?'

Moses looked fearfully at his brother, but Peter was ready with an answer. 'The death of the baby, prophet.'

Moses heard a muffled sob from behind him, so he knew that must be where Judith's mother was standing.

Then he realized the prophet was looking straight at him.

'Why, Moses, are you fortunate?'

He tried to take a breath, but couldn't seem to get the air inside his chest. 'I was spared,' he whispered.

The prophet nodded slowly. 'God spared Moses as a baby, though He could have slain him as punishment for his parents' sins. Instead God allowed the devil to disfigure Moses, as a permanent reminder for all of us. Have you all forgotten so easily what the wrath of God looks like?'

Moses wanted to cover his face with his hands but he knew that would make things worse, so he held his arms stiffly by his sides.

'Make no mistake,' the prophet said. 'God is serious. God is coming for you. As long as you harbour sin, you're slipping into the hands of the devil – destroying the Ark we've worked so hard to build. Jonathan, what are the wages of sin?'

'Death, prophet.'

'*Death*. God is giving you time to mend your ways. A short time. After that, He is coming for you. Ezra, what's hell like?'

Ezra faltered a little in his answer. 'Horrible, prophet. A place of eternal torment. And fire.'

The prophet's eyes burned with a fire of their own. He said, 'Yes. A place of eternal torment and despair. Your skin is scalded off your flesh; your flesh is boiled off your bones. You're put back together only so you can suffer further. You're in agony – *every* – *second*. It doesn't end. It doesn't get better. Do you realize how long eternity lasts? Of course you don't. Human minds can't conceive of it.

One day, you'll know what eternity is, and if you've chosen an eternity of suffering you'll scream and curse and beg for forgiveness. But let me tell you, no forgiveness will come. You had your chance. Your chance is now.' His voice rose to a shout. 'Your chance is now!'

Then he smiled. Moses' breath came like a shudder.

The prophet said, 'Who here doesn't believe me?'

Nobody spoke.

Still, the smile. He said, 'Come with me. There's something I want to show you.'

Nobody stopped to put their waterproofs on. They followed the prophet outside and were soon drenched to the skin.

The rain was so heavy that Moses didn't see it until they were already up close. The forest. He rubbed the water from his face and stared. Someone had cut the forest open. The tangled branches that guarded the entrance had been ripped away leaving a gaping, ugly hole like a wound, a tunnel amongst the trees. Moses turned to Judith. She was frowning, but didn't speak. Moses saw the dead thing before his eyes again; blinked it away.

The prophet said, 'Follow me.'

He stepped in amongst the mutilated trees and the others went after him. Moses could hardly bear it, seeing the adults walk with such ease into their forest. They didn't even have to dip their heads to enter, let alone crawl.

As Moses had thought, the rain had begun to make its way inside the forest, even through the thick canopy of branches. There was a smell of damp earth. But still, the onslaught was lessened by the trees and the drops that made it through were light and half-hearted. It was a relief, being out of the driving rain, but the forest no longer felt like a refuge.

After a while, Moses realized where the prophet was leading them. It was taking longer than it should because, not knowing the forest well, the prophet hadn't chosen the quickest route. But they were sloping gently downhill now, bending towards the left, and soon they would come out at the river. Moses wondered what the prophet wanted them to see. A horrible thought occurred to him, and he looked quickly for Esther, walking alone a little way ahead. The prophet talked a lot about punishment these days. What if he was planning to drown her in the river like the Egyptians? He told himself this was impossible, but nothing seemed impossible any more.

He and Judith had gradually dropped back behind the others, who were almost out of sight ahead. But soon Moses could see light trickling through the trees in front of them so he knew they were close to the edge of the forest. In seconds, the prophet and the grown-ups would be out in the light and rain. He tugged at Judith's arm.

'Come on. We're getting left behind.'

They heard the screams before they reached the edge of the forest. For a moment, both of them stopped dead.

'What the—' Judith began, but Moses couldn't answer, just looked at her wildly. His instinct was to run as fast as he could back the way they'd come. Whatever was happening on the riverbank, he didn't want to see it. But there was another scream, though this time it was closer to a wail. He thought he recognized his mother's voice.

Together they burst out of the forest, and the rain hit them again, fierce and disorientating.

The first thing Moses saw was that no one was in the river. All the grown-ups were standing there on the bank, and the other children, too. As far as he could tell, no one had been hurt, but now he could see that his mother and Deborah were crying. He turned to his father for an explanation, but his father didn't look back at him. His body was rigid.

Very slowly, Moses followed their eyes. It seemed to take him too long, because before he saw it for himself he heard Judith's sharp intake of breath, her muttered 'Oh *God*.'

Between the two dipped banks, the river was running with blood.

Moses stared and stared at the red torrent. In front of it, the prophet stood, his legs planted wide, his arms spread. Moses closed his eyes, but when he opened them again the monstrous sight remained. He thought he could smell it now, stagnant and reeking of slaughter. He saw the Egyptians filling up their pitchers, raising them to their mouths, expecting cool, clear water and finding something thick and warm and metallic spreading across their tongues, staining their lips red.

'Now do you see?' the prophet said. '*Now do you see?*'

Even through the fog of confusion and terror, Moses was shocked by the expression on Nathaniel's face. It seemed strange to him, amongst all the other strange things he had seen, that this most horrifying punishment seemed to have filled the prophet with triumph.

After

Judith hadn't known withdrawal would be this bad. The tight feeling in her chest, the throb of panic as though at any moment things were going to spiral out of control. Her head ached, her eyes ached, all her muscles ached. She had a horrible, constant nausea, but she never threw up.

This was all unexpected.

'You're fucked up,' she remembered Nick saying to her once.

'It's *recreational*.'

'It's only recreational so long as you're actually having fun.'

She would have stayed in bed all day, but every morning at half past seven her gran would arrive outside her door and knock, politely but insistently, until Judith opened it, groggy and irritable. Then they would go downstairs to the kitchen, where her gran would make them both a cup of tea and they'd listen to Radio 4 together.

Her gran, it appeared, was 'taking her in hand'. This didn't delight Judith, but at least she hadn't been chucked out on the street.

'I'll look for another job soon,' she muttered over the porridge that had just been placed in front of her. God, she hated porridge, particularly when she was feeling this queasy. But her gran, who was half Scottish, was adamant on the subject of its restorative qualities.

'You can look for work as soon as you're better,' her gran said. Meaning, presumably, as soon as you've sorted yourself out, and stopped sweating and shuddering over breakfast.

In the meantime, Judith stayed at home under her watchful eye. Throughout the morning they sat together in the small front room, electric fire on, her gran listening to the radio and knitting, or reading another intimidating-looking novel.

In the absence of anything better to do, Judith really had borrowed *Swann's Way*. It was dense and slow, bizarrely out of step with the stuttering rhythm of her own life. She began to lose herself in it, only absorbing about half the words, but finding the experience strangely rest-ful. Although she had been ploughing through it for over a week now, she didn't seem to be making much progress. Comforting, in a way.

In the afternoons, she was permitted to disappear off to her room for a nap. These seemed to be the only occasions she did actually sleep. Night-time was still a write-off, and Judith sought refuge in *Persuasion*. Proust for the day, Austen for the night. (When she'd accompanied her gran to the local library, Judith had originally made a beeline for Dostoyevsky, but her gran had steered her firmly away: 'I recommend something less alarming, Judith.') But the spike of panic was still lodged in her chest, and she won-dered if it would ever ease. Was this what it would always be like without any pills to soothe her, without a sly hit of alcohol to take the edge off? They told you in counselling that it wasn't about forgetting what had happened, but about coming to terms with it – that old cliché. But what did it even *mean*? Precisely nothing, so far as she could see. You went to the sessions obediently enough, and then you walked on razor blades for the rest of your life.

People say this place is beautiful, Moses had written in one of his last letters. *They say I'm lucky to be living by the sea. My mother grew up here, so she likes it. But it doesn't mean anything to me. I can't get away from the Ark. It's with me all the time, the smell of heather and earth, the feel of the wind. I think that must be the problem with growing up in one place, never knowing anything else. When you move on, you can't help but take it all with you, so you find yourself always in the wrong place, the wrong time.*

3

They waited nearly two days after the river turned red before they shut Esther in the prayer room. She'd known it was coming, and didn't struggle or protest. There didn't seem much point.

The room was chilly and dark. They'd hung a cloth in front of the window so she wouldn't be distracted from contemplating her sins. Esther sat in the corner, wrapped in the blanket Rachael had brought her.

'I don't think this will go on for long,' Rachael had murmured as she passed the blanket through the door. 'Just be patient.'

Esther nodded, then listened as Rachael locked the door again behind her. This seemed unnecessary; she wasn't going anywhere. The idea of trying to escape across the moors alone and on foot was ridiculous. And anyway, how could she run from God?

She had known her punishment was coming when she saw the river of blood. Rachael and Deborah had cried out when they saw it, a strange, primal response to horror. Esther's heart had faltered for a few moments before she realized what had happened: the heavy rainfall had washed the reddish-brown clay from the banks into the river. Had the others understood this too? Nobody said. And anyway it didn't matter whether or not it was really blood: it wasn't what it was that was important, but what it represented. Esther wondered, when the session came, how much they would hurt her. The worst she'd suffered before was a broken nose. It had been agony at the time, and had healed crooked. She couldn't even remember now what she'd done to bring it about. Must be more than ten years ago. She no longer noticed the bump in her nose when she looked in the mirror.

She had a feeling that this occasion would be more memorable; that the mark, whatever mark she was left with, would cling to her inside as well as out. She would not be one of them again after this.

The rain was still coming down hard outside. She had to shift her position after a few hours when there was a fresh leak in the roof, the cold drops hitting the back of her neck and running down her collar. She moved a few yards away and watched the puddle forming where she'd been sitting, droplets splashing onto the floor one after another and beginning to band together; a little pool fanning out, glossy and dark in the gloom.

She still found it unbelievable that he had left her. Nothing seemed real these days, and probably it stemmed from this, the fact that he had abandoned her, which was impossible and yet seemed to be true. Though Esther tried not to acknowledge it, part of her was still waiting for him to come back, to say, There's been a mistake – I thought you were with me, and suddenly I looked round and you weren't.

She struggled to make herself give up. The worst part

of her, the part most vulnerable to the devil, thought she might go with him this time, if only he would come back for her. It frightened her, the idea that her love for Thomas could be greater than her love for God or her fear of hell. She didn't want to go to heaven without him. How could it be heaven then?

But he'd left her. He'd said he loved her and then he'd left her.

Ruth came a little while later to escort her to the loo. Esther hadn't realized until then that her bladder was painfully full, an ache low in her gut. She hobbled after Ruth, who waited outside the door as Esther locked herself in and fumbled with her dress.

She followed Ruth back to the prayer room, wondering vaguely how they would have reacted if she'd had an accident on the floor. It would probably be taken as a further sign of her iniquity.

It was difficult to get it straight in her mind, everything that had happened. She could lay out all the pieces in front of her – the river, the wailing; Thomas walking away to the car that last morning, though she hadn't known it was the last; the bundle of bloodstained towels they'd buried at the edge of the forest. But she didn't know what to do with them after that. She couldn't work out how they all came together and brought her here, to the prayer room, alone in the dark. She didn't know how to think. We close down our thoughts to protect ourselves, the prophet said.

It is written in Genesis: the imagination of man's heart is evil from his youth.

He could read minds. He could look into the shadowed places of her heart and see everything. But what did he see? Esther struggled again as she tried to look inside herself. The thoughts seemed to dissolve before they had even formed. She couldn't judge herself guilty or innocent because she couldn't hold it all in her mind for long enough.

It wasn't much of a surprise when they didn't let her out that night. She would, it seemed, be sleeping in the prayer room. Ruth brought her a pillow, and Rachael came later with another blanket. Esther rolled herself up in the blankets as best she could and lay on her side. All through the night as she lay awake, she felt the cold from the floor seeping up into her skin and into her blood and her bones. She listened to the rhythmic plunk of raindrops onto the puddle near her feet.

She remembered the last time Nathaniel had come to her at night, the day after Thomas left and shortly before she was exiled to the big house. She had felt his anger when he touched her. Then, a little later, she'd finally recognized sex for what it was: an act of violence. He thrust into her, even as she tightened her muscles as though, uselessly, to resist him. But it was impossible. Her only role was to submit, to endure this invasion because it was what she was made for. The woman is empty, Nathaniel said; she needs to be filled by the man. Of course. When we get ideas above our station, our biology betrays us. Every penetration is an invasion, an act of rape, because God has designed it that way.

And yet. She remembered those times with Thomas, the drowsy satisfaction, that feeling of meeting halfway. It had been unnatural, Nathaniel said, her relationship with Thomas. They had lost sight of God and looked only at each other. Perhaps it was true, Esther thought. But Thomas had looked away in the end.

Since it was dark in the prayer room already, and since Esther couldn't sleep for more than an hour or two at a time, it was sometimes difficult to tell the night from the day, except that the night was colder. Most of the time she sat with her back to the wall and stared in front of her, watching the darkness. She waited patiently. Nobody came to visit her except for Ruth, who didn't speak as she handed over food and water, and walked with her to the bathroom and back.

'It gets very cold at night,' Esther said on the third morning. 'Do you think I could have another blanket?'

Ruth looked like she was about to say no. But Esther was shivering so much she could hardly hold the plate Ruth had handed to her. An extra blanket appeared with lunch. So she was still worthy of some small kindnesses, then.

It was strange, but more than anything else, it was the physical memory of Thomas she retained. More than she longed to hear his voice or see his face, her body craved his: its warmth and weight, the firmness of his arms and the bulk of his shoulders under her hands. She felt him lying next to her on the mattress, his body touching hers at every point, legs entangled, their faces pressed together – noses, foreheads, lips. 'I love you,' she would whisper, but love was given in the tenderness and familiarity of touch, not in words. Words were weak by comparison. She couldn't even remember their final conversation. She hadn't paid enough attention. She hadn't realized.

Since she was spending so much time in the prayer room, she thought perhaps she ought to pray. She would pray for strength, and focus all her energy on being full of the Spirit so there would be no room for the devil to enter. (Though maybe this would do no good if the devil had already entered? She wrestled with this thought, then decided to put it aside.)

Satan, I refuse you.

Satan, I refuse you.

Over and over she said it, but it didn't bring the calm it once had. When she was finished she felt exhausted rather than refreshed.

After a week, Nathaniel finally came. The rain showed no sign of easing. Esther pushed herself up off the floor when she heard the door and leaned her back against the wall, wanting to be on her feet for whatever was coming. The prophet entered.

He didn't say anything at first, so Esther took the opportunity to study him. Even now he was older, there was something about him that made you want to look at him. Perhaps it was the contrast between the dark hair, now greying, and the pale green eyes. Or the fierceness of his gaze, the way he stared into you, allowing you no opportunity to hide.

'Hello, Esther,' he said.

Seth appeared behind him, carrying a wooden chair in each hand. He came into the room and placed the two chairs facing one another. The prophet stepped forward and sat down. Seth disappeared, closing the door softly behind him.

'Sit,' Nathaniel said.

Esther took up her place opposite him. She couldn't decide how to sit, whether to cross her legs, whether to fold her hands in her lap or leave them hanging at her sides. Everything she did seemed clumsy and unnatural. She felt the prophet's eyes on her as she shifted her position; a glimmer of amusement from him, perhaps.

He said, 'I've come to talk about your sin.'

She couldn't look away. She had thought since she was a teenager that this was the most powerful kind of love. She'd thought love was being chosen. She'd thought it was grand sacrifices, all the time trying to prove he was right to choose her. But no: love was the memory of Thomas's forehead pressed against hers. Love was the feel of his arms, his hips, his feet. Choosing him, even though he hadn't chosen her in the end. The weight of the realization doubled her over.

The prophet said gently, 'Do you need a glass of water?'

She shook her head. He thought it was the sight of him that had done it.

He said, 'You let me down, Esther.'

'I'm sorry.'

'I trusted you. I trusted you above everyone.'

'Nathaniel, I promise I didn't know he was leaving,' she said. She was sure she was telling the truth, if you could ever be sure – because if she had known, how would she have been able to bear it?

'You're lying,' he said. 'Even now, you're lying.'

'I'm not,' she said, but her voice was weak.

He said, 'You could have protected the Ark, but instead you conspired to destroy it.'

He must be right, Esther thought. Of course she should have reported Thomas when he shared his doubts with her, only it had been impossible to betray him. She had betrayed the Ark instead.

'I'm sorry,' she said again.

'Thomas let the devil in, and you helped him.'

She didn't know what to say, so she stayed quiet.

'He'll feel God's anger,' Nathaniel said. 'He'll suffer as he deserves.'

'Please, Nathaniel,' Esther said, frightened out of her silence. 'Ask God to spare him.'

A hard, sharp slap across her face, which happened so fast she barely had time to register him rising from his chair. She turned her head away. He stood over her, breathing hard.

'Don't plead for him,' he said.

Esther looked up into Nathaniel's face and thought that she barely recognized him.

And she saw herself again, standing at the bus stop, many years ago. The past had gained strength and was running alongside the present, so that whilst Esther in the present looked back at him, Esther in the past – Jess, as she was then – turned and saw him for the first time.

She'd been standing at the bus stop for over an hour, but she had nowhere to go. She'd just realized that if she didn't go home at the end of the day, her parents might not actually notice, and even if they did, they wouldn't be shocked or frightened because they had been rendered unshockable and unfrightenable by what had happened to Toby.

It might have seemed suspicious, being approached by an older man like that, but he had a woman with him, smiley, normal-looking, so she hadn't been nervous, just looked the man up and down sullenly when he came over. Pale eyes, dark stubble.

He had said, 'You look cold.'

'I am fucking cold,' Esther – Jess – had said.

'Well, we can't have that,' he said. 'We're just off to a meeting. Why don't you come along? We can at least promise a cup of coffee, maybe a slice of cake if you're lucky.'

She fancied a coffee, but she wasn't an idiot, and she didn't go off with strangers.

'No thanks.'

The man had shrugged. 'Up to you. But it's not a sensible move, standing alone on the street like this. It's getting dark. We're heading round the corner to St Martin's. You could at least come along for twenty minutes, just to warm up, decide your next move.'

She considered. It would serve her parents right if he was a rapist. Then the thought of inflicting any more pain on them winded her, and she turned away from the man in sightless misery.

'What kind of meeting?' she said.

'A Bible study group,' the woman said.

She was glad she had turned her back so they couldn't see her sneer.

But the man seemed to know, because he said with a laugh in his voice, 'Yes, yes, you've got us. We're Bible-bashers. But we can just about manage to make a decent hot drink, and we'll promise not to try and convert you if you'll only come along and warm up.'

'*I* might try and convert you,' the woman said cheerfully. 'But I'm not very good at it. I've only just joined. So you're probably safe.'

Confused and rather charmed, she'd agreed. And it became comforting, after a while, to have somewhere to go after school – people who actually worried about her and waited for her. And more than comforting, once it became clear that Nathaniel had chosen her.

He saved me, she had thought at the time. But that wasn't quite right. Because it had been Thomas, in those early months in the Ark, who'd slowly pulled her out of herself, let her rage and cry when she remembered how Toby died, alone in blood and pain. Thomas's patience allowed her to be obedient and calm with the others. He'd never reported her, though there had been times when he probably should have. It had been Thomas all along.

Nathaniel said, 'I ought to have realized you'd let me down. I should have been clear-sighted enough to see you were tainted in the eyes of God.'

The children thing again, Esther thought. She was so tired. She wanted her husband.

'Aren't you going to ask for God's mercy?' Nathaniel said.

She said, 'I trust God to give it if He thinks I deserve it.'

This seemed to silence him.

Esther thought how strange it was that he'd wanted her so much once. When she was seventeen, he'd told her she was perfect to him. Follow me, he said, and I will free you. You will never know a love like this. (That part, at least, was true.)

Abruptly, Nathaniel stood up.

'Because I'm merciful,' he said, 'because I've *always* been merciful, according to God's will, I'll try to think of a way to save you.'

When he was gone and Seth had returned to take away the chairs, Esther sat down again with her back to the wall. She held her hand to her face where it throbbed and thought of Thomas. Perhaps one day she would see him again, even if not in this lifetime. She thought she understood now, after facing Nathaniel, that he would never come back for her. The strength it would have taken to leave was so great it would be impossible to risk returning.

She wished there were some way to let him know she didn't blame him.

She had always relied on the idea of heaven to ease the fears that came with love, knowing that even after death they would all be reunited in paradise. How did the people of Gehenna love without that hope? But Thomas was barred from heaven now, and she must be too. And perhaps it was better that way; perhaps it meant that in some in-between place, somewhere no one else could reach them, they would find each other again.

4

'She's not one of us,' Nathaniel said. 'She never has been.'

The rain had taken on a vindictive quality, clattering against the windows as if trying to break the glass.

Stephanie was alert, though it was late at night. The children had been in bed for hours, and it was just the adults gathered in the kitchen. The others, she'd noticed, had been looking frayed over the past few days, as jittery and pale as she must look herself. They couldn't endure this rain and the prophet's anger much longer.

'Can't we help her back to the true path, prophet?' Rachael said. 'Surely you—'

'It's too late for that,' Nathaniel said. 'She's infected the Ark with sin, she and Thomas. She doesn't want to be saved. She's beyond it now.'

Rachael opened her mouth again, then closed it. Stephanie watched her wearily. She was tired of other people's weakness, just as she was finally ridding herself of her own. Rachael was too feeble to accept Esther's wickedness, but too cowardly to argue on her behalf when the others were against her. People like this were useless to the prophet. Stephanie did not want to be useless herself. Sarah, she reminded herself. My name is Sarah.

'She's strayed too far,' Nathaniel said. 'It hurts me to admit it, but it's true. She's against us.'

'What do we do?' Joshua said.

Nathaniel shook his head. All at once he appeared subdued. 'I don't know. I don't know if anything can be done. It may be too late for us. Perhaps we can't be saved either.'

She looked round at the others. Deborah and Rachael had their eyes cast down, as though their repentance on another's behalf could still persuade God to spare them, but Ruth looked at the prophet and her gaze was hard. Seth and Joshua shifted uncomfortably on their feet.

After a long silence, Seth said, 'Please, prophet. Tell us what we can do. How can we make the rain stop?'

'*Haven't I told you I don't know?*' His anger was sudden and frightening. 'But tell me now, because it's best we all know, if anyone will stand in our way when God does reveal His will. Tell me if you'll stand in our way and prevent us saving the Ark. Will anyone condemn their friends to suffer rather than be saved? Tell me now if this is the case. Tell me if I'm talking about you.'

Silence except for the beat of rain on glass.

'Do you know what she said about you, Rachael?' the prophet said. 'And you, Deborah?'

They shook their heads, slow, bovine.

'She said you were weak. She said you'd never truly served God or your friends in the Ark because you were too afraid.'

'It's not true,' Deborah whispered, but it wasn't clear which part she was referring to.

'Are you going to be weak,' he asked them, 'when the time comes?'

'No, prophet.'

'What about you, Seth?'

'No, prophet.'

'Are you, Joshua?'

'No, prophet.'

Then he turned to her. 'If there's a way to help your friends, will you do it, Sarah?'

'Yes, prophet.'

'Have you cast off your old weakness?'

Stephanie was weak, she thought. But not Sarah. 'I have, prophet.'

'Well, then,' he said. 'We must wait and we must pray.'

Later, when they were alone in her room, he said, 'I've been so proud of you recently, Sarah. You've finally given yourself up to the true purpose. You've become the person you always should have been.'

'I've done my best,' she said. 'I know I still have a long way to go.'

'No,' he said. 'You've surpassed my expectations. I sometimes think you're more of a true follower even than Seth and Joshua, which I never thought I'd say.'

'Thank you.' Even if it weren't true yet, she would make it become true.

'But I'm sorry you've had to suffer like this,' he said. 'I wish I'd been able to protect you.'

She was better at holding back the tears now, better at turning her misery outwards, into a cold hard point.

Nathaniel said, 'Do you know, I sometimes think I'm to blame for not putting more faith in you early on.' He touched her face. 'You could always see it, couldn't you?'

She kept quiet, waiting for more.

'I don't think you ever trusted her, did you?' he said.

She wasn't sure, she couldn't remember now.

'I should have paid more attention,' Nathaniel said. 'My love, you saw so much further than the rest of us.'

'Yes,' she said. I think I must have done.

The next night, he brought them together in the barn after the children were in bed.

This was a new kind of rain, she thought, as they shivered in the draught from the barn's loose window. It didn't sound like it was made of water but of something solid and sharp. Perhaps when they went outside it would cut into their skin. The only light in the barn was the weak glow cast by a single bulb overhead. They huddled together in its pale-orange pool.

'I've prayed long and hard,' the prophet said. 'And I've finally received an answer. We're being given a way out. I can admit to you, now we have a way to save ourselves, that I was afraid we were going to be thrown out into Gehenna. Deprived forever of our chance of heaven. But we're going to be spared – if we do as God asks. The time has come for a cleansing. We must cleanse the evil from our midst, purify the Ark. That is the will of God.'

He turned to Deborah and Rachael. 'Do you accept the will of God? Will you act in the best interests of your friends?'

'Yes,' Deborah said. After a beat of hesitation, Rachael nodded.

The prophet said, 'That's all I need from you for the time being. Your role in the cleansing will be minimal. You can go to bed now.'

They left without argument.

Now the prophet addressed the rest of them. 'Ruth. Joshua. Seth. You three have always been my closest and most faithful followers. And Sarah – ' his eyes stayed on her a little longer – 'although you're the newest here, you've earned your place amongst us.'

She was proud to have been chosen to remain. She couldn't have survived being cast out like Rachael and Deborah.

'Rachael's faithful,' Seth began, but the prophet held up his hand to silence him.

Sarah thought Nathaniel would be angry, but instead he said gently, 'I know that, Seth. Do you forget that I've known Rachael nearly as long as you? Deborah, too. I don't undervalue them. I love them, and I wouldn't see any harm come to them. I'm leaving them out because some women have a weakness when it comes to each other. There's a danger Deborah and Rachael will let tenderness cloud their judgement. There's no room for uncertainty if we're going to save the Ark. We're under attack. Don't forget this. We are under attack.'

'We'll do whatever you ask of us, prophet,' Ruth murmured.

'Good,' Nathaniel said. 'Let me tell you what's required of you. We only have one chance to save the Ark now. Its beauty is in its simplicity. God's not trying to make things difficult for you. *I'm* not trying to make things difficult for you. The answer was in front of us the whole time, only I was too blinded by misplaced loyalty to see it until it was shown to me.' He took from his pocket a small Bible, bound in rich blue leather. He opened it carefully and found his place. 'Let me read to you from Leviticus – no, actually, Seth, I'd like *you* to read to us. You can hear the words plainly, from one of your own.' He handed the book over, saying, 'Chapter 17, verse 11.'

Seth took the book. He read clearly and slowly, 'For the life of the flesh is in the blood: and I have given it to you upon the altar to make an atonement for your souls: for it is the blood that maketh an atonement for the soul.'

'It is the *blood* that maketh an atonement for the soul,' Nathaniel repeated. 'Do you see?'

It took Sarah a few moments to understand, but then she couldn't help drawing her breath in sharply.

'The cleansing will *save* Esther,' Nathaniel went on, 'as well as the rest of us. It's the only way we have to save her now, the only way to make an atonement for her soul. It's merciful as well as necessary.'

'Prophet—' Seth began, and Nathaniel turned to him, but Seth didn't seem to know what it was he wanted to say.

'It's pure and good,' Nathaniel said. 'And so neat, the solution God's presented to our problem. We will perform

254

the cleansing to save Esther's soul. We will be saved, and so will she.'

'Prophet—' Seth said again.

Nathaniel interrupted him. 'How long have we known each other, Seth?'

'Sixteen years,' Seth said after a pause.

'And have you trusted me all that time?' When Seth didn't reply, Nathaniel reached out and laid his hand on his shoulder. 'Seth, answer me. Have you trusted me all that time?'

Seth looked him in the face at last. 'You know I have.'

'Have I ever led you away from the true path? Have I ever done wrong by you?'

'No.'

The prophet smiled sadly at him. 'Don't deny me now, Seth. Don't forget that I love you. You're closer than a brother to me. I know you trust me, but remember that I trust you too. I'd put my life in your hands.' He gave Seth's shoulder a small shake. 'The path of the righteous isn't always easy. Is it?'

Seth shook his head. There were tears in his eyes.

'Put your faith in me once more,' Nathaniel said. 'I'll take care of you. Of all of you,' he added, opening his words out to the rest of them. 'Seth? Do you believe me? Will you trust me one more time?'

And at last, Seth nodded. The prophet pulled him into an embrace. Held him a few moments, then released him.

Ruth spoke again. 'When?'

*

She wasn't surprised to be told that he'd chosen her. In any case, it didn't matter which of them did it. They would all hold the knife; and none of them would.

Would it be difficult?

She asked him this when they were in bed that night and he said, 'Not in this case, Sarah. God will support your hand.'

'What if I can't do it?'

He looked at her steadily and didn't answer.

'What if I do it badly?'

'You won't,' he said. 'Leave yourself out of this. God will be working through you. They'll be God's actions, and all our actions.'

'Not mine,' she murmured.

He placed two fingers gently on her neck, then took her hand and placed it where his had been. 'Can you feel where your pulse beats?'

'Yes.'

'Pierce here with the blade. It will be quick and easy, so long as you aren't frightened by the sight of blood.'

'Perhaps I am,' she said.

'The stream of blood will be beautiful. It will save her and purify us. Do you trust me?'

'Yes.'

'Can you do what God asks of you? What we all need from you?'

Sarah looked at him. Those eyes. She said, 'Yes.'

5

He'd travelled far but he'd travelled nowhere at all. He'd been so long on the moors that 'the south' had become a fantastical place, something out of a story. Now that Thomas found himself there, he was unreal too, all the colour faded from him; he slunk through these southern streets like a ghost.

Supermarkets were the same down south, though the accents were different. He mastered the work easily enough. The big project of the next few weeks would be transitioning a new store layout with their customers, four self-service checkouts introduced in a neat line by the exit. It was not onerous, but Thomas threw himself into the task. The days were much easier. In the evenings, he returned to the small flat he rented above a shop – he would get himself a car, then he could live out of town, in a village perhaps – and sat and thought of her.

He would get himself a car.

He would drive back up there, four or five hours or however long it took. He would get on the road to the moors and rise up into their ragged folds, and then he'd drive onto the track towards the Ark, and eventually he'd pull up outside the two houses. Esther would be waiting for him because she must know – surely she must know – that he would never leave her for long.

He would be firm, this new, unreal Thomas. He would say, 'I love you and this time I'm not leaving without you. Get in.' And she would, and he'd bring her back here.

Sometimes he thought about it so hard and for so long that he could actually see it – not in his mind's eye, but almost as an external reality, so that if someone else were to come into his flat at that moment he believed they would see it too. He and Esther would get a small house somewhere out of the way, surrounded by fields. Esther would feel safe there. And perhaps they'd find God again, or what they used to mean by God. Perhaps they would be happy.

6

The followers do as they're bid and bring her in at dawn. It's still raining when Sarah comes downstairs a little before six, but it's eased off at some point in the night, lost its fierceness and now it's simply weather.

Rachael and Deborah have been instructed to stay in their rooms, and then later to go to the kitchen to prepare breakfast. Sarah wonders how much they know.

She finds Seth and Joshua waiting by the door of the prayer room. Joshua has his hands in his pockets. Under other circumstances, this stance might look relaxed, but Sarah can see through the fabric of his clothes to the clenched fists.

Seth is shivering. He is not wearing a jumper over his thin shirt.

'You should put an extra layer on,' Sarah tells him. She sounds like his wife, she thinks. Rachael should have told him to wear a jumper.

'The prophet says to wait in the barn,' Joshua says. 'We'll bring her in.'

Sarah goes out into the rain. She has almost forgotten what normal rain is like: this light, effortless drizzle that takes time to soak through her clothes. She wonders what will happen if it stops before they've done it. Would it be a sign from God, like the story Nathaniel told her about Abraham and Isaac? Could they just forget the whole thing and go back to bed, get up later and never mention it again? The thought is unexpected. Weakness, always weakness.

In the barn, it's scarcely lighter than outside. They should have waited till daylight, Sarah thinks, so they wouldn't be reliant on the single bulb, which illuminates only the small area of floor directly below it.

Ruth is already in there, pacing. She gives Sarah a tight smile. Sarah is wondering where the prophet is when he appears. He stands for a moment, a shadow in the doorway; then comes over, kisses her and wordlessly presses something into her hand. The cool, smooth handle of the knife.

Is it really this simple? Gathering at the appointed hour, getting it done before breakfast, most of them half asleep? Sarah looks down at her feet, at the black house shoes she wears beneath her dress. They rest neatly, side by side, on the dirt floor of the barn. She moves her right toe a little, sending up a small cloud of dust. Now she notices that whilst dressing in a rush this morning, she has put on odd socks. This is all wrong. She wonders if she has time to go and change them. She can't perform the cleansing like this.

She is just deciding that she will have to ask Nathaniel to wait for her for a few moments when the barn door opens again and Seth and Joshua come through it. Esther is between them. The men hold her arms on either side, though she is meek and still. They lead her into the splash of light under the bulb. Sarah steps back a little, further into the shadows. Tries not to think about her socks.

Heaven is high. It's difficult to believe what's about to happen. But Sarah feels no ties to Esther, no pity and no sadness. In truth Esther is already gone. It is only the finishing that will happen now, the very end. And even if Sarah did want to change her mind, even if she did want to try and stop it, she knows she couldn't: what's taking place is beyond her. On her own, she doesn't even exist.

Her guard has dropped for a moment; her eyes have met Esther's and Esther is staring back at her. A frightened, questioning look. There's nothing Sarah can tell her.

The prophet says, 'Esther, you've been weighed in the balance and found wanting.'

Esther looks around at them all, as if trying to work out what's going on.

Sarah makes herself step a little closer, comes to stand at the edge of the circle of light. The knife glints and she sees the moment Esther notices it.

Don't worry, she wants to say. It'll be over soon.

But Esther, not understanding it has to happen, not understanding that it is done to save her, begins to struggle wildly. Joshua and Seth are still holding her arms and Sarah thinks how slender Esther is, how fragile she looks between the two men. Esther's eyes never leave the blade in Sarah's hand as she bucks and pulls uselessly for escape.

'Nathaniel—' Esther says, her voice high.

He raises his hand to silence her. He says, 'Esther, the

life of the flesh is in the blood. It is the blood that makes an atonement for the soul.'

'I don't want my soul!' she says. 'Take it. Leave me my body!'

The prophet smiles sadly and Sarah sees that Esther condemns herself with her own words. Nathaniel says, 'No one as lost as you *wants* to be saved. Trust us to act in your best interests.'

Esther continues to struggle, but she is no match for Seth and Joshua, who bend her arms up behind her, causing her to cry out in pain. Her mouth has dropped open, Sarah sees, as though she has lost control of her body. She hopes Esther won't wet herself; vaguely, at the back of her mind, she is aware that this can happen to people in extreme terror.

Then Esther seems to go limp, so the men are no longer holding her still but holding her up. After hanging there weakly for a few moments, she manages to put her weight back on her own feet.

She says, 'So it's decided, then.' Her voice shakes, but all the same, Sarah admires her courage.

'Esther,' the prophet says, his voice infinitely gentle. 'We're giving you the chance of heaven.'

If the rain stops now, Sarah thinks, perhaps it's not too late. We can all go back to bed, Esther included.

But even as she thinks this, she hears it again on the roof, soft and insistent.

And probably it will be easy. She knows what to do. When the prophet nods at her, she takes another step forward. The mechanics of it are so simple, she thinks, as she puts the blade to Esther's neck, the soft part where the pulse shivers. Put the point to the pulse and press. In a moment, that is what she will do, but for now she tries to hold the blade still, the sharp tip not yet pressing into the skin. Esther is trembling violently, and Sarah notices her own hand shaking, as though Esther's trembling is catching. She had pictured the motion of sliding in the blade as delicate and gentle, but now she realizes that with Esther moving like this, she'll have to push the knife in harder to make sure it reaches the right point. It makes her anxious, that her plan has to change.

Joshua and Seth, though still holding Esther's arms, have turned their heads away. Ruth has as well. This is what surprises Sarah the most, that Ruth of all people should prove weak in the end. But this is Ruth's act too, she thinks, as much as it belongs to any of them.

She tries to make Esther look at her. She wants this, needs it, perhaps: a final moment of understanding between the two of them. She wants Esther to know that this is not personal. Sarah is merely the instrument of God. And she wants to say, I'm sorry.

But Esther won't look at her.

Sarah suspects that everything will change when she pushes the point of the knife in. It will be like stepping across an invisible divide into a new world. She wants to take a few moments to say goodbye to the old one. The wooden handle of the blade has grown warm in her hand. It is such a small tool, this knife.

But the prophet, standing behind her, says, 'Do it.' She tries to focus on God as Nathaniel has taught her but her mind remains empty. She pushes on the handle of the knife but doesn't use enough force; the blade nicks the skin, and there is some blood, but only a little. Esther shudders and pulls away, but makes no sound.

A small, impatient noise from the prophet. Sarah realizes with dismay that she is messing everything up. The sight of the blood has startled her and she feels her fingers loosening around the knife. She has only seconds before she will lose control of herself. Help me, God, she thinks, but again God does not come. She gathers herself. Her grip tightens on the handle until her knuckles go white. She drives the blade in with all her strength.

Esther knows she should feel pain, but it's too white-hot to register. She is relieved, because she's always wondered what Toby must have felt in his last moments and now she knows the answer: nothing much at all. Surprise, perhaps – because he was never the sort of person to be in the wrong place at the wrong time. Not like Esther herself. But he would have quickly soared out of pain's reach. She wishes she could tell her parents this.

She is no longer afraid, though her body shakes and jerks because it's been taught to want to preserve itself. Her mind is clear.

Even as she feels the blade in her neck, she raises her eyes to Nathaniel and keeps them there. She thinks she sees him flinch. This time he will be the one who can't look away.

But he is moving, shimmering from side to side. Esther

is on her knees, then on the floor, and there is red everywhere. Blood, she corrects herself vaguely. The pain is coming now, but as quickly as it arrives she seems to be moving away from it. Catch me if you can, she thinks. The words come into her head slowly, stay with her for a moment, then leave her. Her cheek is against the dirt floor. The darkness is coming in. God is nowhere.

So, she thinks. Then: Thomas.

And, at last, she feels his arms go round her. She closes her eyes.

'We should have put plastic sheets down,' Ruth says. 'For the blood.'

VI

Revelation

1

When Moses opened his eyes, he was lying in a pool of sunlight. It must be past eight, but no one had come to get them. He experienced a moment of panic, a residue from early childhood. The old fear that the end times had come and he'd been left behind. But when he moved his leg he felt the reassuring warmth of Peter beside him on the mattress.

Slowly, he sat up. Why hadn't his mother or Deborah called them for breakfast? Something else was troubling him, too. It took a few moments to work out what it was.

'Peter,' he said, shaking his shoulder.

His brother made an indistinct noise, and rolled away from him.

'*Peter*,' Moses said, prodding him insistently. When Peter finally groaned and opened his eyes, Moses said, 'The rain's stopped.'

Now Peter was sitting up as well, rubbing his face and saying through a yawn, 'I think you're right.'

'Is it over, then?' Moses said.

Peter reached for one of his slippers, and hurled it at the top bunk. It caught Jonathan's ear and he woke with a start.

'Listen,' Peter told him.

Jonathan's face creased in confusion.

'What do you hear?' Peter said.

'Nothing.'

'Exactly.'

Comprehension dawned, and Jonathan swung down the ladder to wake Ezra. 'The storm's over,' he said. 'We've been spared the flood—'

He faltered and gave Peter a quick, questioning look. Peter replied in exasperation, 'Well, we're not floating, are we?'

'So where are the grown-ups?' Moses said as they pulled their clothes on.

'Praying?' Ezra said.

They crept along the corridor to the girls' room and knocked on the door. Abigail opened it, already dressed.

'Did someone come to get you up?' she said. 'I think they forgot us.'

'We haven't seen anyone,' Peter said. 'But the rain's stopped.'

Judith and Mary appeared behind Abigail at the door, Mary attached to Judith by the end of her hair as she finished plaiting it.

In a small crowd they headed down the stairs to the kitchen. Judith dropped back to walk beside Moses. She had her plait over her shoulder and was chewing the end.

He said, 'Do you think things will go back to normal now?'

'This place was never very normal,' Judith said.

The others' voices fell away as they entered the kitchen. When Moses and Judith reached the door, Moses sensed it too. There was something strange in the atmosphere of the room. The air felt different, as if they'd suddenly gone deep down below the earth. But the kitchen looked the same as always. The strangeness, whatever it was, was silent and hidden. Nevertheless, it dissolved their words even before they spoke them.

Moses looked at his mother for reassurance. She was standing by the stove putting food onto plates, but she didn't turn as they came in. There was a rhythm to her movements as she dished out sausages, then toast, then eggs. He watched her a few moments longer, thinking that perhaps she couldn't break off or the rhythm would be lost. Then he turned to his father, who was sitting at the kitchen table. His father's face was very white. He didn't look back at Moses.

Joshua was sitting opposite but he wasn't talking. No one was talking. Deborah was washing up pans at the sink, with Ruth doing the drying.

The grown-ups had forgotten themselves. They had forgotten how they were supposed to behave, the things they normally did.

Only Judith's mother remembered. She turned to smile at them as they entered the room and Moses was relieved.

'Good morning,' she said. 'Did you sleep well?'

'Yeah, OK,' Judith said.

'Will you take the plates through to the dining room? The table's already laid.'

'But that's our job,' Abigail said. 'Laying the table is our job.'

Moses thought of all the times in the past when Abigail

had grumbled about this; but he understood that she, too, was afraid, that she wanted this feeling of unfamiliarity to go away as much as he did.

'We thought it would be nice to let you sleep in today,' Judith's mother said.

So, in a quiet procession, the children carried the loaded plates through to the dining room and set them down amongst the cutlery. Unsure what to do next, they took their places at the table and waited.

After a long silence, Ezra said, 'Nobody mentioned it. About the rain stopping.'

'They must be waiting for the prophet,' Peter said.

Moses sat beside Judith and looked at his plate. The yolk of the egg was hardening, grease standing out in drops on the sausages.

'There aren't enough places,' Mary said suddenly. 'They haven't laid enough places.'

'Esther's still in the prayer room, stupid,' Ezra said.

Eventually the grown-ups came in, the prophet amongst them now, dressed neatly in his usual white shirt and dark trousers. When they were all in their seats, he said, 'Thank you, Lord, for providing this delicious food.'

Moses waited, expecting a longer prayer, but apparently this was to be all. Nathaniel nodded at them to begin, and for a while the only sound was the scraping of cutlery on plates. The food was almost cold, but nobody commented. Moses wondered if the grown-ups had even noticed; they seemed so quiet and odd. Perhaps they didn't remember food was supposed to be hot. He felt a surge of panic at the thought, the irrational fear that all their meals would be cold from now on.

At length, the prophet said, 'You'll all have noticed by now that the rain's stopped.' He raised his fork and put a piece of sausage in his mouth, looking round at them as he chewed. When nobody answered, he said, 'That's because we've done what the Lord asked. We've cleansed the Ark of sin.'

Perhaps this was what the strange feeling was, Moses thought. The absence of sin.

Into the silence, Judith said, 'Does that mean Esther can come out of the prayer room?'

Moses was amazed at her daring, but knew he shouldn't be. If someone asked him to say one thing about Judith, one single thing you noticed before anything else – well then, he would say that she was brave.

Then he realized the prophet had spoken and he hadn't taken it in properly because he was thinking about Judith. He retraced the prophet's words in his mind: 'Esther is no longer amongst us.'

Again, Judith was the only one who spoke, though her voice was quieter now. 'She's left?'

The prophet said, 'God has removed her. *For evildoers shall be cut off: but those that wait upon the Lord, they shall inherit the earth.* We'll spend today in prayers of thanksgiving to God for sparing us, for saving us from the harm Esther and Thomas brought upon us. And then after today – ' his eyes swept across them – 'nobody will mention either of them again. That's God's condition. Abide by it, or you'll be punished.'

Moses kept his eyes on his plate. He knew he should be joyful – they all should. It was difficult to explain the feeling that had come over him. He glanced up at his mother, but she didn't look back.

It was a long morning. They spent three hours in the prayer room giving thanks for God's mercy and the end of the deluge. Moses had thought that during the prayers they might at least find out where Esther had gone, but it was never made clear. An almost silent lunch followed, then three more hours of prayer, repeating the words of the prophet over and over again.

O God, we thank You for Your mercy.

O God, see how we have cleansed the Ark.

Moses was almost asleep on his feet by the time the light began to fade. The children were sent away to play whilst supper was being prepared, but they were too exhausted to do much except sit in the schoolroom. Peter, Ezra and Jonathan played a half-hearted game of marbles, whilst Mary and Abigail began a new drawing. Moses and Judith sat quietly in the corner.

'Where do you think she went?' Judith murmured.

'We're not supposed to talk about it.'

'After today,' Judith said. 'And besides, it's only you.'

'Well, I don't know. Maybe she left across the moors.'

Judith frowned. 'I hope she made it.' After a moment, she added, 'We've been stuck inside all day. Let's go for a walk before it gets too dark.'

The light was already dim when they stepped outside, stretching and yawning in the chill air.

'Too dark for the forest,' Moses said. Secretly, he was

relieved. The forest was ruined now it had been broken open.

'That's OK. I just wanted to stretch my legs.' Judith broke into a run, shooting away from Moses and then circling back, doing a quick lap around him and stopping again beside him.

'What on *earth* are you doing?' Moses said, in his best imitation of Ruth.

'*Stretching* them. My legs.'

They were both laughing, mainly in relief at being outside, shaking off the heaviness of the air inside the houses. Moses did a quick run too, back and forth along the side of the barn, and then they both leaned against the wall, getting their breath back.

He wasn't sure what made Judith go into the barn. They hadn't been told to stay away from it. If they had, Judith wanting to go in there would have made more sense. Judith pushed against what was right, Nathaniel said, like the devil pushing against God. But as much as Moses had tried to listen to the prophet, he could never make the words seem true. He didn't think Judith was like the devil. She was only like Judith.

And now she opened the barn door idly and wandered inside. Moses followed.

It was the smell they noticed first. Unfamiliar, but somehow Moses recognized it. For a moment he was standing again on the banks of the river as it flowed red, though he knew that smell had been in his head; Judith had explained about the clay.

He blinked away the river, and the next moment he was

beside his mother in the kitchen as she seasoned a slab of raw meat.

The barn smelt of slaughter.

'Why—' he began to say, but Judith had already reached up to put on the light. The bulb lit up only a small patch of the floor, but enough for them to see that it was discoloured, the pale dirt stained a deep brownish-red.

For a while, neither of them spoke; they just stared.

'What's that?' Judith said eventually. Her voice was distant.

Moses didn't reply, just kept looking because he couldn't do anything else. The red fanned out on all sides, its edges blurring into the gloom where the light stopped. Moses felt the cold creeping inside him. Without realizing it, he had moved closer to Judith, and now his arm touched hers. He felt her shivers passing into his own body.

Suddenly she seemed to come back to life. She reached up and tugged at the light cord again, covering the stain with darkness. Then she grabbed his arm, pulled him out of the barn and back into the sharp, clean air. She closed the door behind them, shutting the smell inside.

They started to walk away from the barn and away from the houses, stopping only when they had gone a little way onto the moors. It was too dark and the ground too damp to risk going further.

'We have to go back,' Moses said, not moving.

Beside him, Judith was silent. They looked out across the moors, bluish and shadowed in the fading light.

At last, Judith said, 'We never went into the barn. Do you understand, Moses? We were never there.' When he didn't immediately reply, she said again, more fiercely now, 'Do you understand?'

'Yes.'

My parents, he thought. Were my parents in the barn? And he thought of Esther, who had always been kind to him.

'It's OK,' Judith said. She patted him gently on the back as he threw up. He had managed to lean forward just enough to avoid his shoes, which was good, he thought. He crouched down when it was over, wiping his sleeve across his mouth. He waited for Judith to tell him again that it was OK, but she didn't speak.

2

Yes, she had expected the world to look different. Sarah didn't know whether to be reassured or alarmed by the fact that it didn't. It was hard to get her head round what it all meant. She tried to focus on it, sometimes, in a concentrated way. She would set aside a few moments when she was by herself at night, or whilst going out to get the firewood; and then she would lie still in her bed or lean against the wall outside and try to *think* about what she had done. But it shimmered and scurried away from her vision.

It would probably be easy to be overwhelmed by it, if you let yourself. She tried, sometimes, to be overwhelmed. She placed the facts before her one by one. Esther was dead. She had killed her. Esther was dead. But most of the time Sarah found it difficult to react at all. Such a small thing it had been, pushing in the blade. A little, sharp moment that surged forward then dissolved and was lost. Just another passing action like all the other actions you completed every day: brushing your teeth, walking from room to room, kissing someone.

It didn't change you. It didn't change anything. Sometimes, she forgot to think about it. When she did remember, the fact of it seemed curious, but somehow not shocking. There even seemed to be an ease to the idea, a naturalness. She thought, perhaps we are all killers underneath.

'I'm having another baby,' she said to Rachael as they cleaned the bathroom.

Rachael didn't seem to hear her for a few moments. She was scrubbing away at the bath, but now Sarah noticed her sponge was moving over the same area again and again, even though it was already clean. Rachael's eyes were unfocused, the way they were when you were no longer seeing the world in front of you.

'*Rachael*,' she said.

Rachael's head came up quickly. She looked awful, Sarah thought. Her face was puffy, sagging a little round the cheeks like an old woman.

'I'm going to have another baby,' she repeated.

A smile from Rachael, but it looked like it caused her pain. 'That's wonderful. Congratulations. We can have a lovely supper to celebrate.'

'I'm not pregnant yet,' Sarah said.

'Oh, but I thought—'

'I was just telling you. I will be soon. God's going to send me another baby now the danger's passed.'

'Well – that's nice to hear,' Rachael said. 'I hope so.'

'You don't need to hope. He will.'

Sarah watched as Rachael resumed her scrubbing, but she herself relaxed for a few moments, holding the mop loosely in her hand. When she was pregnant, there would be no more dwelling on what she had done. It would be a new chapter.

She said, 'God only sends children to you if He thinks you're worthy. Esther was never worthy.'

Rachael's hand slowed for a moment, then continued its rhythmic back and forth motion.

'God always knew she wasn't,' Sarah said.

Finally, Rachael answered. 'I suppose He did.'

I killed her, Sarah reminded herself, watching for her own reaction. But again, there was only this blankness, this slight feeling that she had been cheated out of something.

She'd tried to explain it to Nathaniel the night before, but he didn't seem to grasp what she was saying, how difficult it was to get it straight in her head.

He had kissed her passionately, his tongue slipping between her lips so she couldn't speak any more. When he pulled back, he said, 'It's rare for a person to be able to say they've served God as you've served Him. You're first amongst the followers of the Ark.'

She had felt proud at his words, but a little lonely, too. Nathaniel had no trouble understanding what had happened. If she felt any confusion, it must be a further sign of her weakness. Once, she might have confided in Rachael, but the days when she talked to Rachael about her fears were gone.

Still, she was not suffering. She knew Seth had nightmares, could sometimes be heard shouting out; knew, because Ruth had told her. Ruth relayed this information with scarcely suppressed rage, as further evidence of Seth's failings. Sarah was surprised at Ruth's anger; she might have expected disdain perhaps, but this hiss of fury seemed out of character. Ruth was tightly wound these days, sharp, unfamiliar things jumping below the surface of her skin. Still, Sarah had faith in her. Ruth would get herself back under control soon enough. But it might have been better to have left Seth out of it altogether, as they'd done with Rachael and Deborah. Not everyone had the strength to do God's work.

Going down the corridor to the kitchen later, Sarah heard Seth and Rachael talking – arguing, even – in low voices. She paused by the door to listen, but couldn't make out the words. Then their voices broke off, and Sarah decided to take her moment to enter the room. When she pushed the door open, she saw that Seth had his arms around his wife, who was crying again. Rachael cried too much these days. Sarah nodded to them, then filled a glass of water at the sink and drank it. She began to watch them more closely after that. Soon she realized that Nathaniel was watching them too.

When she confided in Nathaniel her hopes of getting pregnant, he raised his eyebrows and said, 'God will send us a child in His own time.'

'I know.'

'He'll need to see first that the Ark is truly free from sin,' Nathaniel said. 'There may still be certain – elements holding us back.'

Sarah nodded, but she felt tired. She wasn't sure she could manage to hold the knife again.

Occasionally, old memories came back to her, odds and ends from the past. Helen and Liz in the coffee shop. Her mum's cramped front room. The mouse she'd had to stamp on, the bright blood smear inside the plastic bag. The person she'd been back then seemed like a stranger. But she knew better than to be surprised at how far she'd come. That was the mistake other people made, thinking things were fixed in place. Nothing was fixed. You might have thought you had one self, and you took it everywhere with you. But the truth was, you were fluid and shifting. You had no edges, no outline at all.

3

'We can't stay here,' Judith said. 'We have to escape. Don't you see that, Moses?'

He tried to understand what she was saying. He saw that at some point the two of them had become 'we', which was perhaps what he had wanted ever since he'd watched the strange red-haired girl climb out of the car so many months before. But that was another life.

They sat in their usual clearing in the forest. It wasn't the same, of course, not now the forest was cut open, but they returned to it from time to time, as though it might still be possible to discover somewhere safe. It was difficult for Moses to remember what life had felt like before they'd gone into the barn. It was as though the flood had come after all, unseen and dreadful.

The earth at the edge of the forest, near the baby's grave, was freshly disturbed.

Judith held her arms across her body. She was rocking slightly, backwards and forwards, as though it were dangerous to be still. 'It's not safe here,' she said.

Moses thought of Nathaniel, eating sausages the morning they'd seen the stain. 'But there's nowhere to go,' he said.

'We'll find somewhere. We could go to my gran. She'd look after us.'

'What about my parents? And Peter?'

'We can't tell them,' Judith said. 'It's not safe to trust anyone. Not my mum, not yours. Not even Peter.' Seeing his face, she added, 'But they could join us afterwards. Once we're there and we're safe. When no one can hurt us.'

'The prophet would find us,' Moses said. 'If he wanted to, he could easily find us.'

'He isn't a prophet,' Judith said.

'He is. He was anointed by God.'

'Who told you that?' Judith said.

'The grown-ups.'

'And who told them?'

'The prophet.'

Judith said nothing.

Moses searched and searched for the truth, but he no longer knew what that meant. 'I don't understand,' he said.

'Of course you don't,' Judith said. 'You don't know how.'

Perhaps she was the devil after all. Anything was possible now. But it hardly mattered if she was, Moses thought; it was too late. He already loved her.

He said, 'Are you the devil?'

'Not that I know of,' Judith said.

Going into the kitchen later, Moses came across his mother. She was standing by the sink, unmoving. She had washing-up gloves on and he could see the pile of dirty plates, but his mother's hands were still and she didn't turn as he came in, didn't appear to hear the door. Lot's wife, transformed utterly.

He said, 'Mum.'

When she did turn round, Moses saw her trying to smile at him. He wondered again, without wanting to, if she had been in the barn; if she had tried to smile at Esther, too.

He was about to mutter an excuse and slip away again, but something in her rigid posture and the quietness of the room unsettled him. So instead he made himself pause, and say, 'What are you doing?'

'Just – washing up,' she said, but there was a little break between the words as though she had struggled to form them in her head, struggled even to remember what washing-up was. The dirty plates remained untouched.

'Would you like some help?'

His mother shook her head. 'No.' Then, softly, 'No help, thanks.'

She looked like she might cry again, and Moses realized he didn't want to see this. She didn't seem like his mother any longer. She had become someone else entirely. I feel very old, he thought suddenly. I feel a hundred years old.

'We'll have to go across the moors,' Judith whispered to him that evening. They knelt side by side in the sitting room, laying the fire.

'It's too far,' Moses said.

'We'll manage. You know them better than me.'

'I've never been as far as Gehenna,' he said. 'I've never been anywhere near it.' He had a terrible, sad feeling: the knowledge that now of all times, when she trusted him to help her, he was going to fail. 'I'm sorry,' he said.

Judith had been assembling a pyramid of twigs in the grate, pushing smaller twigs and balls of paper into the middle, but now she stopped and put her hands to her face.

Helplessly, he touched her arm. 'Don't cry.'

'Just say it, if you're not coming,' Judith said, her voice muffled. 'Don't be a coward. Just say it.'

He tried to imagine staying in the Ark without her. 'Please don't cry,' he said again.

She wiped her hands roughly across her face and reached for the logs in the basket next to them, beginning to lay them around the base of the pyramid. 'Well?' she said. 'Are you going to report me?'

Shock prevented him speaking for a few moments. 'Of course not.'

'They'd kill me, wouldn't they?' Judith said. 'My mum wouldn't stop them. And if they knew you hadn't reported me, they'd kill you as well.' Her hands were shaking so much she knocked over the tower when she tried to add the final log.

Moses said, 'I'd never report you.'

'Why not?' Her voice had grown louder and he made a gesture with his hands to shush her.

'I don't know,' he said. 'I just wouldn't.'

'How can you be sure?'

'I don't know. But I am.'

'*I don't believe you.*' Judith hurled the log she was holding back down with such force it knocked the basket over. 'Everyone's a *liar!*'

Moses tried to calm himself so he could calm her. But it was impossible to make her see how clear she was in his head, how she was the only clear thing now. Impossible to make her see that she stood in front of everything, even in front of the prophet and in front of all his words about the devil and hell.

'I wouldn't report you,' he said, 'because you're my friend. It's – the main thing.'

Judith stared at him. At last, she nodded and wiped her eyes on her sleeve.

Gently, they relaid the logs around the pyramid. Moses handed Judith the box of matches and she struck one and held it against the paper. It flared, and fire surged over the smaller kindling.

Moses said, 'We'll find a way across the moors. We'll manage.'

She let out her breath. 'So you're coming?'

'Yes,' he said.

'I think we should go tomorrow.'

Moses hesitated, but only for a moment. He nodded.

'Shall we go after lessons in the afternoon?' Judith said. 'We'll have a couple of hours before they notice. And the light will be fading so it'll be harder for him to catch us.'

What about bogs? Moses wanted to say, but he could

see that bogs were the least of their problems. He didn't think they'd make it. But he would go with her anyway.

'We'll manage,' he said again.

They watched as the flames began to trickle up the tower and grab onto the larger logs.

'I'll tell you something,' Judith said.

'Alright.'

'You're my best friend,' she said. 'It was Megan once. Now it's you.'

He turned quickly to her. He thought she had gone red, but it might have been the heat from the flames, or the fact that she'd been crying.

'You needn't look so pleased with yourself,' she added. 'It's not like you had loads of competition.'

4

Moses struggled to fall asleep that night. He listened to the gentle breathing of the other boys, and wondered how they could be so peaceful when the Ark had fallen away, leaving them high on the moors in the cold wind. But the others hadn't been in the barn, he thought.

Judith was right. They had to escape, even if they couldn't reach Gehenna. Perhaps God would help them. Moses tried to decide if this was likely, but God wouldn't speak to him when he was on his own. Still, he tried to cling on to what he had always believed. My God is a good God.

He must have fallen asleep eventually, because it was a shock to feel Peter pulling at his arm, to open his eyes and for it to be morning.

Ruth was standing in the doorway, and Moses blundered upright, seized with terror, knowing at once they had been discovered.

But Peter said, 'It's Mum.'

Moses was so unused to seeing his brother at a loss that it took him a few moments to recognize the expression.

'What about her?'

'She's missing,' Peter said. He looked at Moses with a desperate, beseeching confusion, as if he expected Moses to be able to explain what had happened, though he'd only just been pulled awake. Moses felt the bed heave beneath him, like the great earthquake promised at the end of days.

Ruth said, 'Get dressed and come downstairs. Both of you.'

They pulled on their clothes in silence as she waited outside the door, and stumbled downstairs after her. Behind them, Jonathan and Ezra slept on.

In the kitchen they found their father sitting at the table, his shoulders slumped.

'I don't know where she is,' he said. 'I don't know. I just woke up—'

Deborah was at the stove. She said, 'It'll all turn out fine, Seth. I know it will.' She came over to the table and sat down, then got up again.

'I'm making porridge,' she said, to no one in particular.

When Nathaniel came in, Moses stared at him as though he were seeing him for the first time. The unkempt hair, the shadows under his eyes. *What have you done to my mother?* Moses wanted to say. But he couldn't speak.

Nathaniel took the cup of tea Deborah proffered, but his hand was trembling and he spilled it.

'Nathaniel—' Deborah began, but he spoke over her.

'Be *quiet*.'

He strode out again.

Deborah stirred the porridge rapidly. 'It'll all be fine, Seth,' she said again. 'Just have faith.'

Moses and Peter sat down at the table, because there seemed to be nothing else to do, and Deborah placed bowls of porridge in front of them.

'You can have honey in it today,' she said.

'I'm not hungry,' Peter said.

'Eat it,' their father said, though not angrily, and because they were afraid he might cry – unthinkable – they did, drizzling in honey from the pot Deborah pushed towards them. Moses didn't twist the spoon quickly enough and dribbled honey down the side of the jar. He wiped it away with his finger, hating the stickiness.

A short while later, the other children trailed in.

'Your mother's gone,' Abigail said to Moses and Peter in wonder.

'Yes, I think they know that,' Judith snapped at her. She laid her hand on Moses' arm.

'Porridge, everyone!' Deborah said. 'You can have honey today.'

Stiffly, Seth stood up and went out of the kitchen. Peter and Moses got up to follow him, but their father headed upstairs without looking back at them, so they remained in the hallway. They could still hear voices from the kitchen, Mary saying, 'Did she sin?' and Judith saying, 'Shut *up*, Mary.'

'Let's go outside,' Peter said. 'I can't stand it in there.'

Together, they slipped out of the front door and walked away from the houses. It was a bright, clear morning. The wind sent the long grass reaching for their feet.

'I don't understand,' Peter said. 'She hasn't done any-thing wrong.'

Moses wondered if his brother knew about Esther after all. He stared out across the moors, tried to take it all in at once. He'd looked at this view every day of his life, but it no longer seemed familiar. The moors couldn't have changed, not when they hadn't changed in a thousand years, as his father said. It must be Moses himself who'd changed.

He turned when Peter made a small sound, a quick intake of breath.

'What?'

'The car's gone,' Peter said.

'What do you mean?'

'The car's gone,' Peter said again. 'But all the men are here. Don't you understand?'

And then Moses did understand.

His mother's plan had been so much better than his and Judith's. And he found he was hardly even surprised, in this terrifying new landscape, that she hadn't tried to take her children with her.

Later that morning, they stood in the prayer room as Nathaniel prayed for their souls. The prophet's anger pulsed through the room. His voice was louder than usual.

'The devil is tearing the Ark apart!' he said. 'You let him in! You did this!'

It wasn't clear if he was addressing one of them or all of them. Moses held himself very still, trying his best – as the others were surely doing as well – to avoid attracting attention.

Nathaniel ran his hands through his hair, making it stand up wildly. He spread his arms.

'There will be retribution!' he said. 'There will be wailing and gnashing of teeth.'

There was no lunch served that day. Nobody was hungry, and in any case Nathaniel said they must fast to show God their repentance. Ruth led the children to the schoolroom, where they would have lessons as normal.

Moses sat beside Judith and tried to concentrate on his sums. The numbers and symbols meant nothing to him and wouldn't even stay still on the page. Judith waited until Ruth had turned away and then quickly swapped her sheet with his.

They all staggered outside at break time, and stood in a small cluster.

Ezra broke the silence. 'God will punish her,' he said.

'Shut up,' Peter said. 'Or I'll thump you.'

'Then God will punish you, too.'

'You know, Ezra,' Judith said, 'I bet you're God's least favourite.'

'I'll tell the prophet you said that,' Ezra said.

'I don't care.'

Moses was hardly listening. There was a lurching feeling in his chest. Someone was going to be punished in his mother's place. It would be Moses, or his father, or Peter. And even if Moses lived through this, he and Judith could never try to escape, because it was obvious – it should have been obvious before – that if they left, more people would be punished. Cleansing after cleansing. There was no way out.

'Are you alright, Moses?' Judith said, stepping closer to him.

He swayed on his feet, and she caught his arm. 'Are you going to faint?'

Moses sat down on the ground.

Judith crouched beside him. 'Take deep breaths,' she said.

'God's punishment,' Ezra muttered, but Abigail shoved him and said, 'Be *quiet*, Ezra.'

'I'm alright,' Moses said.

There was a distant thrum, so faint at first that he wasn't sure if he was really hearing it. The throbbing of an engine. Slowly, he stood up. Judith copied him.

The noise became louder, and now Moses could see the others had heard it too. Abigail said, 'She's coming back!'

They all turned towards the direction of the sound. The car was a dark shape in the distance, but it was quickly growing larger as it moved along the moor road and turned onto the track that led towards the houses.

My mother will be killed, Moses thought. She's coming back to be killed.

'It looks wrong,' Mary said suddenly.

They screwed up their eyes and stared. As it came closer, Moses realized she was right. It was similar enough to their car to know that it *was* a car – but it was a different shape.

And there were more of them.

They could make out a steady procession behind the

first car, emerging snake-like from the dust of the track: five cars in total, moving sedately towards them. As the cars came closer still, Moses saw that they were white on the front, with flashes of bright yellow and blue.

Nobody spoke now. It was impossible to describe what they were seeing.

Then Deborah was there, and Ruth as well, saying, 'Back into the schoolroom. *Now.*'

Deborah pushed their shoulders, forcing them back inside. They allowed themselves to be herded, too confused to resist, and huddled together at one end of the schoolroom. Deborah stayed with them, whilst Ruth strode out again.

Moses turned to Judith for reassurance. She was covering her mouth with her hand, but he could feel her excitement all the same. Then she hit his arm, hard enough to hurt, and said, 'Don't you get it?'

He turned to look out of the schoolroom window, from which he could observe strange men and women getting out of the cars. They were dressed in black and white, and he thought of the chessboard in the sitting room.

'It's the police,' Judith said.

'Who's the police?' Mary said, but at the same time Deborah said, 'Be quiet, Judith,' and for once Judith obeyed.

Ruth came back into the room, moving fast. 'Take the children upstairs,' she said to Deborah. 'Keep them there.'

'Come on, my loves,' Deborah said, and began to usher them out into the hallway.

But then the front door opened and a strange man was standing there.

'Leave the children and come outside with me,' the man said to Deborah.

Ruth appeared behind them, saying, 'Take them upstairs, Deborah,' as though the man hadn't spoken.

The man said, 'Do as I say, please, madam.'

Through his terror, Moses thought how foolish the man was to think he could defeat Ruth.

But the next moment, Deborah was stepping away from them, stepping towards the man.

Ruth said to them, 'Go *upstairs*,' and they obeyed, running up to the landing as fast as they could. The others went to hide in the boys' bedroom, but Judith stopped and pulled Moses back with her. Moses watched the door to the boys' room close.

'We need to go back downstairs,' Judith said. 'We have to make sure.'

Make sure of what? he thought. There was a strange expression on Judith's face, but he recognized it. The old fierceness and fury were back, as though no time had passed since she had climbed out of the car that first day. He wanted to go and hide with the others, but instead he followed her down to the now empty hallway and out of the front door.

There were many strangers, some standing around the cars, some moving towards the small house, and another group striding towards the edge of the forest. A woman hurried up to Moses and Judith.

'What are your names?' she said. She had blonde hair like Esther's. She seemed distracted, glancing around as if she had too many names to find out at once, though Moses and Judith were the only children in sight.

'I'm Judith and he's Moses,' Judith told the woman. 'Have you come to take us away?'

The woman hesitated. 'We need to have a bit of a chat with everyone. OK? Nothing to be scared of.'

'We're not scared,' Judith said. 'But you can't leave us here.'

The woman was giving Judith her full attention now. 'We won't, love. OK? We won't leave you.'

'But do you promise?' Judith said.

The woman met Judith's gaze. 'I promise. You're coming with us.'

Judith made a strange, shaky sound, halfway between a sob and a laugh. She took Moses' hand.

Moses looked past them both. Out of the small house came two of the chessboard men. They were leading his father between them, walking along in a strange trio. Moses stared at his father, but his father didn't look back at him. One of the men opened the back door of a car, and his father climbed in. Then they closed the door.

'Where's my father going?' Moses said.

'It's alright, sweetheart,' said the woman with hair like Esther's. 'We just need to ask the adults some questions.'

Moses felt tears in his eyes, because 'sweetheart' was what his mother used to call him, back before the rain came and the river turned to blood.

'It's alright,' the woman said again.

When he looked harder, he could just make out Ruth in the back of another of the cars.

'I need to go and find the other children,' the woman said to Judith. 'I need to make sure they're OK.'

'They're fine,' Judith said. 'Only they're hiding, because they think you're the devil.'

The woman smiled nervously.

Then Judith went very still and Moses saw that her mother was being brought out, walking between a man and a woman. Sarah turned at the last moment, when they were almost at the car, and looked over at them.

'Judith,' she said, but Judith didn't say anything back. She watched as her mother was put into the back of the car.

And finally, the strangest sight of all. Here was Nathaniel, being led out to the cars from behind the barn. He wasn't walking meekly like the others. He was struggling and cursing at the men on either side of him and he had his hands tied behind his back with something that looked like metal.

'You'll be punished for this,' he was shouting. 'God will curse you! God will kill your children!'

Moses stared at the prophet. Nathaniel's face was red and screwed up as he shouted. His voice sounded high and harsh, not soothing as it had once been. It was as though a different Nathaniel had stepped out from behind the old one.

One of the men opened the back door of a car, and Nathaniel was pushed inside, another man placing his hand on Nathaniel's head to stop him bumping it.

Beside Moses, Judith spoke very softly. '*Good.*'

Inside the car, Nathaniel turned and looked straight at Moses. Moses looked back.

So this is what the end times look like, he thought.

VII

Gehenna

1

Moses wasn't sure how long he'd been standing at the window. There was no movement along the street now, not a single person. But from this position he could see a little way into the first-floor rooms of the houses opposite: glimpses of a mirror, a sofa, a wardrobe. The houses were scrunched together in a line, with no space in between. Moses was amazed at how close to one another people lived in Gehenna.

Peter came back into the room. 'Stop looking,' he said. 'It's better not to look.'

Moses ignored him, but suddenly a light went on in one of the windows facing them and the room came into bright focus. He could see a young woman framed in light, opening a drawer, pulling out a jumper. Moses stepped quickly back from the window.

He surveyed their new bedroom again. Two beds, side by side. A wardrobe, a pale carpet. Not exactly the fires of hell, though it was true that evil rarely came dressed in its own clothes.

He had been brave up to this point, but his courage was beginning to fail him. When they drove down off the moors in the line of cars, he'd watched unflinchingly as the familiar sights moved past him and disappeared. The ragged grass, the slumped rocks – all pulled smoothly away, like someone winding up a piece of ribbon. And as they descended into the valley and left the moors behind, still he had looked, even as the world collapsed around him. Fields and woodland curved up on either side, guarded by skeletal hedgerows. A sprinkling of sheep on the tiered landscape. Peter and Ezra sat beside him in the police car in silence, except for Peter asking once, 'Is our mother alright?'

'She's fine,' the woman in the passenger seat had said. 'She's just answering some questions at the moment.'

'When will we see our parents again?' Ezra said.

'Soon, I hope,' the woman said. 'The police need to talk to them, and I'm not sure how long it'll take. In the meantime, we're trying to contact other family members for all of you. Please try not to worry. We're taking you somewhere safe whilst we get everything sorted out.'

Her name, she had said, was Melissa. An odd name, Moses thought, but he managed not to comment. Melissa wasn't wearing black and white. She was in dark trousers and a pink cardigan. Moses had tried not to stare too much at the trousers. The man driving the car, dressed in black and white like the others, hadn't said a word since they'd set off.

Peter was staring at the back of the seat in front of him, and Ezra was looking down at his lap, despite the extraordinary sights passing by the window. Everything was becoming softer now, and strangely flat – where was the savage sweep of the moors? The grass down here was clipped and low and green. Look, Moses wanted to say, look!

But when they reached the edge of the town, he couldn't look any longer. First one house appeared, then another, and another. The fields ran out, and everything was hard and grey. If Moses turned and craned his neck to look out of the back window he could still see the crest of the moors behind them, but he knew all the same that he had come to the burning place, the valley of the son of Hinnom.

He had seen grey on the moors before, when the wind rose and the sky changed, but the grey of Gehenna had no life in it. And there were more cars now, in front of them, behind them, beside them. Gehenna was pulling the breath out of his lungs. He wished Judith were with them, not in the other police car with the girls and Jonathan. He closed his eyes.

The car jolted slightly as they turned a corner, and Moses fell against Ezra, who was trembling.

'Almost there!' Melissa said.

Almost where? Moses thought.

They reached it in the end, whether they wanted to or not. When the noise of the engine died, Moses opened his eyes. A narrow grey road, lined with houses on either side.

They were ushered up a short path and into the nearest house. Moses kept his eyes on the ground. But even that looked wrong, and felt wrong beneath his feet. It had no give like the ground on the moors – it pushed back at you. There was no sign of the other police car, and Moses was afraid Judith was being taken somewhere else. But he'd used up all his panic on the journey and now he felt nothing.

As Melissa stood back to let them through the door ('This is only temporary, guys, whilst we get a few things sorted out, OK?'), Moses glanced round and saw a man in the garden next to theirs. He was watching them, and he didn't look away when Moses met his eye. It occurred to Moses that perhaps the man was noticing the mark on his face. Would it make him stand out in Gehenna as it had in the Ark? But he decided he didn't care. He knew enough now to understand that the adults had been wrong; it didn't matter if your face was stained. Everybody was marked.

Inside the house, Melissa took them up some stairs covered in brown carpet. 'You'll be sleeping in here tonight,' she said to Moses and Peter, gesturing to a door. 'And you, love – ' to Ezra, who seemed on the verge of tears – 'will be in here, just next door. The other boy – Jonathan, isn't it? – will join you when he gets here. Alright?' She smiled at them. 'I'll give you a bit of time to get settled in.'

Now, standing just inside the door of their bedroom, Peter repeated, 'It's better not to look.'

Of course he was right. 'There's so much of it,' Moses said. 'So much stuff.'

Peter went and sat down on one of the beds. He

bounced up and down a few times. 'It's really springy,' he said.

Moses went to join him. 'Do you think all the beds in Gehenna are like this?'

'Don't know.' Peter paused, then added, 'The bathroom's along the corridor. The water comes out hot straight away. You should try it.'

Moses nodded, but along the corridor seemed a long way to go.

The sound of a car outside. Please, he thought. Please let it be Judith.

They heard the front door opening, voices, then footsteps thundering up the stairs. Surely they could only belong to her.

And the next moment, Judith burst in.

'Hi! This is weird, isn't it? You OK?'

Moses nodded, weak with relief at seeing her. There were more voices out in the corridor, and then Jonathan, Mary and Abigail crowded in, Ezra behind them.

'Did you see all the cars on the way?' Jonathan said.

The others nodded.

'And the sinners,' Ezra said. 'Their houses. There are so many.'

'It's not what I pictured,' Mary said shakily. 'It's not how I pictured Gehenna.'

'Lunchtime!' Melissa called from downstairs.

In the kitchen, small sandwiches were laid out on plates. The man in black and white was standing by the counter, and so was another woman whom Melissa introduced as Kerry.

'Have a seat,' Melissa said. 'And tuck in.'

Obediently, they took up their places round the table, but didn't make any move to reach for the sandwiches.

'What's wrong?' Melissa said. 'Come on, guys. You need to eat something.'

Moses looked at Peter, who eventually spoke up. 'But who's going to say the prayer?'

The adults' expressions seemed to freeze. The woman called Kerry said, 'Well – would one of you like to?'

Peter said, 'We're not supposed to. Not without the – not without Nathaniel here.'

'Well, can you go without, just this once?' Melissa said. 'I'm sure it's OK just once. I'm sure – God will understand. It's not your fault, is it?'

'We can't eat without saying the prayer,' Mary said.

Moses had realized by now that he was starving, and thought the others probably were too. Melissa and Kerry and the silent man didn't seem to know what to suggest, so Moses said, 'I'll do it. And if it's wrong, I'll be the one who gets punished.'

'No one's going to punish you, love,' Melissa said gently.

'God might,' Ezra said, sounding a bit more like himself.

'Shut up, Ezra,' Judith said, turning on him. To Moses, she said, 'Want me to say it instead? I don't care.'

'I'm not eating anything if she's said it,' Ezra muttered.

'Shut *up*, Ezra,' Judith said again.

'Come on, guys,' Kerry said, but they all ignored her.

'I'll say it,' Moses said. 'It's fine. I think it's probably fine.' For his own part, he found he wasn't really afraid. He waited till they'd all bowed their heads – Ezra still looked doubtful, but after a moment he copied the others – then began: 'O God. Thank you for the food you've placed before us. Thank you for the Ark you've built to house us.' He faltered. The last part was, 'Thank you for the prophet you've sent to lead us,' but he wasn't sure he could say it. There was an agonizing pause.

'Amen,' Judith said firmly. She reached for a sandwich, and then Peter did too. This was enough to prompt the others, and soon they were all eating. Moses was beginning to feel calmer now. The fizz of unease in the room seemed to have died down. You didn't have to let the world grow bigger around you. You could shrink it again, until it consisted only of this house, nothing beyond.

'Now,' Melissa said when they'd almost finished eating. 'There are some people coming to talk to you this afternoon. Nothing to worry about – they're very nice. They just have one or two things to ask you about. OK? And then the doctor will be here after that, just to check you over, make sure you're all OK. We thought it would be best if everyone came here, rather than taking you back into town. You've had enough moving about today, haven't you?'

Nobody answered her.

'We've got an hour or two free before they get here,' she said. 'How about a game of something? There are some great board games in the cupboard.'

Jonathan pushed his plate away and looked up at the grown-ups. 'When can we go home?'

There was a silence.

'I'm afraid we don't know,' Melissa said. 'I wish we could tell you more. We're just working a few things out. We want to do what's best for you all. And this is a – slightly unusual situation. For all of us. It might take a day or two before things are sorted.'

Moses looked across at Judith, who met his eye. She gave a small shrug. Moses was starting to see that they were never going home. And anyway, it didn't exist any longer. The prophet had created a world, and then he'd destroyed it.

The next two hours seemed long. The rules to the games Melissa produced were complicated and nobody could summon up the energy to understand them. They eventually trailed upstairs to their rooms, only able to shake Melissa off by saying they all wanted a nap. Then, since she kept asking if they needed anything, they really did have to go into their separate rooms and get into bed in their clothes. Once Melissa had gone downstairs again, Moses and Peter stayed where they were, exhausted by the events of the day. They might really have fallen asleep if they hadn't heard a scream from next door.

In the girls' room, they found Mary and Abigail huddled together on one of the beds, whilst Judith shook her head scornfully at them.

'I tried to tell them,' she said. 'It's just the TV. It was in the cupboard. I warned them I was going to turn it on.'

Moses watched, transfixed. He was vaguely familiar with the concept of TV, as Judith had talked him through it in some detail whilst they were in the Ark, but it hadn't prepared him for seeing the real thing. The dark box sitting in the cupboard was lit up, and there was a picture of a person inside it. The picture moved, and the person was speaking to them quietly, as though she had been shrunk and trapped inside the box.

'Wow,' Peter murmured beside him, stepping forward and putting out his hand to touch the picture. 'How do they do that?'

'Not sure,' Judith said. 'But it's not a miracle or magic or anything like that. It's just TV. Everyone has one. It's – something to do with electricity. Something like that. It's *science*.'

Nobody answered her because suddenly the woman was gone and instead there was a picture of the big house and the small house.

'What on—' Peter began, but Judith shushed him.

A voice was still speaking, but Moses didn't take in much of it. He heard the word 'police', but mainly he just looked at the tiny Ark locked away inside the box.

Then it vanished.

Melissa was in the doorway, holding something in her hand which she was pointing at the TV. The screen had gone black.

She said, 'Guys, it's best if you don't watch television right now. To be honest, I didn't realize it was in here. I'm going to take it out.'

'We're not stupid,' Judith said. 'We'd rather know what's going on.'

'I know you're not stupid, Judith,' Melissa said. 'But

311

things get jumbled by reporters and I don't think that's going to be very helpful.' When Judith didn't answer, she added, 'I'll keep you in the loop as much as I can. Alright?'

'Alright,' Judith said. She sounded sullen, but Moses could tell she didn't hate Melissa the way she hated Ruth.

When Melissa had wheeled the cupboard with the TV out of the room, the girls and Peter and Moses sat together on the beds. Soon after, Ezra and Jonathan came in as well. No one said much, but Moses was glad they were together. It was odd, not being able to picture the future.

The people who came to talk to them were another strange man and a woman, though this pair weren't dressed in black and white. The woman wore trousers like Melissa, and she had such short hair that Moses thought she was a man when he saw her from the top of the stairs, except that her body was wrong for a man's (this thought made him blush as soon as it occurred to him).

They went into the sitting room, and then Melissa brought the children in one at a time. Peter was called first. The rest of them stayed where they were in the girls' room, eating the biscuits Melissa had given them.

'What do you think they're talking about?' Abigail asked. It was almost the first thing she'd said since coming to Gehenna.

'They'll be trying to make him curse God,' Ezra said. 'And if he lets them corrupt him, he'll go to hell.'

'Don't pretend to know what you're talking about when you don't,' Judith snapped. They all looked at her, since she was the expert on Gehenna.

'Well, I don't really know either,' she said. 'But I think they're going to ask us about Nathaniel. And – about Esther.'

A silence.

Jonathan said, 'About – how she sinned?'

'No,' Judith said. 'About what happened to her.' She got up and went to the window.

Abigail said, 'I want to see Mum. When can I see Mum?'

Nobody spoke. Ezra had turned away and was rubbing his hands over his face. Moses almost felt sorry for him.

When Moses' own turn came, the man and woman in the living room told him their names and a bit about themselves, but Moses found it hard to listen. There had been too many unfamiliar people already today. He held his hands together tightly.

'We'll keep this short, Moses,' the man said. 'We'll need to talk to you a bit more another time, but I know you've been through a lot already. This is just a quick chat, OK?'

Moses nodded.

'To start us off, can you tell us your parents' names?'

'Rachael and Seth,' Moses said – he had almost answered 'Mum and Dad'.

The man wrote something down, and the short-haired woman said, 'You're doing brilliantly, Moses.'

This confused him, since he had only said three words so far.

A series of questions followed, mostly delivered in the man's soft voice, with the woman adding bits in occasionally. Moses wasn't sure at first whether he should answer their questions, whether he was supposed to do as the people of Gehenna asked. He knew Ezra wouldn't say much. But right and wrong were jumbled together now.

The man was asking him about Nathaniel. He said, 'Did he ever hurt you?'

Moses thought about it. He had been hit once or twice during sessions, but that had mainly been Ruth, and he said so.

'Hit you round the face?' the man said, writing again.

'Yes.'

'Did it hurt a lot?'

'No.'

'A bit?'

'Yes.'

'Did either of your parents ever hit you?'

Moses shook his head.

'What did they do when Ruth hit you?'

'They were upset.'

'Did they try to stop it?'

Moses was about to shake his head again, but he had an anxious feeling, like he was facing some hidden danger. After a pause, he said 'Yes', and was interested to see that the man didn't detect the lie.

The woman asked him some odd questions then about the grown-ups touching him, and Moses said his mother hugged him sometimes, but not so often since he was older.

He saw the man and woman glance at each other, and then back at him.

'We're nearly finished, Moses,' the man said. 'You're doing really well, and in a moment we'll leave it for today. But can you just tell me, as truthfully as you can, if you know what happened to Jess Sadler?' He corrected himself: 'Esther.'

Moses stared down at his hands for a while and tried not to see the bloodstain again. He thought, *I must protect the Ark against the sinners of Gehenna.* But it was an automatic thought, and brought with it no emotion.

His next thought was sharper and clearer: there's nothing left to protect. So instead, he listened to his own feeling, which might have been God or might have been the devil, or something else entirely. He didn't know if he could trust it, but he didn't know if he could trust anything now, and it seemed better, after everything, to be led astray by yourself than by someone else.

So after a moment he looked up at the man. 'They killed her,' he said.

2

Thomas met Rachael in the corridor at the police station. It was a shock, seeing her like that, though he'd known she was somewhere in the building, being asked a few final questions – there seemed to be endless questions. He himself had answered so many by then that he felt muddled and exhausted, far less certain of his replies than when he started.

Rachael didn't speak except to say his name, and then she stopped dead in the middle of the corridor.

Thomas tried to recover himself. Rachael didn't belong in the world of police stations and paperwork and styrofoam cups of tea. This thought had obviously occurred to her as well. She looked almost transparent, as though willing herself to fade away and reappear somewhere else, somewhere safe. Her hair was lank, and she was oddly dressed, presumably in clothes lent to her by the social workers or police: a red skirt and shapeless white T-shirt; clumpy lace-up shoes. Some kind of insane compromise between Gehenna's dress code and her own. She looked ugly, Thomas thought, and then was surprised at himself. But thoughts, as he knew so well, rarely did what you wanted or expected them to do.

'Please,' he said to the officer accompanying him. 'Can we have a minute? Is there somewhere we can talk?'

Another officer was fetched, along with the liaison officer, an inappropriately cheerful woman called Sally. Eventually Rachael and Thomas were ushered into a small, peach-coloured room with an orange sofa and arm-chair.

'I don't need to tell you not to discuss your statements.' Sally beamed at them.

'No,' Thomas said. 'You don't need to tell us.'

Rachael had gone quickly to the sofa and sat down. When he stared at her, she seemed to fade a little further.

And he found he couldn't say anything at all, just felt his way to the chair and sat down as well, suddenly an old man.

Neither of them spoke. Thomas didn't know what he'd wanted to talk about. He knew everything already. Perhaps he'd just wanted to look at her.

Then Rachael said, as though he'd asked her, 'I didn't know it was going to happen. Thomas, I didn't know.'

He nodded slowly. No use trying to work out whether she was telling the truth. She probably didn't even know herself. Her face was taut, like she was in pain. Thomas saw that it was in his power to help her; that perhaps, since he was able to, he should.

He said, 'They'll be punished, thanks to you. Nathaniel will be punished.' A pause, then he brought out with dif-ficulty, 'It was brave of you.'

Her mouth twisted. 'I hardly knew what I was doing. I just found that I – had to. I barely remembered how to drive. Managed it, though.' Another silence, then she added, 'They're all being charged with murder. All of them. Except Deborah. And me.'

'I know.'

'I thought it would only be him. Nathaniel. I didn't think it would be the others as well.'

'Why not?'

'I don't know. I think – I'd got so used to the idea that we didn't decide things. That only he decided things, so if something happened it was because of him, and not because of anyone else. I know now that's not true.' Obediently, she added, 'I know none of us are innocent.'

'Would you still have left,' Thomas said, 'if you'd known Seth would be charged?'

'Yes.' Unblinking. 'That doesn't make any difference.'

There was a long silence. Thomas stared down at the carpet. Pale orange, flecks of red.

'I can't seem to make myself feel the things I ought to feel,' he said. 'I try to hate Seth, but it's difficult. It doesn't feel real. I *want* to hate him. He was part of it.'

'Do you know what he said to me?' Rachael said after a few moments. 'What Seth said to me?'

'What?'

'He said that you don't realize until it happens to you, how easy it is to – forget yourself. I'm not defending him,' she added. 'Just – he knew it was wrong. Or he knows now. He'll live with it forever.'

Perhaps he will, Thomas thought. And either way, Seth was right – it *was* easy. There was a time when Thomas, too, would have done anything for Nathaniel. That was the horror of it; the word 'anything' had come to mean so little. Beyond a certain point, all acts were the same.

'Do you still love him?' he asked. It was difficult to say the word 'love'.

'He's my husband,' Rachael said.

'Yes.'

She paused, then went on, 'Do you remember, Thomas, what it felt like in the beginning? It was so pure, wasn't it? But we went too far. We got lost. So – maybe that was one reason why I had to do it. It was the only way to save him. And to save all of us.'

'Too late to save Esther.'

He must have meant to hurt her, and he could see he had. She'd been dry-eyed until now, but suddenly the tears were coming, and she bent over as if winded.

'I'm sorry,' she said.

There were stories he could tell himself to make it bearable. He told himself he couldn't have guessed. He told himself he never suspected, not in a million years. But here was the truth, ugly and insistent: the moment he'd seen the barn on the front page of the newspaper – just the building, nothing more – he'd known. Which means the knowledge must have been there already, patiently awaiting its time. In any case, it didn't matter what stories he told himself. Nothing made it bearable.

'He'll suffer for what he did,' Rachael said. 'They all will.'

'Not as much as she suffered.' And without warning, he felt himself beginning to cry as well. He didn't realize what was happening at first; it felt like his whole body was convulsing, and then, after a few struggling, panicked moments, the sobs burst out. Rachael didn't try to comfort him.

'I try not to picture it,' he said. 'I try not to let myself think of what her last moments must have been like. But I can't help it.' He cried and cried, and in rhythm with his sobs his mind threw out *Esther, Esther, Esther.*

'I met her parents,' he said, when he'd regained some control. 'Met them last week. They're just – *destroyed*. They waited for her to come home—' He broke off.

Rachael was still crying too, but softly.

When Thomas spoke again, his voice was almost steady. 'I told her I loved her.'

'You did,' Rachael said.

'No, not enough. I didn't love her enough to stay.' He rubbed his hands over his eyes. Gave one more dry sob. 'Fourteen years in the Ark. Fourteen years of trying to break myself, trying to obey God, and all I've learnt is this. You never love anyone enough.'

They sat quietly after that. Sally came in at one point to offer them tea – more styrofoam cups – which they both declined. After their misery had burned itself out, a kind of deadness seemed to come over them. They struggled to push the conversation back onto its rails, to get to the moment when they could say goodbye and not see each other again.

'What will you do now?' Thomas said at last.

'I'll go to my parents. In Cornwall. I hope the boys will like it.'

'By the sea?'

'Yes. I'm lucky,' she added, 'that they'll take me in. Deborah's parents are already dead.'

'What will she do?'

'There's some money left for her and the children. She's going to Derbyshire, I think. Where she grew up.'

'Everyone returning home,' Thomas said.

'But there is no home now, is there?' Rachael said.

After he had said goodbye, he got into the car to drive back down south. He wouldn't be needed again until the trial started. He would put distance between himself and what had happened. He would return to his small flat and close the curtains and go to sleep. The next day he'd get up and return to work, where no one would question him. He would not think of her. He would think of her constantly.

It felt too big to confront, the terrible mistake they'd made. Too big even to see properly. The Gehenna they had feared before, the one blighted with suffering and sin: that was nothing more than shadows on the wall. The real Gehenna was something else entirely. It was this sense of wrongness, of having gone so far away from what you intended that now you would never get back. It was this feeling of dislocation you carried about with you, so that wherever you were was Gehenna, and Gehenna was you yourself. He knew that Rachael understood this too.

As the motorway opened up before him, he tried to trace it all back to where it started, as he would often do during the years that followed. It would be tempting to blame God, but of course that was no good now. Difficult to remember what it was like to believe the way he once had. Slowly, over time, God had moved further and further away, until He was eventually nothing more than an idea – and someone else's idea, at that. A decoy, intended to distract you from what was really before you. Just someone throwing their voice.

After

'I was worried about you,' Stephanie said. 'When you didn't show up last time. Did Gran tell you I rang?'

'Yes,' Judith said.

'She said you were unwell.'

'I was.'

'Are you feeling better?'

'A bit.'

A long pause, then her mother said, 'Have you seen *Despicable Me*?'

Judith was startled out of her silence. 'What?'

'It's an animated film.' Her mother thought for a moment. 'Computer animated.'

'Yes, I've seen it.'

'It was our film last week.'

'Weird choice.'

'Yes, I thought so too,' her mother said. 'But everyone seemed to like it. It was fun. I like those – little yellow creatures.'

'Minions,' Judith said absently.

'I was thinking,' her mother said, 'that it's just the kind of film I'd have loved to take you to see when you were little.' When Judith didn't answer, she added, 'Perhaps one day we could go to the cinema again together.'

'Yeah,' Judith said. 'Maybe.' She glanced over to the window, all the way across the room. A bright square of light. She found herself unable to look back at her mother. Her eyes were beginning to water as she kept them on the brightness. She considered telling her mother about *Let the Right One In*, which she'd watched the night before. But instead she said softly, 'If Nathaniel had asked you to kill me, would you have done it?'

A shocked pause, as they both absorbed her question. Judith was amazed at herself, but full of a strange, savage delight.

Stephanie's voice was tight when she finally answered. 'Of course not. How can you ask that?'

'Well, how can you say "of course not"? How do you know you wouldn't have?'

'Judith—'

'You would have done anything he asked,' Judith said. 'Not that.'

Judith made herself meet her mother's eye.

Stephanie said, 'I don't know what to say. Tell me what to say to you.'

'Say that you ruined my life. Stop pretending it's going to be OK. Admit that everything's ruined. Admit it'll never be OK.'

'No,' Stephanie said. 'I won't admit that, because it isn't true.'

'Of course not.'

'No,' Stephanie said again. She had tears in her eyes, but her voice had taken on a sharpness, and it reminded

Judith of being a child again, being scolded for being too loud, too rude, too much for her mother to handle.

'I'm sorry,' her mother said. 'But I'm not going to let you pretend it's all over for you. It's not.'

'You don't know what you're talking about.'

'I know you. And you're not like other people. Not – breakable like everyone else. Nathaniel didn't realize that. But I do.'

'You're wrong,' Judith said.

Stephanie wiped her face, quickly, discreetly. She said, 'You don't have to keep visiting me. I think – you find it hard. It might be better for you to stop.'

Judith didn't reply. Yes, it would be better, she thought.

Her mother reached out tentatively to take her hand. 'It would be OK, if you stopped. I'd understand.'

Judith pulled her hand away and leaned against the hard back of the chair. Briefly, she closed her eyes. She would walk out of this bleak space into the sunlight and never come back.

When she opened her eyes, her mother was still there, still waiting. Stephanie had her hands together in her lap, as though they needed something to hold on to. Judith couldn't bear to look at her face again, so she stared at her mother's clasped hands instead. They were dry, the skin cracked around the knuckles. Her mum had used hand cream all the time when Judith was a child, greasy and sweet-scented. Judith pictured Stephanie being led back to her cell, sitting alone in that small room, tuning the radio, unable to bear the silence. Imagined her sitting in the dark watching that week's film, storing up small details to talk to her daughter about.

There was a long pause. Judith took a breath.

She said, 'I watched *Let the Right One In* last night.'

Her mum leaned forward a little. Her hands moved apart in her lap. 'What's it about?'

'Vampires,' Judith said. 'But it's better than it sounds. Actually, I loved it.'

'Would I like it?'

'I think so,' Judith said. She began to explain.

3

Whilst Judith's grandmother was downstairs talking to Melissa, Judith and Moses stood together on the landing. They were alone for the first time that day. Peter, Jonathan, Abigail and Mary were in the living room, having finally succumbed to one of Melissa's board games. Ezra had been taken away the previous morning by a mysterious aunt, who bore an unsettling, thin-lipped resemblance to Ruth.

No one was there to listen to their conversation, but they were still finding it difficult to speak to one other. Judith pushed her hands into her pockets, and almost without realizing it, Moses copied her.

'My gran wrote down her address,' Judith said. 'So you can write to me. Your mum will show you what to do.'

Moses nodded.

There was another silence, then Judith said abruptly, 'They're probably going to prison for a long time.'

'I know.' He knew too, what prison was: a place where you were kept for years and couldn't leave. But there was no promise that it would earn you heaven.

'They deserve it,' Judith said. 'I'm never going to speak to my mum again. I hate her.'

'But she's your mother,' Moses said.

'Still.'

Moses had been trying to decide how he felt about his own mother. He settled for saying, 'You can write to me too. We're going south.'

'Yeah. Cornwall. It's nice there,' Judith said, though he knew she'd never been.

A fresh start, his mother had said. Melissa said it too. As though you could begin your whole life again, without it even mattering what had gone before. Looking at his mother's exhausted face, he knew she didn't believe it either.

'It'll be alright,' Peter had said.

'How?' Moses said.

'Don't know.'

But Peter really would be alright, Moses thought. He could see his brother more clearly now, as though his outline had grown sharper and bolder. Peter looked at nothing but what was in front of him. He would cope.

'Do you think God exists?' he asked Judith.

Judith looked at him carefully. 'No.'

A world without God was unimaginable once. Now it was here. Inside his chest where he thought his soul had been, there was emptiness and silence. All this struggle and pain for nothing. No promised land to make it all worthwhile. Nobody was going to be saved.

'I'll tell you one thing, though,' Judith said. 'If I *had* believed in God, I wouldn't let Nathaniel take it away from me.'

'But he lied,' Moses said.

'So what? Nathaniel has nothing to do with God. I don't think he believes in God.'

Moses nodded. In any case, he thought the heaviness that had come over him wasn't just the loss of heaven.

As if reading his mind, Judith said, 'We'll see each other again. Before we know it.'

Moses tried to think of all the things he ought to be saying. Downstairs they heard the sound of the kitchen door opening, the voices of the women growing louder, and Moses knew that their time was nearly up. Then the door closed again and the voices were muffled once more: a false alarm.

'It's horrible,' Judith said at last. 'Being able to see how different things could have been, but not being able to go back and change them. If my mum had never met him. If she hadn't agreed to join him.'

Moses was finding it hard to follow what she was saying. He'd never been able to see another life. He watched her instead: the red hair, the frown. He thought, if you hadn't come, I'd never have known what it is people live for, apart from heaven. But he didn't say this out loud.

The kitchen door opened again. The voices became louder and this time they didn't fade.

'Judith, are you ready?' Her grandmother's voice, calling up the stairs. Stiff, covering its awkwardness.

Judith took her hands out of her pockets. 'I'll miss you,' she said.

'But we'll see each other again,' Moses said, trying to believe it. 'Very soon.'

She smiled at him, an unusually gentle smile for her. But he didn't see it for long because she was already turning away.

After

Judith sat at the kitchen table whilst her gran made tea. Laid out in front of her was the Sunday magazine featuring Jo Hooper's story, a four-page spread entitled *God's Slaughter*. It had been so long since her encounter with the journalist that Judith had stopped thinking about her. But Jo Hooper had clearly just been taking her time to make sure she got the story exactly right.

A large and rather unflattering picture of Judith's mother stared out at her, above a blurry image of a smiling, blonde-haired teenager who could only be a young Esther. On the next page, there was a full-length shot of Nathaniel being led away from the courtroom after sentencing. *Adrian Fisher*, the caption said, *known to his followers as Nathaniel*. There was a small picture below of his parents at the trial, a faded, elderly couple who looked bewildered to be there.

'A load of dross,' her grandmother said when Judith brought the magazine home. 'Throw it away.'

But Judith had to look.

'They mention me by name,' she said now. 'But not the other kids. Not Moses.'

Her gran didn't reply. She was wiping down the counter with fierce concentration.

Judith stared at the photograph of Esther. *Jess Sadler, pictured before she joined the group.* Poor Esther. She turned the page, hoping Moses, all the way down in Cornwall, hadn't seen it.

She studied the picture of Nathaniel again. It was strange seeing him like this, dressed in a rumpled suit, eyes on the ground. He looked shockingly ordinary. She peered closer, trying to work out what it was that had given him such power, where that weird magnetism had come from. She had never felt it herself, but there seemed no denying other people had.

She said, 'Do you think he's got a new band of followers around him in prison?'

Her gran paused in her scrubbing. 'That's a nasty thought,' she said.

'I hope he dies in there.'

'If he doesn't, he'll be a very old man by the time he's released.'

'Mum will be out soon, though. A few more years.' She paused, trying to imagine it. 'What then?'

'We'll try to help her,' her gran said shortly, 'as best we can.'

'I always thought they should have got as long as him,' Judith said. 'They're all guilty. I didn't see what difference it made, whether or not he told them to do it.'

She waited for a comment from her gran, but none was forthcoming.

'Anyway, I don't know any more,' Judith murmured. She returned to the article. 'She makes it sound like a freak show, this Jo Hooper woman. Maybe it was. But nobody who wasn't there understands it.'

'Of course not,' her gran said.

Judith turned to the beginning of the article and looked at her mother's face. Despair was creeping in again.

'But what about the people who were there?' her gran said.

When Judith pretended not to hear, her gran came over to the table and sat down opposite her. She said crisply, 'I'm not one for blind optimism, but I do think unpleasant circumstances can be outweighed by other things.'

Judith raised her eyebrows.

'The strongest bonds,' her grandmother added, 'are often forged in fire.'

'You don't have to be so cryptic,' Judith said. 'We're not at Bletchley Park.'

'It's a pity to spend your whole life missing someone when there's no need.'

Judith thought of her grandfather, who'd died in a road accident in his thirties. She knew none of the details. It was never mentioned.

'I'm trying to move forward,' she said blandly.

'Well,' her grandmother remarked, 'you're certainly making an excellent job of that.' She got up and went back to the counter, picking up her cloth again.

A week later, Judith sat on the train and watched the countryside moving past. She had already eaten the cheese sandwich she'd found slipped into her bag. It had taken her about thirty miles of the journey just to wrestle it free from the cling film, but all the same, she was touched. Now she had nothing to do but look at the scenery. Should've brought *Swann's Way* with her.

She took out her phone and typed a text to Nick. *Sorry I was such a dick.* She pressed Send before she could change her mind. He would reply, or he wouldn't. At least she'd said it.

She thought of Moses making this same journey by car years before, shocked and disorientated, seeing all this for the first time. Seeing any landscape that wasn't moorland for the first time. Now she saw the courage that lay behind those quiet, stoical letters he'd written her. He always ended by saying he hoped she was OK. He never talked about God, and rarely mentioned what he'd lost. There were other kinds of heroism besides the sort that held its fists up.

Once the bus had dropped her at the edge of the village, she followed the directions she'd written down. The coastal path was easy to find and soon the whitewashed house rose up before her. It looked strangely familiar, a bit like the big house perhaps, only infinitely fresher and cleaner. She thought of them then, the two old houses and the barn, battered in the wind and abandoned on the moors. They were infamous now, their image reproduced often in newspapers and on TV news during the trial. It was unlikely anyone would live there again.

She rang the bell and waited, twisting her fingers together, too nervous to keep still. Nobody came, and she was beginning to think she'd left it too late, that it was all for nothing now. But then the door opened and a woman stood there. She was wearing jeans and an old sweatshirt, and her greying hair was cut short, so it took Judith a few seconds to realize it was Rachael.

'It's me,' Judith said, unnecessarily, because even as she said it Rachael had given a small cry and put her hand to her mouth. Judith was afraid she'd upset her, brought with her reminders Rachael would rather avoid, but the next moment Rachael's arms were round her. There was a keen relief in laying her head against Rachael's shoulder and allowing herself to be folded into this solid warmth, even as she reminded herself Rachael wasn't to be trusted – none of them were, except for Moses. You were in danger the moment you forgot how easily people lost themselves. She felt Rachael's tears on her face.

'Is he here?' she said.

Rachael was still holding her by the shoulders, but she took one hand away now to wipe her eyes. 'Yes. He's in the garden. I'll show you.'

So Judith followed her through the narrow hallway, through the light, neat living room into the kitchen, and then she was being ushered out of the French windows into the garden.

Rachael seemed to melt away.

And there he was, his back to her, feeding the chickens. Taller, of course, his shoulders broader. She wondered what she should say, and could think of nothing.

But she didn't need to speak. He turned, as though he'd been called. His eyes fixed on hers. The stain on his face, the dark hair. Perhaps he looked different, he surely looked older, but to Judith he looked like no one but himself.

Not knowing what to do, Judith took a step towards him.

'Hi, Moses.'

It was difficult to see what he was thinking behind the shock on his face. It didn't help that he wasn't saying anything. He was angry with her, probably, for ignoring him for so long, for acting as though they'd never been friends. In his place, she would have been furious.

'I'm sorry I didn't write to you,' she said hopelessly. 'I'm sorry I didn't come to see you before.'

He just stared at her. It reminded her of that first day she'd been taken to the Ark, when he kept offering her orange squash.

She tried to make herself see things clearly so she could explain them to him. At last, she said, 'I thought it would be alright, but none of it was. I thought I'd cope, but I didn't.'

She was waiting for his anger to break. But she should have known him better. The shock on his face was becoming something else. His eyes were bright.

He said, 'Judith!' And he walked towards her, his smile growing wider and wider.

Judith took a step forward. She opened her arms.

Acknowledgements

It takes a village to write a book. I'm so grateful for the support I've had. Thank you once again to my superb editors Francesca Main and Sophie Jonathan, who helped me unpick the tangle of my intentions to end up with the book I wanted to write. Thank you to my agent Caroline Hardman, whose calm and common sense can always be relied on, and to Jo Swainson, whose support has been invaluable. Most writers are lucky to have one brilliant agent; over the past few months, I've had two. Thanks also to the rest of the Picador team – it's a pleasure to work with you.

For huge generosity in giving up their time to deal with my legal queries, I'd like to thank Carolina Bracken, and also Jae Carwardine of Russell-Cooke Solicitors. My plot veered wildly as I wrote the book, and so, therefore, did my questions – they showed saint-like patience. Any inconsistencies or liberties taken are, of course, my own. Thank you, as well, to staff of the British Geological Survey: an amazing resource.

Several friends have helped with this novel in diverse ways. Helen Wyatt shared my brush with recruitment when we were teenagers ('Jesus is coming on a white horse, and he is NOT HAPPY!'), and was an enthusiastic reader of early drafts. Suzie Chamberlain provided detailed information on supermarkets, which I will carry to my grave. When it comes to cults, Katie Nairne has the gleam of the fanatic in her eye, and has been on hand throughout for in-depth discussion. Clare Garbett went out of her way to get answers to some of my stranger questions and Archie Davies provided characteristically incisive comments on the manuscript. Issy Sudbury, Briony Newman, Helen Wyatt and Katie Nairne gave me the beautiful writing desk at which I wrote most of the novel. It kept me going on hard days. Thanks, all of you.

Finally, thank you to the long-suffering triumvirate: Dave Young, a bastion of sanity in a mad world; my mum, who is always at the end of the phone, and has never given up on her dream of ensuring I don't go out without a cardigan; and my dad, who made me a table, and came round to the idea of reading.